She was so familiar...

Jake watched the tall blonde, her shapely curves ripe in a body-hugging sweater and skintight leggings. Adrenaline pumped through him, pooling in his groin as he took in the soft flaxen hair, the lush red lips. "Lookit, Ms. Jones or Devlin, or whatever your real name is," he said as she got into his car, "do I know you?"

"Intimately."

She tugged off the blond hair. A wig. As her sable hair fell around her face, the air leapt from Jake's lungs. He hadn't seen this woman since she'd left him at the altar.

"Hello, Jake."

White-hot fury coursed through his veins. "Get out of my car, Laura."

"But you have to help me."

He wasn't about to, not after the way she'd cut out on their wedding day. "Why?"

"Because someone's trying to kill me."

ABOUT THE AUTHOR

Seattle-area native Adrianne Lee started her career writing mainstream mysteries, but her romantic heart soon led her to Harlequin Intrigue. She says, "Family and love are very important to me, and I hope you enjoy the way I weave them through my stories." Adrianne's own life has been wonderfully romantic; she married her high school sweetheart and became the mother of three beautiful daughters. She loves to hear from readers, and can be reached at: P.O. Box 3835, Sequim, WA 98382. Please include an SASE for response.

Books by Adrianne Lee

HARLEQUIN INTRIGUE
296—SOMETHING BORROWED, SOMETHING BLUE
354—MIDNIGHT COWBOY
383—EDEN'S BABY
422—ALIAS: DADDY
438—LITTLE GIRL LOST

The Runaway Bride
Adrianne Lee

HARLEQUIN®

TORONTO • NEW YORK • LONDON
AMSTERDAM • PARIS • SYDNEY • HAMBURG
STOCKHOLM • ATHENS • TOKYO • MILAN • MADRID
PRAGUE • WARSAW • BUDAPEST • AUCKLAND

For Susan and Don Baumann, who are always in my corner rooting me on and making the highs higher.

Special thanks to Jennifer Malone, Delta Airlines, Boston Reservations; Gerri Muley, R.N.; the nagging gang at Tuffit for understanding what a deadline means; and always, Anne Martin, Kelly McKillip, Susan Skaggs, Gayle Webster and Larry.

ISBN 0-373-22479-6

THE RUNAWAY BRIDE

Copyright © 1998 by Adrianne Lee Undsderfer

Printed in U.S.A.

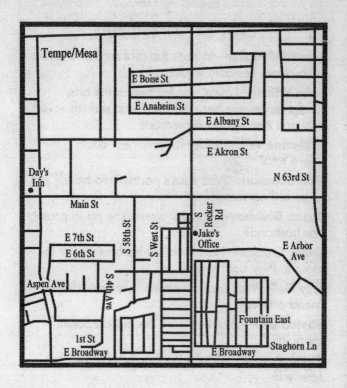

CAST OF CHARACTERS

Laura Whittaker—What's the real reason she ran away from her own wedding?

Jake Wilder—Laura had left him at the altar. Could he believe her when she said she still loved him and needed his protection?

Ruthanne Wilder—Her forgetfulness could prove fatal.

Don Bowman—Was Jake's partner too hostile not to be hiding something?

Susan Bowman—How far would she go to protect her husband?

Travis Crocker—Had he killed his brother for the woman they both loved?

Izzy Dell—Was Laura's emotionally wounded ex-friend a killer?

Payton Dell—Had he stolen the million-dollar formula?

Ralph Russell—Was he the honest cop he seemed?

Cullen Crocker—Had Laura's friendship cost him his life?

Chapter One

Fire trucks and police cars blocked Highway 101, stalling traffic. An odd prickling started at her neck. Instinctively, she knew whatever was going on ahead somehow involved her. But how?

Smoke burned her nostrils, blotting out the moon and stars as she emerged from the stranger's car and began running toward the commotion of people and vehicles. Flames shot into the night sky. Winning out over the stream of water pouring from the fire hoses, they engulfed the pitched roof, the main frame of the tiny beach house.

Her house.

She staggered to a stop. Shock held her in the shadows of a giant fire truck. Two people were passing. Talking. "Poor woman. Didn't have a chance."

She found her own voice. "W-what happened?"

In the dark, with all the confusion, she knew these neighbors wouldn't recognize her. To most Californians, one leggy, blue-eyed blonde looked much like another. She'd counted on that. Kept to herself. Discouraged any and all who'd found their way to her doorstep.

But she'd paid careful attention to her neighbors, where they lived, their comings and goings, their visitors. This couple lived across the street.

The woman shook her head, her hennaed hair bobbing in the night air. "Just heard a god-awful explosion. It knocked out all the windows in our house, all the windows on both sides of her house." She sniffed into a hankie.

"Gas leak," the man said, a slight lisp to the words. "Lit a cigarette the second she went inside and *boom* that's all she heard."

Laura's gaze flew to the house. Her Taurus was parked in the driveway—crushed from the impact of the explosion. Sunny had been driving it. Sunny was dead. An innocent victim in this nightmare that had become Laura's life. Horror and guilt sent ice through her veins, into her stomach.

She stepped back, repulsed by the sights and smells and sounds. By the abomination that had occurred. *She* had been the intended victim. Not Sunny Devlin. Whoever had flattened Sunny's two rear tires thought he'd kept her from following Laura home. He didn't know Sunny and she had traded cars.

Laura's knees wobbled. He'd tried to kill her. Again. Thought he *had* killed her. Again. The warm night air felt chilly. Was he here somewhere now? Savoring his handiwork? Thinking he'd silenced her at long last? Would he spot her and realize his error?

With bile climbing her throat, Laura ducked her head, darted back across the street to Sunny's Corvette, climbed inside and sank onto the leather seat. What was she going to do? She started the car and drove away. She'd have a few days before *he* discovered the remains in the house weren't hers.

She drove to a busy street and into a deserted bank lot, made certain no one lurked nearby, then hurried to the ATM machine and withdrew all the money from her account. One hundred sixty dollars. It wouldn't last two weeks.

Back inside the Corvette, she caught her reflection in the rearview mirror. Panic glistened in her eyes. What the hell was she going to do? A sob exploded in her throat. Hot tears burned her cheeks. What else could she do but what she'd always done? Run.

She swiped at her eyes. Crying helped nothing. It wouldn't bring Sunny and the others back. She had to think. *Think!* She sniffed and drew in a jerky breath. She knew the drill. The police wouldn't act on any missing-person reports for Sunny Devlin for at least twenty-four hours. She couldn't stay at Sunny's residence. The woman might not have lived alone. But the Corvette offered a convenient, if temporary, haven, transportation, and the added bonus of a car phone.

And tomorrow…or the day after, it would all start anew. She swallowed hard. How long would it be before *he* found her again?

Weariness washed through Laura, heavy and draining, pulling at her arms, her legs, weighing her down. She loathed running. Hiding. Changing identities. Starting new jobs. Beginning to feel safe again. Then watching some innocent someone killed in her place.

She screamed, one loud, long howl of impotent rage. Afterward, she felt no better. With her chest heaving, she started the engine and drove back onto the busy thoroughfare. The car swerved as wildly as her pulse. This horror had to end. One way or the other. That meant returning. That meant getting the evidence to the police.

A cold, mirthless laugh sprang from her throat.

She didn't even know if the evidence still existed. Or if it was still in Riverdell. The thought of her childhood hometown chilled her. Had she lost what little remained of her sanity? As long as she didn't know who was after her, she might as well parade in front of targets on a rifle range as show up in Riverdell, Washington, and contact the local law.

A dull ache drummed at her temple. The knot in her stomach tightened. But a sense of purpose settled over her like a coat of armor. If the evidence still existed, she would risk anything, everything; whatever it took, wherever it took her, to end the nightmare.

First, however, she had to track down Jake Wilder. His name sang through her head like a bittersweet tune she'd once loved, but had grown to hate. And now he held her fate in his hands. Her heart twisted at the irony.

"I DON'T KNOW any woman named Bunny." Jake Wilder shoved his long blunt fingers through his short golden hair and frowned at his partner.

Don Bowman, all six foot four of him, hitched a muscled thigh onto the edge of Jake's oak desk. Don wore his dark-brown hair long, held at his nape with a leather thong. He reminded Jake of the Grand Canyon, his size impressive, imposing, his face craggy and sharp planed, with eyes as muddy as the Colorado during spring runoff.

His voice was deceptively gentle, the soft drawling tone disarming. "She asked for you specifically, pal. Sounded like she knew you."

"Anyone named Bunny would take one look at my ugly mug and hightail it straight for the desert." Jake smirked, feeling the skin tauten the entire length of the scar that sliced the left side of his face. He kicked back in his chair and crossed his own long legs at the ankles. His snakeskin Tony Lamas collided with a soft thwack. "Believe me, I don't know her."

Don scratched his head. "Bunny. Who'd name a kid Bunny? Someone from Tinsel Town, maybe?"

Jake shook his head and scowled at Don. They'd grown up together in Riverdell, Washington, been partners for three years with the local police, until Jake transferred to the Los Angeles police force last year. He'd loved the California weather, but hated the frequent earthquakes. Loved the casual lifestyle, but the violence in the City of Angels had sickened him.

When he'd signed on with the LAPD, he'd thought himself cynical enough to deal with the depravities that one human being could inflict on another. Not for the first time in his life, he'd been wrong. He touched his scarred cheek. Three months with the force and he'd resigned. No job waiting, no idea what he'd do next.

An unexpected windfall from a fortuitous investment he'd backed some months earlier saved him from being evicted. Within five more months, it had made him financially secure enough to write his own ticket to just about anything he wanted to do. He decided he wanted to own his own company. A business that suited his restless spirit, an occupation that kept him on the move, meeting new people and new challenges, a job well suited to his law enforcement background.

Four months ago, he'd talked Don into joining him in Mesa, Arizona. They'd opened BMW Securities with Don's longtime girlfriend, Susan Meade.

Now Don and Susan were married, new parents, and BMW Securities was a going concern. Their clients ranged from rock stars to rock collectors, anyone in need of a temporary bodyguard.

Jake shook his head more firmly this time. "I said I don't know any women named Bunny."

Susan Meade-Bowman strolled in from the hall that led to her and Don's offices and a large conference room and tiny kitchen. She held her squirming three-month-old daughter, Jake's goddaughter. Both females had curly, soft blond hair and bright blue eyes. Susan smirked at Jake. "Are you sure she's not someone from your Hollywood days?"

"Positive. Your husband already suggested that." Jake blinked hard. Heat climbed his neck. Don and Susan knew more than he liked about the women in his past. The woman. And they both knew this was sensitive territory. Not to push him too far. He strove to keep his temper level. "I swear I never met anyone named Bunny. Can we drop it, please?"

Susan smiled apologetically. "Maybe a former client recommended you."

Don stroked his chin. "She didn't mention anyone."

"What's her story?" Jake asked, his temper cooling.

"All she'd tell me was that she needed someone to see her safely home," Don said.

"Which is where?" Jake sat straighter.

Don shrugged. "Wouldn't say over the phone. She did tell me that someone is trying to stop her from returning and that she'd explain everything to you in person."

"Why didn't she come here?" Susan asked.

"She sounded scared, so I didn't push it," Don explained.

The baby let out a gentle gurgle and Jake leaned forward, tenderly stroked the back of her tiny hand with one finger and smiled at Susan. Deep inside him, regret throbbed like a nasty bruise. A godfather was as close as he would ever come to being a parent. He'd permanently closed the door last year on marriage. Love was for soft-headed, softhearted fools.

And...those few lucky ones like Susan and Don.

With an effort, he refocused his mind to his new assignment. To the mystery woman who'd asked for him specifically. "Where can I find this Bunny what's-her-name?"

"Jones. She's at the Days Inn on East Main," Don said. "She's expecting you in about ten minutes."

Jake stood, crossed to the coat hook near the door and reached for his bomber jacket. This was likely some kind of joke. Bunny Jones indeed. It did sound like the name of some X-rated-film star. He told Don, "I'll call after our meeting. Let you know the particulars and how I'll be proceeding."

BMW SECURITIES WAS near the Fiesta Mall on Broadway Road. Traffic noise attacked Jake as he walked outside into the frosty, sunlit January morning. He'd come to love Mesa. Sure, it got hot in summer, but if a guy planned his assignments right, he could be elsewhere during the worst heat waves.

He slowed his pace, enjoying the vivid sky, the clean, crisp air. A new assignment always invigorated him. And this time was no exception, in spite of his partners' teasing.

He started his Cherokee and pulled onto Broadway, turned left onto Country Club Drive, then right onto Main, heading east. The Days Inn parking lot was nearly empty. He drove slowly around the two-story building, finally spotting the number he sought on the second floor end, near the stairs.

He parked next to a Corvette with California license plates, climbed out of his car and surveyed his surroundings, his instincts alert for anything that seemed out of place, out of sync. A maid's cart stood in front of an open room at the opposite end of the landing. Nothing irregular or abnormal about that.

He started toward the stairs. A car door opened behind him. Jake lurched around. His heart hammered. His hand gripped the Glock in his jacket pocket.

A tall blonde, her shapely curves ripe in a body-hugging, black sweater and skintight leggings, rose from behind the wheel of the Corvette. He hadn't seen her through the tinted windows. Adrenaline pumped through his veins, some of it pooling in his groin as he took in the soft flaxen hair that hung past her shoulders, the lush red lips beneath large sunglasses that hid the rest of her face.

She looked like she'd stepped off the silver screen, as sexy and innocent as a ripe ingenue. But Jake never trusted looks. Never underestimated women. Especially gorgeous women. He flicked off the safety on his gun and curled his fingers around the trigger.

She strode toward him, hitching the strap of an over-sized leather bag on her shoulder. "Mr. Wilder?"

She spoke just above a whisper, her voice throaty. Jake didn't answer. "Who are you?"

"Bunny Jones. I called your agency. Could we talk in your car?"

Without waiting for an answer, she hurried furtively over to the driver's side. "Please…"

A second later, she was inside his car, closing the door.

Jake's mouth dropped open. What the hell? He had his keys. She wasn't taking his car anywhere, but he didn't like the feel of this. With his nerves jumping, he surveyed the parking lot and motel again. What had he missed? Five heart-tripping seconds passed.

Spotting nothing, he pivoted. His gaze landed on the Corvette. He approached it with caution. Jerked open the door. No one was inside. He blew out a hard breath, then leaned in and found the registration. She'd lied about her name. The car belonged to a Sunny Devlin. Not Bunny Jones.

Jake stalked to the Cherokee, wondering what the hell she was up to. What else had she lied about? He tightened his hold on the gun and yanked open the passenger door.

Again she pleaded with him, "Please, get in. Quickly."

Against his better judgment, Jake reluctantly did as

asked. Maybe this woman's fright steered her actions. Maybe not. "Lookit, Ms. Jones or Ms. Devlin, whichever it is, why don't you let me take you somewhere a little less…vulnerable? Then we can talk."

"We can talk here," she said in a more normal voice. She removed the sunglasses and gazed directly at him.

To his surprise, there was something familiar about her stormy, smoke-gray eyes, something his mind wanted to reject. *Had* he met her before? "Do I know you?"

"Intimately." She tugged off the blond hair.

A wig. Sable, chin-length hair, as rich as mink, as shiny as silk, as haunting as a bad dream, fell around her heart-shaped face. And recognition slammed into him. The air leaped from his lungs. "Laura?"

"Hello, Jake," she said, in a voice that was now distinctly recognizable.

His chest ached as though he'd been slugged by a heavyweight boxer. This wasn't how he'd pictured her. He'd seen her so often in white lace with a veil perched atop that glorious hair, pictured himself putting his ring on her finger, pictured them exchanging vows of love.

But those were just the images of his nightmares.

Laura Whittaker had broken his heart, had made him Riverdell's reigning fool. She'd thought so little of him she hadn't even had the decency to tell him that she'd changed her mind about marrying him—just left him waiting at the church with all their friends and family in attendance, on what was to have been the happiest day of his life.

What did she want with him now—after twelve months of silence?

His distress and shock jetted away on a wave of white-hot fury. He tugged the gun from his pocket and waved it at her, only half-conscious that he still held it. "What the hell kind of bad joke is this?"

She reared back, her smoky eyes widening, shifting from his gaze to his hand. The color dropped from her face. "It's no joke. You *have* to help me, Jake."

Desperation and terror leapfrogged across her face. Jake tensed. Desperate women were unpredictable. This was over. Right now. "Get out of my car."

"Put the gun away first."

He frowned. He'd forgotten all about the gun. Without looking away from her, he flipped the safety on and tucked the weapon back into his jacket pocket. "Out. Now."

"Please, Jake, just hear me—"

"You don't have anything I want to hear. Get out."

Her desperation returned, darkening her eyes to a deep pewter. "You *have* to help me."

"'*Have*' to?" He laughed, a sound as bitter as his memories. "Lady, and I use the term only in its broadest meaning, if you were on fire I wouldn't spit on you. Now, get out of my car."

"Okay, but I'm sorry it has to be this way."

The words seemed to choke her. Or was she also remembering what she'd done to him? She ran her tongue across her lush red lips. The action drew his gaze even as he struggled not to be affected by it. He missed seeing her hand come out of her purse. She lifted her chin and let out a wobbly breath.

"But you *are* going to help me."

In a lightning move, Laura jammed a small stun gun against his solar plexus and fired.

Chapter Two

"Oh, God, oh, God." Laura cringed at the surprised look in Jake's eyes, wilted momentarily as his face went slack and he slumped in the seat beside her. She'd been prepared to use the stun gun, prepared to cope with the effect it would have on him. She hadn't counted on feeling bad about hurting him. But her heart ached with such pain she nearly buckled. "I'm sorry, Jake. You gave me no choice."

She reminded herself that Jake Wilder could well be the enemy. The very one trying to kill her. Adrenaline burst through Laura. She had mere seconds before he revived, before his anger exploded.

Moving nimbly, she found the car keys, disarmed Jake, dropped his gun into her purse and extracted a length of rope and a roll of duct tape. In her former life as head of product acquisitions for Dell Pharmaceuticals, she'd never imagined herself doing anything this intrepid. This brutal. But survival had forced her to learn and execute skills to counteract those of her pursuer. She lashed Jake's ankles, then knotted the rope around his wrists. After tearing off a length of tape, she smoothed it over his lips.

Touching him was her undoing. Her fingers faltered as they contacted his warm, familiar jaw, his wide, sculpted mouth. A wealth of unbidden images, deliciously wicked remembrances of things that mouth had done to her, stole from the secret trove deep within her mind. The memories riveted her. Filled her with bittersweet longing for what might have been. What should have been.

Her gaze caressed his beloved face, landing on the scar that ran from his temple to his jaw. When, where, had he gotten this? Except for his thick, richly golden hair, Jake had never been male-model handsome. His features were too irregular, his nose too large, his chin too strong, his teal-blue eyes deep set and serious.

On another man, the scar would have been ugly. On Jake, conversely, it enhanced his looks, said he could be vulnerable. And dangerous. Was he dangerous? To her? The possibility unnerved Laura as she realized the effects of the stun gun were wearing off with the speed of her accelerating pulse.

Fury danced in Jake's teal eyes. She snatched the seat belt and rammed the catch home just as he lurched straighter in the seat—as straight as the rope allowed. He railed at her, one long, mumbling vociferation, each indistinguishable word punctuated with a jerk of his head, a yank on his restraints.

Laura started the engine, left the parking lot of the motel and turned away from town, toward Superstition Mountain. "You think I wanted it this way?"

He nodded furiously.

"No. Not at all. If you'd been reasonable this wouldn't be necessary."

He bucked against the seat belt, muttered something that, even through the tape, sounded like a string of curses. Somehow, she had to get him to calm down and listen to her before they reached their destination. She drove faster, grateful that traffic was light, that the windows of his Cherokee were opaque. The last thing she wanted was someone noticing the tape on her hostage's mouth.

Beside her, Jake continued mumbling against the tape. He'd stopped wrenching against the ropes, stopped jarring the bench seat, but his chest lifted and fell with the unmistakable beat of a man in the throes of anger.

"I swear, Jake, I'll let you go soon. As soon as you agree to help me."

His muffled response amplified several decibels. From the hard, cold glint in his eyes, she suspected he'd reiterated his refusal to help her. This wasn't going as she'd planned. She spotted the dirt road she wanted and slowed, then pulled onto it. It seemed to meander through flat, cactus-dotted desert toward a sweep of low, rolling hills. Jake muttered something that sounded like a question.

She glanced at him. "We're going to a cabin I know about out here."

A dark frown furrowed his brow, puckered the scar, and she knew his distrust of her grew with every pothole on this godforsaken road. Maybe if she removed the tape he'd be more cooperative. Would listen to reason. Would hear her out.

Besides, there wasn't anyone out here who could hear him holler for help. She caught an edge of the tape. Again, the touch of her skin against his jarred Laura. She swallowed hard, ignored the unwanted sensations, gripped tighter and ripped the tape free.

Cursing, Jake wrenched back against the headrest. "Ahh."

"Sorry." Even to herself, she didn't sound as though she meant it.

"Yeah, right. What the hell do you think you're doing? Where are you taking me?"

"I told you. It's a cabin. A place where we can talk without interruption."

"I don't want to talk to you. I don't want anything to do with you."

The remark stung Laura; how badly it hurt surprised her. She pressed her lips together and stared at the road. Had she expected Jake would feel the same about her as he had before she'd run away from their wedding? Hardly. But she supposed a teeny part of her must have hoped for exactly that. Otherwise her heart wouldn't feel as though he'd just stomped on it.

Keeping the pain from her face, she glanced at him. "I'd hoped by now you'd realize how important this is to me."

He opened his mouth, undoubtedly to tell her how unimportant that fact was to him, but instead, he heaved a sigh, shut his eyes and turned toward the window. An angry red rash surrounded his mouth where the tape had been. A nerve jumped at his temple.

FURIOUS. Horrified. Humiliated. Jake tried reining in his stampeding temper. He'd thought being left at the church was mortifying, but this... This was crazed. Psychotic. How could he ever have loved this woman? No normal, sane person used a stun gun on another, trussed him up like a wrangled calf, stole his car and kidnapped him.

He glanced at the barren stretch of land ahead. Uninhabited. Unhabitable. Was she going to leave him out here? Tied up? His mouth dried. He had to think. Had to get free. Overpower her.

He shifted in the seat again and realized with a start that he could no longer feel the weight of the Glock in his pocket. A chill shivered through him. Dear God, was she planning to kill him? No. What possible reason could she have? Then again, what reason did she have for abducting him?

Ahead, nestled in a stand of bent mesquite trees, he spied a dilapidated shack. The cabin? It might once have been the hangout of some long-gone seeker of the Lost Dutchman Mine, but he suspected the only residents these days were unfriendly desert critters who would just as soon bite or sting trespassers. "You don't really plan on using this run-down rattler ranch for a 'chat'?"

She parked in front of the "cabin," cut the engine and shifted toward him. Apparently she did.

She said, "I'm going to come around and help you out of the car, then we're going to go inside and talk."

"Untie me." His pulse ticked to the beat of the cooling engine.

"Will you hear me out...with an open mind?"

His nerves were as unsettled as the dust swirling around the car. His gaze met and held hers, and he recognized in those glorious pewter orbs the same desperation he'd seen there earlier. *Desperate women were dangerous. Unpredictable.* Laura had just proven that to him in spades. He decided the best thing, the only thing, he could do at the moment was humor her. "Yes."

She considered a moment, then reached into her purse and withdrew his gun. He swallowed hard, pressed reflexively against his door. The bright sun stole through the heavily tinted windows, heating his neck, but outside he knew the temperature hovered near freezing. Inside the cabin it would be even colder.

Laura pulled the keys from the ignition, gathered her purse and exited the car. She came around to the passenger side and yanked open the door. He stared up at her, at the gun she now held to her side. The morning sun glinted off its silver snout. His stomach clenched.

Laura leaned into the car, her body stretched over his in an exaggerated arch that precluded touching, as she unlatched his seat belt. The fragrance of wildflowers filled his nostrils and he realized the scent was new, as different and aberrant as the wig she'd worn earlier.

Why the change? Then again, what *hadn't* changed about her? She caught him by the elbow, their noses inches apart, and he realized to his severe annoyance what hadn't changed was his ardor to bed this woman. Her thick, silken sable hair danced about her face, imbuing the air with her dizzying wildflower scent. Jagged spears of heartache pierced him. "Untie me."

"Inside."

"Now."

She stood erect and brought the gun up level with his temple. "Why must you make everything so difficult?"

"Me?" Jake stamped down his returning fury, cautioning himself to keep a cool head. He struggled out of the car and stood hunched forward in the soft sand, his balance precarious. Laura motioned him toward the cabin. Jake stood firm. "I told you I'd listen to you...with an open mind. So start talking."

She hugged herself against the chill. She had no coat, had to be even colder than he was. She glared at him. "And I told you I'd untie you when we get inside."

He warned himself against losing his temper. She was crazy. *She had his gun.* But he'd had enough. "I'm not going into that scorpion sand castle."

Her eyebrows arched and she waved the gun at him. "But I—I'll shoot you."

"Go ahead. If I'm going to die today, I'd prefer it be swiftly."

She grabbed him by the elbow and jerked hard. Jake lost his balance. He toppled toward her. Laura realized it too late. She yelped. He rammed into her. She pitched backward, arms flailing. She hit the ground landing sprawled on her back with her arms flung outward. The gun skittered free.

Jake crashed on top of her. He heard the breath whoosh from her lungs, felt the rush of air on his face, felt Laura wriggle beneath him, and realized that his tied hands cupped the vee of her legs, that he could feel her firm breasts mounded against his chest. Their lips were centimeters apart. Their gazes locked.

Something electric traveled his veins, heated his senses, and for one heady second he forgot the heartache she'd caused him, her craziness this morning. He wanted to ravish her mouth, her body, make her cry out with release, with desire for only him.

Then she glared at him and wheezed, "Get...off...me."

The charged moment vanished, leaving him shaken and disoriented.

Laura grunted and pushed at his shoulders. But with his wrists and ankles bound, he couldn't gain leverage. And every failed attempt to disentangle himself from her only made him more aware of the feel of her. Finally, he bunched his muscles and rolled to his side.

Panting, Laura sat up. She glared at him. "Damn you. You did that on purpose."

Jake laughed. His confidence and anger returned in a rush, twin devils vying for control of him. "Untie me."

She scrambled up, brushed herself off and dug around in her purse. She produced a pocketknife and cut the rope at Jake's wrists, then gathered up the gun again and waved it at him. "You do the rest."

He complied, rapidly considering and rejecting ways to disarm her without either of them getting shot. He rubbed his wrists and then his ankles. He rose gingerly, mounted the front bumper of the car and sat on the hood. To his dismay, he could still feel the sensation of her body beneath his. He fought the desire pooling in his groin. Tried not to notice the way the sweater cleaved her full breasts, tried not to remember the feel of those breasts, the taste of them. "Start talking."

Laura gazed up at him, keeping her distance. She sighed. "I need the evidence I sent your mother."

Jake blinked and shook his head, puzzled. What the hell was she talking about? This made about as much sense as her kidnapping him. "You sent my mother some... evidence?"

"Yes. As a present."

He pressed his elbows to his thighs and buried his head in his hands. Demented. She *was* demented. His chest squeezed. He glanced at her. "A present?"

Laura shoved her free hand through her hair, then let it fall like spilled chocolate silk about her shoulders. "I'm not explaining this well. I disguised the evidence—gift-wrapped it like one of our wedding presents."

Jake blanched at the mention of the wedding. He didn't want any reminders of that day. "I don't have anything that you sent my mother."

She frowned as though she thought he was lying. His anger sparked anew. Where did she get off not believing him? He wasn't the liar. The betrayer.

Laura said, "Are you sure Ruthanne didn't give it to you?"

She *did* think he was lying. Jake glared at her. "Positive. What the hell is this evidence anyway? Evidence of what?"

"It's proof that Uncle Murphy and Aunt May were murdered."

He just stared at her. He couldn't believe his ears. Murdered? Her aunt and uncle had raised her, were the only folks she'd known. Had their deaths sent her over the edge, zapped her sanity? "The explosion was an accident, Laura. I thought you had accepted that."

"It was not an accident. Someone at Dell Pharmaceuticals killed them."

"For what reason?"

"For Uncle Murphy's new formula."

Jake felt like a man wandering in a dense fog. Every time he thought he was stepping clear of it, it grew thicker. His patience waned. "Don and I were the investigating officers on your aunt and uncle's case. It was tragic, but it was an accident." She knew all this, but apparently needed reminding. "The point of origin of the explosion was the basement lab. Your uncle just put the wrong chemicals together."

"My uncle wouldn't be that careless."

Jake snickered. "Murphy Whittaker worked on a shoe-string budget. His lab was slipshod. You know damned well that he took shortcuts from lack of cash. Reused old containers—"

"Recycled!" she interrupted, indignation in her voice, in the set of her lovely jaw.

"Whatever."

"If I'm lying, Jake, why has someone been trying to kill me for a year?"

"What!" This was the most preposterous thing she'd said yet.

"Since the day of our wedding. Why do you think I left you at the altar?"

He knew why she'd left. She'd run off with another man. How dared she claim that was a lie? That her note to him was a lie? His patience snapped. He jumped down off the car. "I've had enough of this. Give me my keys."

"Please, Jake. It's the truth."

"No, the truth is that you're an insensitive witch who never gave a fig about anyone but yourself." His accusation hung between them like a filthy word. Jake knew it didn't describe the Laura he'd grown up with, fallen in love with, wanted to spend the rest of his life with.

It did, however, describe the Laura who'd run off with Cullen Crocker, a man whose handsome face could grace the covers of the world's best-selling men's and women's magazines. Jake's insides felt clammy. He held his hand out to her. "My keys."

Laura stood her ground, squaring her shoulders. The desperate gleam had returned to her eyes, along with a spark of determination. "Jake, I swear I can prove my aunt and uncle were murdered *and* that someone has been trying to kill me ever since I discovered that truth. I just have to retrieve the package I sent your mother."

Jake leveled his gaze on her. "All the wedding presents were returned."

"Not this one. Ruthanne didn't know where to send it."

"Then she probably disposed of it."

"But you don't know that for certain. And I can't return to Riverdell. I don't dare call her, either. The last time I did, someone tracked me down and killed a woman who looked like me in the parking lot of my motel."

He shook his head. Not for one minute did he believe this story. "If you won't give me the keys, I'll just hot-wire the car."

He started toward the driver's side. Laura caught up with him. She held out the keys. "Please, Jake, would you call Ruthanne and ask her about the package?"

He took the keys, then motioned for his gun. She turned it over to him. He made sure the safety was on and slipped it back in his jacket pocket.

Laura had begun to shiver. "Please, Jake. You're my only hope."

He blew out a heavy breath. "Ruthanne's not living in Riverdell anymore. I moved her to Mesa. Not far from here." He wasn't sure about the wisdom of the suggestion he was about to make, but maybe it would get Laura back on track. And out of his life for good. "Would you like to ask her about the package, yourself?"

Chapter Three

"I—I suppose if you were going to kill me," Laura said, her voice shaky with cold and nerves, "you'd have done it a second ago. After all, what better place to leave a body than out here?"

Jake growled low in his throat. "Let's get one thing straight—I haven't been trying to kill you. I don't believe anyone has. But if you try using that stun gun on me again, I will shoot you. Now, get in the car before you freeze to death."

Laura was in the car with her seat belt buckled before he started the engine. The warmth of the heater, along with the bouncing jostle as they traveled the dirt road, stirred her languid circulation, making her painfully aware of how chilled she'd gotten standing out in the desert in only a sweater and leggings. "If you don't believe me, why are you helping me?"

Jake glanced at her, his teal eyes icy with loathing. He opened his mouth, then snapped it shut as though he'd been going to lash out at her but had changed his mind. Looking back at the road, he said, "I'm not doing much. But when it's done, I don't want to hear from you again. Not ever. Understand?"

Laura fell silent. They'd once been best friends, once

shared their deepest, darkest secrets and desires, but now being civil strained their tempers. If he'd sliced her heart open with a rusty knife it couldn't have hurt worse. She had loved this man with all her soul. God, help her, she loved him still. But she didn't like him much. And she hoped she wasn't making a mistake by asking for his help.

She gazed away from him. Life had kicked them both hard. She doubted she'd ever truly trust anyone again. Perhaps he was equally disillusioned. But his folks hadn't been murdered. *She* hadn't bungled the investigation into their deaths. The old resentment swirled through her. She'd been forced on the run not because Jake was a dirty cop, just a bad one. She'd tried telling him Uncle Murphy and Aunt May were murdered. He hadn't believed her then.

He didn't believe her now.

Love and marriage should be based on trust. On belief in each other. For the first time in a year, she was glad she'd missed her own wedding.

They gained the main road again, merging with the noon-hour traffic. Laura scanned cars in front, beside and behind them, an automatic reflex these days, but as she settled back in her seat, she paid little attention to which roads Jake took. Her thoughts drifted to Ruthanne, to what his mother living in Mesa might mean to her.

Ruthanne Wilder, a genuine pack rat, never threw out anything. Had she kept the package? Had she brought it with her from Riverdell? Hope heated a small corner of Laura's ice-encrusted heart. If so, it was the best news she could receive. It meant she wouldn't have to go back to Riverdell. That she could recover the evidence against her aunt and uncle's killer without putting herself—or anyone else—in further jeopardy.

Doubts attacked her seedling hope. Could it really be this easy? This simple? The past year she'd acquired new respect for caution, no longer taking anything or anyone at face value. Had she trusted Jake too readily? Was he really taking her to his mother?

Or had he lured her into the car so he could drive her to the nearest police station and have her arrested for abducting him? The thought riveted her. Despite his threat, she pushed her hand into her purse and curled her fingers around the stun gun. Its cold metal against her hot palm felt reassuring.

Jake slowed the car, then turned into a moderately crowded parking lot. Laura's nerves leaped and her gaze shifted to the low-slung adobe building. A sign above the front entrance identified it as Sunshine Vista Estates. Definitely not a police station. She released a taut breath and eased her hand out of her purse.

Jake found a parking space.

Laura unlatched her seat belt. "How does Ruthanne like Mesa?"

"She manages." Jake opened his car door.

Manages? What did that mean? Laura scrambled out of the car and hurried to Jake's side. She eyed the building critically. "I'd think your mom would have preferred a small bungalow surrounded with mounds of desert flowers, or a mobile home in one of those trailer parks along Main Street where she'd be surrounded by friends."

"She's surrounded by friends here, and she has a tiny garden off her terrace." He kept his face turned straight ahead.

"This is an apartment building, then?"

"Sort of."

Sort of? Laura frowned. Curiosity raged through her, but Jake's brusque retorts discouraged further questioning. With her pulse skittering, she followed him up the entrance walkway and into a wide foyer. The smell of freshly cooked food greeted them. Straight ahead was a large formal room with its doors hanging open. From the people milling in the open doorway and those seated at clothed tables, being served, inside, Laura realized Sunshine Vista Estates was a senior complex.

Jake passed the dining room without looking in and strode toward a long hallway.

Laura hurried to catch up to him. "How do you know Ruthanne isn't in the dining room?"

"I don't. But first we'll check her quarters."

They traveled the long hallway, then turned into another. Laura wished Jake would slow down. She'd dipped deep into her well of courage today already, but the toughest undertaking lay ahead. Facing Ruthanne. The last time they'd spoken, she had been cool to Laura. Understandably so, considering Laura had left her son at the altar two weeks earlier. Ruthanne's disappointment in her still hurt. She'd tried explaining to Ruthanne why she'd run off, but hadn't wanted to alarm her or put the woman's life in danger.

In the end, she'd borne the disappointment in an effort to convince Ruthanne to pass her message and the package along to Jake. But instead of help arriving, someone had shown up at the motel in Idaho intent on murdering her. Until today, she'd harbored a fear that that someone was Jake. She knew now she'd been wrong. He'd have killed her in the desert this morning otherwise. Ended this hell for once and all.

So, what about the package? Jake seemed truly not to know about it. Had Ruthanne given it to someone else? Had she given it to anyone at all? Ruthanne tended toward forgetfulness, a trait Laura had once thought endearing. Had it proven deadly in this instance?

On the other hand, if Ruthanne had forgotten to tell

anyone about the package or her telephone call, how had she been traced to the Idaho motel? Had someone bugged the Wilder telephone?

Jake stopped before a door with a red heart taped to it. His mother's name was written in white across the center of the paper valentine. The butterflies in Laura's stomach fluttered with new life. This would be easy if Ruthanne had been nothing more to her than a mother-in-law-to-be. But she was so much more. Jake's mom had given her the only real mothering she'd ever known.

Laura leaned against the wall as Jake knocked on the door. She shut her eyes, recalling the couple who'd raised her. Murphy Whittaker, who'd been preoccupied with his work, had neglected his wife. Most women in May's place would have doted on a child. But Aunt May, well meaning but flighty, was intimidated by the young niece who'd come to her grieving over the loss of her parents. She decided immediately that it would be better if she was Laura's friend instead of her parent.

What Laura had needed was a mother. She'd found that in Ruthanne Wilder.

Jake opened the door. "Mom?"

Laura's heart fluttered. She trailed after Jake, the knot in her stomach tightening with every step. But once she was inside, her eyes widened with dismay as she took in the eleven-by-eleven room. Granted the two-story house in Riverdell was getting too large for Ruthanne, but reducing her living quarters to a single room seemed extreme. And wrong.

Yet all was not unfamiliar. The bedspread and curtains, for as far back as she could recall, had graced the Wilders' master bedroom. Her heart squeezed. There were other recognized treasures, too: framed photographs and a favorite planter, which now held a Christmas cactus in full bloom.

She felt Jake's eyes on her and looked up to catch him staring at her. Something about this alien room, perhaps the few things that identified it as his mother's, felt too intimate, stirred long-denied memories. Laura took a step toward him. He swallowed and spun away from her, strode toward a patio door.

Laura spied a tall woman in a housedress and cardigan on the minuscule deck, bent over a window box. Her gunmetal-gray hair was cropped close to her head and flattened into an unflattering nest of tight curls.

Jake opened the door. "Mom?"

The woman's head snapped up. With a start Laura realized it was Ruthanne. In twelve months time the woman had changed so much she would not have known her. Laura froze, her mind reeling.

Jake's mother had always prided herself on her appearance, exercised, dieted and dressed younger than her fifty-plus years. For the past ten years, she'd worn her pale-golden hair in the same softly flattering pageboy. But this new color, new style aged her dreadfully. She looked nearer eighty than sixty.

Ruthanne blinked at Jake as though she didn't know him. Laura saw that her usually warm and lively teal eyes seemed dull. Medication? Was Ruthanne ill?

But Laura's concern vanished instantly as a smile spread across Ruthanne's face and she exclaimed, "J.J., what a nice surprise!"

Jake said something to her, and Ruthanne's attention swung to Laura. Laura held her breath, but Ruthanne's smile widened. She hurried inside, brushing past Jake. "It's about time you brought Laura to see me. How wonderful."

She crossed to Laura and hugged her. Laura wanted to melt in the embrace of this woman whom she considered mother and friend. But Ruthanne stepped back quickly and caught her by the hands. Ruthanne's hands felt dry, but her eyes were watery. She studied Laura.

"You've done something different with your hair."

"Well, ah, it's a little longer is all." Actually, it was much longer than it had been last year, and in dire need of a decent cut. But she'd avoided beauty parlors, spending whatever cash she garnered on essentials: rent, food, disguises, devices like the stun gun.

She smiled tentatively. "You've changed your hair, too, I see."

"Have I?" Ruthanne touched the hair at her nape and frowned, as though surprised at its shorter length. "Kim says this is easier."

Kim, Laura supposed, was Kim Durant, Ruthanne's brother Larry's girl. Besides being Jake's cousin, Kim was also Laura's friend, a close enough friend that Laura had asked her to be one of her bridesmaids. "How do you like living here…in Arizona?"

"It's nice. I miss my house. My garden. But we have tea in the afternoon and I play bridge, you know, with Milly down the hall and…and…Phyllis and…and the others. Goodness, I can't seem to remember their names."

Laura nodded. She saw a flicker of pain cross Jake's eyes and wondered at it.

"Sit down, you two." Ruthanne motioned Jake and Laura into a love seat that hugged the wall beneath the window.

Jake grimaced, causing the scar to stand out. It gave him a menacing mien that so opposed his true nature. Laura's pulse faltered. God, he could still steal her breath. How was it possible to love a man and detest him at the same time? She swallowed hard over the knot in her throat.

Jake dropped onto the tiny sofa, his gaze locked with

hers, and patted the seat beside him. The space left by his powerful body would barely accommodate her. She balked. She didn't want to sit within touching distance of Jake. Would have sworn he wanted it that way, too. Then why the sham? What was going on that she was missing?

Jake said, "Laura didn't come to talk about bridge and hairdos, Mom."

"Well, of course not." Ruthanne sank onto her bed, opened the top drawer of her nightstand, stuck her hand inside, then pulled it out and began rubbing her hands together, applying lotion. She looked at Laura expectantly. "You're wound tight as a drum, girl. Sit down and tell me what's bothering you."

Reluctantly, Laura joined Jake on the love seat, but held herself away from him—an impossibility. Their shoulders brushed and her heartbeat skipped.

She forced her mind to the package, but all hope that Ruthanne had it here had vanished ten minutes ago. If she'd been living in a house... But she wasn't. This room held nothing but the bare essentials. Ruthanne's other possessions had either been disposed of or put in storage.

Why hadn't Jake just told her that? Because he wanted to torture her, if only a little, she realized. Her resentment of him deepened a notch.

His mother steadied her gaze on Laura, eyes narrowed. "What are you doing in Mesa, dear?"

Trying to get my life back, Laura wanted to shout. The life that had been snatched from her by her aunt and uncle's murderer. By Jake not believing her.

"Dear?" Ruthanne prodded.

Laura ran her tongue across her dry lips. "Do you still have the package I sent you?"

"Package?" Ruthanne frowned and her expression grew

thoughtful. "They bring all my packages to me. I don't recall anything from you, Laura, dear."

"I sent it to your house in Riverdell. It was wrapped in wedding paper."

"Oh, you mean the present."

Hope leaped in Laura's chest. Jake moved closer to the edge of his seat. Another quarter inch and he'd land on the floor. Laura resisted the urge to help him along. "Yes. The one for Jake."

"Oh." Ruthanne clasped her hands together. "So many lovely things have come for you and Jake."

Perplexed, Laura said, "What?"

She felt Jake wince. But Ruthanne nodded and smiled. "You and J.J. are going to start your marriage off with a bang."

Laura stiffened. Start their marriage? "Ruthanne, I—"

"We have to go, Mom." Jake cut Laura off and lurched to his feet.

But without missing a beat, Ruthanne said, "I know you're going to be a beautiful bride. It's a pity Murphy won't be there to give you away. I suppose Ralph will have to do."

Laura's mouth dropped open. Ralph had been Jake's boss in Riverdell, the chief of police. He *had* been going to give her away. Last year. But Ruthanne sounded as though she believed the wedding was about to take place. Dismay dragged her stomach to her toes.

She glanced at Jake, seeking reassurance that Ruthanne was well. One hundred percent sane. His face was as hard as granite. But the awful pain in his eyes ripped at her heart. He spun on his heel and stalked to the door, then closed it behind him with a firm thud.

Laura found her feet, and Ruthanne came off the bed with a start. "Why, where is J.J. going? You two have a little lovers' spat? Don't you worry, darling. He's a bit hotheaded, but he loves you. You're going to have a wonderful life together."

Apprehension shivered through Laura. How dared Jake run out on her? She deserved an explanation. She needed to know that her suspicions about Ruthanne were unfounded. She kissed Ruthanne goodbye and hurried into the hall. She expected that Jake had abandoned her and that she'd have to chase him down. But he was there. Leaning against the wall. Agony etched in every line of his glorious face.

Laura couldn't swallow. "What's the matter with her Jake? Is—is it Alzheimer's?"

He nodded, then said in a voice taut with stifled emotion, "It came on fast. Most days she doesn't know me. Today was a good day."

Laura's chest heaved, her breath coming in huge gasps as though she'd just stopped running at full out speed. "W-why didn't you tell me?" She wanted to hit him. To slam her fists into his chest and just keep pounding on him until her fear and anger subsided. "I love her, too, you know. Letting me find out this way was cruel. You didn't used to be cruel, Jake."

His gaze narrowed. "I didn't used to be a lot of things."

Tears blurred her vision. Her heart ached as though it had been fileted. She'd lost her birth parents, her adopted parents, Jake and now Ruthanne. She hugged herself, feeling lost and alone in a strange town, a strange building where former loved ones were strangers to her now.

JAKE DIDN'T WANT to feel anything warm and fuzzy for Laura, but damned if this didn't hit him where he lived. She looked stunned by the devastation of his mother's illness. Had his animosity for Laura erased all thought that she'd care this deeply? Or had he shoved it out of his mind, not wanting to face the fact that she cared more for his mother than she ever had for him?

He shut his eyes, recalling the first time he'd seen Laura. A vision filled his mind of a lost little angel with sable braids and wide gray eyes. A typical third-grade boy, he'd teased her horribly, been a real brat. He opened his eyes. He'd made her cry. As she was crying now. But this time the tears were for his mother.

Ruthanne's gentle guidance had given Laura confidence and self-respect. She'd flourished, grown into a proud and beautiful woman. Laura loved his mother as unselfishly as he'd thought she'd love him. Now he had the overpowering urge to pull her to him. To offer her comfort. To accept some in return.

Laura wiped at her eyes and lifted her chin. Determination dominated her expression. "What became of Ruthanne's possessions?"

Jake tensed. One minute Laura was bereft over his mother, the next she was harping on that package again. In the past, she wouldn't have shifted gears so swiftly. So heartlessly. She had changed. Suddenly. Inexplicably. And his mother didn't need this unstable woman in her life. He gestured toward the hallway. "Come on. I'll take you back to your motel."

Laura fell into step with him. "First tell me what became of Ruthanne's possessions."

"In storage." He started down the hall.

She caught him by the arm. He stopped and glared at her. She glowered right back at him. "Where?"

"Riverdell."

Laura drew a sharp breath. Satisfaction curled the corners of his mouth. He started walking again.

She hurriedly fell into step beside him. "Did—did you keep everything?"

"I couldn't tell you." He didn't stop this time, but strolled through the lobby and outside.

"You can't tell me, or you won't tell me?"

"Can't." Jake eyed her across the roof of his Cherokee. Right after Laura's betrayal, he'd quit the police force and left Riverdell for good. A man could take only so much pity and lampooning from friends and co-workers. He wasn't ever going back to that stinking one-horse town. "Kim packed up Mom's house, held the garage sale and put everything else in storage."

LAURA FELT COLD again. She was back to square one. The cream might or might not exist. Might have been, of all the awful things, sold at a garage sale. She rammed her hand through her hair. At least the killer didn't have the lotion. He wouldn't still be after her if he did.

Her gaze flitted through the heavy traffic, but she saw little, registered less. Worry for Ruthanne blunted her usual wary edge. Jake said Ruthanne didn't always recognize him. But how long would it be before she didn't know him at all?

Sorrow grabbed Laura's stomach and twisted it into a tight knot. This visit with Ruthanne mustn't be the last. Laura had to get her life back. Had to be able to come and go at Sunshine Vista Estates for as long as Ruthanne remembered her and needed her.

Laura's motel loomed and she eyed it with icy resolution. She wouldn't be staying there this night. No. She'd be in the Corvette, headed for Riverdell, Washington, returning to the scene of the first crime, the stomping grounds of an unknown murderer. Shards of terror spiked her.

But they wouldn't deter her. If the cream was in Ruthanne's belongings, she would find it. Had to find it. "Will you give me permission to go through Ruthanne's storage in Riverdell?"

He arched an eyebrow at her and shook his head in disbelief. "You want me to call Kim?"

"N-no."

"Oh, don't tell me, you think Kim is a killer?" He rolled his eyes and pulled to a stop near the Corvette.

"I—I just don't want anyone to know I'm returning." And Kim Durant was the biggest gossip in town.

He blew out a big breath. "Sorry. Request denied. I took you to see Mom. And that's the last favor I'm doing for you. Get out of the car...and my life."

"Favor? You call that a favor?" Laura glared at him. She needed to get into Ruthanne's storage unit, but Jake wasn't the only one who could grant her that right. "Fine, don't help me. I'll get permission from your mother."

"The hell you will. You stay away from her."

"Okay." Laura squared her shoulders. "Help me, then."

Jake reached into the pocket that held the Glock. "The only thing I'm going to help you with is getting out of my car."

Laura raised her hands. "Okay, okay. I'm going."

She scrambled out of the car, slammed the door and stepped back. She didn't need Jake Wilder to help her with anything. She would just go back and visit Ruthanne on her own.

His tires squealed as he sped away too fast.

Laura watched his taillights round the building. She stood in the empty parking lot, one woman, one car. The sense of loneliness crept over her again. "The hell with you, Jake Wilder. I'll find out who killed my aunt and uncle all by myself.''

Laura dug through her purse, found the keys and swung toward the Corvette, which stood ten feet away. Forgetting she hadn't locked the car, she palmed the tiny black security device and depressed the automatic lock-release. It made the usual chirping noise that sounded to Laura like the high-pitched yip of a tiny dog.

She took a step forward.

The car exploded.

Chapter Four

Anger at Laura burned hot and bitter in Jake's gut. He slammed the gas pedal to the floor. The Cherokee's tires dug into the pavement with a satisfying yelp as he left her behind, an ever-diminishing dot of reflection in his rearview mirror.

He'd fantasized coming face-to-face with her again. Knew exactly what he'd say. Do. But nothing he'd dreamed even approached the past four hours. Obviously his imagination lacked color and depth. He swore, disgusted with himself.

She'd gained control of the situation from the outset, and though he'd taken the reins back halfway through the ordeal, she'd still come out on top. Damn her. Why had he ever softened toward her? Taken her to see his mother?

He hit the steering wheel and slammed on his brakes. A couple coming out of the Days Inn office eyed him suspiciously. He swiped his hand down the side of his face, self-conscious of the scar and how sinister it made him look. He stared at the traffic cruising Main Street and pulled in several deep breaths. He needed to calm down. To think. To anticipate Laura's next move.

He supposed the first thing he'd better do was make certain she stayed the hell away from his mother. He reached for his car phone, and noticed it was switched off. He frowned. He always kept it on. Laura. She'd been in the car alone while he'd checked out the Corvette. Damn. He hit the activate button, but before he could punch in the number for Sunshine Vista Estates, the phone began ringing.

"Jake Wilder," he answered.

"It's about time, buddy." It was Don. "Where the hell have you been?"

With Laura, he thought, wincing. But that was something he wouldn't tell Don. His partner wouldn't approve. Wouldn't understand. He wasn't sure he understood. "Let's just say Ms. Bunny Jones had a few surprises for me."

"Such as?"

"Nothing important enough to repeat."

"She's not a client, then?"

"Definitely not."

"Good."

"Good? Why do you say that?"

"Well, for starters, because her name's not Bunny Jones."

"How do you know?" Disquiet chattered through Jake. What he really wondered was how much his partner knew.

"When we couldn't rouse you, I ran over to Days Inn and checked her out."

"And...?" Jake held his breath.

"She registered at the motel as Bunny Jones and paid cash for her room, but the car in the parking lot, which matches the one she signed in, is licensed to a Sunny Devlin."

"Yeah, I know."

Don fell silent for a long moment, then said, "Look, if

I'm repeating what you've spent the past four hours learning, then I'll shut up and let you talk.''

"You're doing fine." Jake slouched in the seat. "Don't clam up on me now."

Don made an indeterminate noise. "Do you also know this Devlin woman is a private investigator from Malibu?"

"No." Jake sat straighter. Before now, he hadn't cared about the car. Or that Laura was using an alias. Everything about her had been a lie from the first time she'd said "I love you, Jake" to that blond wig she'd been wearing today and that outrageous tale of someone trying to kill—

An explosion rocked the Cherokee.

The cell phone went dead in Jake's white-knuckled grip. He jerked around in his seat. Smoke rose from behind the motel. His heart froze. "Laura."

He jammed the gearshift into reverse, tires squealing again, and raced to the back of the motel.

What was left of the Corvette was consumed in flames. Twisted auto parts littered the parking lot. Shattered glass lay everywhere. He spotted Laura about forty feet from the burning car. She sprawled on the tarmac like a discarded rag doll, her head pillowed by her large purse. She might be a waif sleeping in a junkyard.

Jake's scalp prickled. He scrambled out of the Cherokee and rushed to her. She was unconscious, her pulse thready. Her face had numerous scrapes, and blood oozed from a nasty-looking cut on her calf. Thinking to apply pressure, he tugged the clean handkerchief from his pants pocket, but as he did so, he drew in a ragged breath, inhaling the rank smoke…and another pungent stench. Alarms went off in his head. Gas fumes.

Terrified, Jake dropped the handkerchief and scooped Laura, purse and all, off the pavement and into the Cherokee. As he rounded the car, a couple arrived to investigate the smoke. He shooed them away. "Get out of here! The gas tank is going to explode!"

The couple turned and sprinted off in the direction of the motel office. Jake landed in the Cherokee on the run. As he drove around the corner of the building, he saw a flash of light in his driver's side mirror. The ensuing blast quaked the car.

He didn't slow down, but sped onto Main Street, missing a collision by inches and eliciting horn blasts of protest from the outraged motorist. Driving like a fiend, he sped ahead, swerved from lane to lane, the urgency to get Laura to the nearest hospital controlling him.

He shouldn't have moved her. He hadn't had any choice, but it might have worsened her condition. He glanced down at her, at the blood issuing from her calf. His chest tightened with fear. He pressed his hand to the cut. She didn't respond. He spoke to her anyway. "It's all right, Laura. I'll have you at the hospital in a few minutes. Hang on, babe."

A fire truck was coming toward them, its sirens blaring. Cars moved to the shoulder, making way for it and the other emergency vehicles following. Jake zoomed on, taking advantage of the cleared road.

Laura felt so fragile beneath his big hand, so tiny and vulnerable, no longer the tough woman who'd used a stun gun on him earlier. No longer the betraying witch who'd left him humiliated in Riverdell. Who'd haunted his dreams the past twelve months.

With her thick lashes grazing her cheeks, she so resembled the sweet girl he'd fallen in love with in junior high school he couldn't rouse an ounce of anger at her. A pinch of hatred. He wanted only for her to be well. To survive this awful thing. The cut on her leg didn't worry him—it seemed superficial. But she wasn't waking up. His fear leaped a notch higher. *He* shouldn't have moved her. Was her neck broken? Was she bleeding internally?

Saguaro County General loomed into view. An aged adobe structure, it hugged the edge of the desert, with Camelback Mountain as a distant backdrop. SC General was neither the biggest nor best-equipped hospital in the area. Nor was it the one most likely to be used by the rescue crew at the motel. But it was the closest.

Jake plowed through the parking lot, past the palm and orange trees and saguaro cacti that served as landscaping, around to the back of the building.

He braked outside the emergency room entrance, left the motor running and summoned help. A minute later, Laura was wheeled away on a gurney.

Watching, he felt a mixture of relief and deepening anxiety. She was in capable, skilled hands, but what would they discover? The car phone rang, jarring him from his bleak thoughts. "Jake Wilder."

"We were disconnected, but you didn't call back." Don again. "Did you hear the Days Inn blew up?"

"I was there."

Don swore.

"I'm fine, and except for the loss of most of its windows, the motel is intact."

"What happened?"

"I'm not sure. I can't talk now. I'll call you later and fill you in."

"Do that."

Jake disconnected, parked his car and ran back inside the hospital.

"Sir?" A compact, gray-haired woman in a white nurse's uniform and thick-soled shoes stopped him. She was short, reaching just about to the middle of his stomach. She reminded Jake of a much-loved cat he'd had as a child—the same tiny pink nose and keen blue eyes, her hair as fluffy as angora fur. "You brought in the young woman just now?"

"Yes." He frowned. Had something happened to Laura in the time he'd taken to talk to Don, park and lock his car? A tinny taste coated his tongue. "How is she?"

"Well, we don't know yet." The nurse, whose name tag identified her as S. I. Ames, strode around the reception desk and plopped herself down before a computer, positioning her hands on the keyboard. "But I'll need some admittance information from you."

"Of course." He knew the routine. As an L.A. cop, taking people to emergency rooms had been as much a part of his job description as investigating crimes. He moved to the counter.

"Her name?"

S. I. Ames stared up at him as expectantly as a cat awaiting a bowl of cream, her gaze sweeping his face. Jake was used to people who encountered him for the first time being either put off by or curious about his scar. It drew neither reaction from this nurse. He supposed she'd seen as much of the seamier side of life as he had. "Laura Jean Whittaker—with two *t*s."

"Address?"

"I—er…" Their reunion this morning hadn't included exchanging addresses. He shrugged. "I don't know."

"Okay. Can you tell me what happened? What caused her injuries?"

"She was standing near a car that exploded."

The nurse's eyes widened at this. "Drive-by shootings, exploding cars." She tsked. "World's tough enough without folks making it worse on themselves and all their neighbors."

As she typed, Jake recalled a car bombing he'd seen in

L.A. He'd need confirmation, but if pressed now he'd say that was exactly the fate met by the Corvette. The fact rattled his solid belief that Laura had lied at every turn. Was there a grain of truth in what she'd said about someone trying to kill her for the past twelve months?

Was that the reason she'd run away from their wedding? The thought pained him. God, how he wished he could believe it. But it just didn't explain the note she'd written him when she eloped with Cullen. And her behavior this morning proved her mental instability. For all he knew, she was deranged enough to blow up the Corvette herself.

The nurse cleared her throat. "I said, I don't suppose you'd know if Ms. Whittaker is allergic to any medications?"

"Actually, I do know that—she's allergic to penicillin."

The nurse's gray eyebrows lifted slightly. She was likely wondering why he didn't know something as mundane as where Laura lived, but did know something as personal as what drugs she should avoid.

He squirmed inwardly. "How soon before we know something?"

"In a little while. Would you also know if Ms. Whittaker has medical insurance?"

Last year she'd been covered by the company policy held by Dell Pharmaceuticals. That wouldn't be viable now. He shook his head. "Sorry."

"She didn't happen to have a purse with her? You see, we could look in her wallet for her address and insurance information. Someone she'd like notified."

Jake's stomach lurched. Laura's purse was in his car. He could easily hand it over to this woman. But what would she find inside? The stun gun? The wig? False identities? Better to hold off on that. He lied, "No. I didn't see one."

"Well, I guess that's it for now. Why don't you have a seat. I'm sure the doctor will be out to speak with you soon."

Jake turned toward the empty row of plastic chairs lined against the wall. Impatience and worry nipped at him. He settled on the edge of the seat closest to the exit. He should go out to the Cherokee and look through Laura's purse himself. If her injuries were as serious as he feared, she'd probably want Cullen notified. It would be the right thing to do. The decent thing.

LAURA FELT as though she'd collided with a wall of concrete. Her head ached, her ears rang, her eyes seemed swollen shut. She tried prying them open, but the bright shaft of light she encountered stung. She slammed them shut again. Oddly, she imagined she'd seen someone standing over her, someone with the face she'd missed every day for a whole year.

Jake's face.

Dear God, was she dreaming? Or dead? She prayed she was dreaming. If she was dead and seeing Jake, that meant he was dead, too.

Her heart squeezed at the thought and she pried her eyes open again, determined to keep them open this time. Her gaze landed on the figure beside the bed. It *was* Jake. She murmured, "Are we dead?"

He looked startled at the question. Then he burst out laughing. The sound echoed with relief, as though he'd dreaded receiving bad news and been given the opposite. "No. We're in a hospital."

She glanced beyond him. She was in the bed nearest the hallway door of a four-bed ward. The other beds were empty. The style and structure of the room told her this was not one of the modern facilities being built these days, but someone had attempted to make it cheery by painting the walls a mellow green and adding splashes of pastel in the patterned curtains.

A bathroom door hung open between the two beds facing hers. Bright sunlight poked through the blinds covering the single large window, splintering soft yellow rays across everything.

Jake said, "You've got a few stitches in your leg and a slight concussion."

Brutal memory flooded her. She lurched forward, thinking to sit up, and instantly regretted it as pain zinged through her skull. Sinking back on the pillow, she clutched her head in both hands. "The car..."

"Yes." There was something guarded yet speculative in his voice. "If I'm not mistaken...it was a bomb."

"A...a bomb?" Her throat constricted. She shuddered. No wonder Jake had been worried. A few steps closer to the Corvette and she might not have awakened.

She struggled to her elbows. Her head protested, the pain a hammer at each temple. But fear drove her through it. She'd been expecting *him*. Just not this soon. Had *he* followed them to the hospital?

Ignoring her splitting headache, she tossed aside the covers. "We've got to get out of here."

"Whoa." Jake lunged forward, catching her as she pitched from the bed. "Where do you think you're going?"

"'Where' doesn't matter—just away from here. Quickly. Secretly." She shook off his grip and stepped away from him. The room spun. She blinked and flailed her arms, seeking balance. One of her open hands connected with Jake's chest, but the leverage was precarious.

"You aren't leaving." He pulled her to him. Her head

swam, and her hand caught, splayed on his chest. He held her still, close in his solid embrace.

In that moment, she felt a rush of relief, felt safer than she had in a year. She gave in to the encompassing warmth, pressing against him. Gradually her equilibrium steadied, but her body trembled with a new, more frightening emotion: longing. She knew the danger of this was as life-threatening as the man determined to kill her.

"The doctor," Jake said, his voice husky against her ear, "wants you to stay put tonight. I'd say that's a wise idea."

She felt his heart hammering against her palm. She lifted her head and as their gazes met the beat leaped, marching in rhythm with her pulse. There was genuine concern in his eyes, in every hard line of his face, and in that moment she forgot all about the need to flee.

She stammered, "I—I didn't think you cared what happened to me."

He stiffened. "I don't."

But she could see it was a lie. A lie he might never admit. Her throat ached. Could he ever love her as he once had? As she still loved him? Could either of them ever trust that completely again? The terrifying urgency overwhelmed her anew. She shoved from Jake's arms. The room reeled, then went black.

IN AN EVER-BLACKENING rage, Laura's pursuer dialed the last number on the list of hospitals and morgues, then listened impatiently to the ringing phone.

"Saguaro County General." The woman's voice sounded young, bored. "Emergency."

The pursuer pressed the cloth over the cell phone, speaking in a husky tone that might be male or female. "Have you admitted a woman today by the name of Laura Whittaker?''

A snapping noise, as though the nurse were chewing bubble gum, issued through the line. "Laura Whittaker? Let's see."

Hurry up! The killer scowled as the moon crept higher into the evening sky.

Finally the nurse said, "Yes, she's been admitted and will be spending the night for observation. She's in room 304, bed 1. Would you like me to connect you?''

"I'd rather pay her a visit."

"Okay…um, I'm sorry, though. Visiting hours ended ten minutes ago.''

But the killer had hung up. Observation? Laura was basically unharmed? The damned woman had more lives than a cat. Well, no more. The killer growled. She'd just reached number nine.

A glance at the map located the quickest route to Saguaro County General. The engine of the stolen florist's delivery van hummed to life. A gun rested within easy reach. "I'm through fooling with you, Laura. The only thing the doctor will be observing about you tonight is your dead body.''

Chapter Five

Laura opened her eyes. She was tucked into the hospital bed, the covers pulled to her chin. Night pressed the window and a faint light crept beneath the closed bathroom door. The dim bulb over her bed cast the large room in shadow, but she could see the bed across from her had been disturbed.

Dear God, had she been out for hours? Certainly long enough and hard enough so that another patient moving into the bed across from hers hadn't disturbed her. Where was her new roommate? How long had she been gone? How soon before she returned? Panic washed over her. She probably had mere minutes to get out of here without being caught.

She lurched forward, relieved to find her headache mellowed to a dull throb, the room no longer tilting with every movement. She swept aside the covers. Except for a faded hospital gown, she was naked.

Was this all she'd worn when Jake held her earlier? The thought brought back memories she couldn't deal with right now—no more than she could deal with the fact that Jake had once more abandoned her to the mercy of a determined killer. There wasn't time for self-pity. She had to get dressed.

A man moved from behind the curtain of the next bed.
She yelped. Her heart kicked her rib cage. For a split second, she couldn't move. Thought she was dead. Then recognition hit, and she nearly buckled with relief. "Jake!
Thank God!"

He stepped toward her. "I've been waiting for you to
wake up."

"Good. I'm better." She swung her legs over the bed
and stood, becoming aware for the first time of the stinging
pain on her calf. A bandage covered the achy area. God,
when she thought of how much worse she could have been
hurt... She shook herself. "It'll only take me a minute to
dress."

"I told you you aren't going anywhere tonight. You
have a lot of questions to answer." His soft expression
hardened.

He sounded more like a jailer than a concerned friend.
The thought gave her pause. Questions to answer? To him?
Or someone else? Had he called the cops? Her panic
climbed.

"With or without your help, I'm leaving here as soon
as I'm dressed." Conscious of her backless gown, she bent
toward the metal closet separating her bed from the next
one. The only thing in it was her high heels. "Where are
my clothes?"

"They had to cut them off."

She swore. "What am I supposed to wear?"

"If you'll give me your motel room key, I'll go and get
you another outfit."

She blanched and glanced down at the hospital gown.
"Those were the only clothes I had." He muttered something she didn't catch as she grabbed her shoes and put
them on. Feeling totally silly in pumps and regulation hos-

pital garb, she spun to face him, one hand outstretched. "Give me your jacket. Hurry! We have to leave now."

He crossed his arms, but seemed to struggle to keep his expression stern. His gaze traveled the length of her, an old warmth lighting their teal depths. "I'm not lending you my jacket and I'm not taking you out of here tonight. But I will pick you up some sweats and tennis shoes in the morning. After that you're on your own."

"The hell with that." She swept past him, rushed to the locker of her new roommate and flung the door open. A brightly colored polyester pantsuit hung there. She reached for it.

"Hey," Jake protested, grabbing her arm. "What are you doing?"

She glared at him. "I'm borrowing some clothes."

"No, you're not." He grabbed the hanger from her, returned it to the hook and closed the closet door firmly.

She blew out a breath and shifted her weight to one hip, holding the gown together at the back. "Why are you being so uncooperative? Don't tell me you *still* don't believe someone is after me."

Jake sobered. He started to say something, then clamped his mouth shut. He was blocking her path to the door. She took a step to the side. He matched it. She heard noises in the hallway, voices coming their way.

Alarmed, she pleaded, "Jake, please. It could be him." Or, she thought trembling inside, the cops.

"Get back into bed."

"No." She tried getting around him again. He was too quick. Too determined to keep her there. Laura's impatience and fear ignited her temper. "Is this because I didn't marry you last year?"

He blanched. "No. It's not."

She pursed her lips. He was lying as surely as she was

half-naked. She understood he'd been angry and probably embarrassed as hell when she hadn't shown up at the church, but she'd run away only to keep herself from being murdered. How could that be unforgivable?

She bit down her anxiety. But couldn't swallow her temper as readily. "Then what is it, Jake? You say you don't want anything to do with me, and yet you've spent the afternoon beside my hospital bed as though I might expire at any moment. What are you still doing here?"

He blinked as if she'd struck a nerve. "I—I want to find out what happened at the motel."

She grabbed the opportunity to duck around him. She hurried to the door, but he grasped her upper arm, stopping her completely, whirling her to face him.

She shook free of his grip, careening back, bumping her bare bottom against the cold doorknob. She flinched. "Damn it, I told you what happened. Someone tried killing me. And if you don't let me leave, he'll try again."

Disbelief reddened Jake's face.

Renewed desperation tore at Laura. The voices were getting louder. Coming closer. She cracked the door open and peered out. A gurney was being wheeled into a neighboring room by a man in surgical garb. Two nurses followed. From the sound of it, they were settling the patient into the room. Laura let out a whimper of relief.

She pulled the door open farther. Jake caught her arm again. "Get back into bed."

"No." She tugged out of his grasp.

"If you don't get back in that bed now, I'll put you there myself."

Her anxiety doubled. She knew he could overpower her any time he wanted. Where was the stun gun when she needed it? Still nestled in her purse. But her purse hadn't been in the hospital closet. God knows what had become of it. And her meager cash.

She took a step toward him, scrambling for a plan, pretending to give in to him. "Okay."

Behind him, the door to the bathroom banged open. An elderly woman stood outlined there, hanging on to the jamb, apparently the new roommate. "Young man, I'm ready. Could you help me back to the bed now?"

Jake wheeled around.

Laura slipped into the hall. A nurse was entering a room two doors farther down, her back to Laura. Laura took off in the other direction. Ahead she could see a deserted nurses' station. Someone with an armload of flowers emerged from one of the elevators beyond.

From this distance, she couldn't tell if it was man or woman. Weren't visiting hours over? Wasn't it too late for floral deliveries? Fear galvanized her. Trapped her like a caged animal. Danger was ahead and behind.

Desperate, she ducked into the nearest doorway and leaned against the wall. Her pulse raced out of control. She closed her eyes, willing herself to calm down. As her heartbeat steadied, she opened her eyes and took in her surroundings, realizing she was in the very place she'd sought. A supply closet.

With a grin tugging her mouth, she hastened over to a shelf piled high with more gowns like the one she wore and with pajamas and scrubs.

Behind her, the door opened. Laura froze, her heart climbing her throat as the door shut with a click as soft and final as the lid of a coffin. Cold flushed her skin.

"There you are," Jake growled.

She wheeled around, relief tripping through her, followed by the urge to do him bodily harm. "Dear God,

Jake," she railed at him in a fierce whisper. "Stop sneaking up on me!"

He crossed to her and caught her by the arm, his grip tighter than before, his voice, too. "Do I have to call security?"

Laura blew out a taut breath. "Jake, think! Would I be this determined to leave if I wasn't terrified?"

He frowned hard, appearing finally to realize she meant what she said. He studied her face for a moment, holding her as tight as ever, as though releasing her would somehow mean relinquishing his grip on this situation. "Would it make you feel better if I stayed outside your room all night?"

"No." How did she make him understand? Neither of them controlled what would happen if she stayed here long enough to be caught. "He'll go through anyone to get to me. I don't want your blood on my conscience, too."

"Stubborn…" He bit out the word, then let it hang between them, a judgment to her tenacity. *Stubborn as Farmer Handley's mule.* That's what he'd called her since she was ten. It was the first sign that she'd finally dented his resistance.

He released a sigh of his own, longer, louder and more full of resignation than hers. "Fine. I'm tired of arguing with you. I'll take you wherever you want to go."

"Really?" She glanced at his hand that still held her upper arm in a death grip.

He released her and stepped back. "Really."

"Thank you." Rubbing her arm, she turned back toward the clothes shelf.

"Pick something quick," Jake said, a grin in his voice. "Your, um, best asset is flapping in the wind."

A heated blush swept Laura and she grabbed the back of the gown together. "A gentleman wouldn't notice."

"I quit being a gentleman a year ago."

No, you haven't, she thought, glancing over her shoulder to find he'd turned his back. *You just don't realize it.* A twinge for what they'd lost tweaked her heart. Perhaps he coped better believing himself as tough and ornery as he looked. But somewhere beneath the hard exterior her old Jake still existed. Would he ever emerge again?

"I thought you were in a hurry," he said, startling her out of her dark reverie.

She returned to the shelf, gathering a pair of green pants with a drawstring closure and a matching pullover top. She stepped into the pants, then tossed aside the gown and lifted the top over her head. She still felt silly in her pumps, but at least now she could travel the streets without being arrested for indecent exposure. "Let's go."

"Wait a minute." Jake slipped off his jacket and offered it to her.

She raised her eyebrows questioningly.

"It will look more like you're getting off work," he explained.

"Thanks." Touched by his unexpected gesture, Laura accepted the coat and slipped it on. It hung to her mid-thigh, the sleeves to the middle of her hands, but she shoved the cuffs over her wrists and squared her shoulders. She'd adopted an array of personae the past year, "surgical-nurse-in-bomber-jacket" should be one of the easier ones to carry off.

The difficulty came with her first breath. The jacket not only held Jake's warmth, it held his scent, a mind-jarring mixture of mint and man. Her man. And therein lay the trouble. He wasn't her man. Not anymore. Their gazes met and something tentative passed between them, something that made him swallow hard enough to jostle his Adam's apple.

His eyes darkened and he reached for the door. "Ready?"

Alarmed, she sprang forward and stopped him, her hand landing on his. "Careful."

What was he thinking? Caution was his business. Second nature to him. He drew his hand from beneath hers as though she'd burned him. "Lead on."

Hurt brushed her heart. She ignored it. Her life was at stake. Later, she could feel sorry for all that she'd lost. As long as she hadn't lost her life. She nudged the door open a couple of inches and peered out into the hallway.

Again it was deserted. But footsteps were coming toward them, clipping along the hall from the direction of her abandoned room. The image of the florist who'd arrived after visiting hours flashed inexplicably into her mind. Someone to fear? Someone looking for her? Was it *him?* Or was she being paranoid?

"Come on." She tugged Jake by the arm, hurrying him into the hall. She'd rather be wrong than dead.

A nurse sat behind the station desk, talking softly into the phone. She glanced up absently, then bent her head back to the chart she was writing on. Laura's pulse echoed in her ears as loudly as her heels clicking the hard, polished floor.

Near the elevators a second nurse emerged from the pharmacy, pushing a cart loaded with little white paper cups, the kind used to deliver prescribed medications to patients. She also gave them only a cursory once-over. Her mind was obviously on her job.

Laura stole a glance behind them and spotted someone shuffling covertly into a door near the nurses' station. The same supply closet they'd just vacated. Her skin prickled.

She pulled Jake into the stairwell. "I think I just saw him."

"What?" Jake jerked back toward the stairway door. "Where?"

"Ducking into the supply closet."

Jake's face darkened and a keen glint shone from his eyes. As though his instincts had finally kicked in, he took a solid grip of her arm and rushed her faster down the concrete stairs. Scrambling to keep from stumbling, Laura felt the blood singing through her head. Somehow she managed to keep her balance and actually welcomed the cold night air on her face as they exited the building.

She scanned the lit parking area. "Where's your car?"

"In back. By emergency. That way." Jake hurried her around the side of the building.

A bright-yellow florist's van sat near the emergency room entrance, a Saguaro County police car parked to block its departure. Two uniformed cops stepped toward them.

Laura released a tight yip. She rammed to a stop, began pivoting, meant to run back the way they'd just come.

"No." Jake caught her elbow and cautioned in a hissing whisper, "You'll look suspicious. Keep moving."

He propelled her forward. Her feet moved clumsily. As she and Jake came alongside the police car, one of the cops waylaid them.

"Evening, sir, ma'am."

"Officers." Jake smiled.

"You folks see the person driving this van?"

Laura's legs felt as wobbly as a toddler's. The cops weren't here looking for her. But were they looking for the florist? She didn't know whether to be relieved or more frightened.

"Nope," Jake said. "That van wasn't here when I arrived to pick her up from work. That's my car. Third one down."

The policeman glanced over to where he pointed and nodded.

"I'm Jake Wilder. BMW Securities." He handed the cop his credentials. "What's the problem?"

The cop studied his papers, then returned his wallet. "It's a stolen vehicle."

"I see. Well, I guess we should get out of your way." Jake reached for Laura's arm again, and realized she was shivering.

"Why don't you give me your card, Mr. Wilder," the taller of the cops said. "In case we need to talk to you further."

"Sure." Jake turned to Laura and handed her his keys. "Go get in the car. I'll be right there."

"No," she mouthed, fear bright in her eyes.

"You're freezing," he whispered, curling her fingers over the keys. "Quit being stubborn and listen to me for once."

She glanced nervously back at the hospital, at the cops, then spun on her heel, hurried to his car and let herself in.

A moment later, he was opening the driver's door. The interior light illuminated the inside of the car. The keys hung in the ignition. But Laura's purse was gone.

And so was she.

Chapter Six

Headlights swept the expansive adobe house that seemed sculpted from the desert hillside it hugged. The circular drive was framed by tall cacti and shorter flowering scrub brush. No lawn, no grass like the Wilder house in Riverdell; this yard grew huge rock formations, their designs man-made, calculated, artistic, resplendent.

Shivering in the cold night, Laura hunkered behind a plump saguaro, the beams of light brushing the air around her. The garage door rumbled open. The car slowed. A dim light from within spilled across the tarmac, illuminating the car and its driver, both of them known to her.

She released a shuddery breath.

Brake lights glowed red as the vehicle edged into the garage. She stole in behind it, ducking quickly beneath the descending door. Her heart thundered against her chest, making swallowing difficult.

He shut off the engine, but continued sitting in the car. She saw reflected in the rearview mirror that his eyebrows were drawn into a tight frown as though his thoughts consumed him. The only sound in the garage: the ticktock of the cooling motor. Then the door latch clicked, and she ran her tongue across her dry lips, shrugging deeper into his jacket.

He stepped out.

"Jake?"

He jolted around. His eyes widened then narrowed. "Where...the...hell...?" Each word choked from him, bitten off, bitter. His warm eyes grew glacial, turning dark blue, like the center of an icicle.

She'd expected he'd be ticked, offended even, but this was so much more it startled her.

He moved toward her, deliberately, one step at a time, a stalking wild cat, an avenging devil. Although she'd seen him angry before, never had the anger been directed at her. "Jake, I—"

The words died on her tongue. He seemed ready to throttle her, his fingers curling and uncurling at his side. His eyes opened wider, the teal now hot as a storm-roiled sea, dazzling and dangerous, churning with hate and fury and even an inexplicable speck of fear.

She wondered at the fear. Heat climbed her face. Cold swept from her neck downward. She felt as though she were drowning, a hapless swimmer who'd wandered into unsafe waters and was now being sucked into the undertow. She'd crossed some invisible line tonight. Pushed him too far. Set him off. She moved away from him, shoved backward by his silent rage, the force of it like giant hands thrusting her away. "You have to understand..."

He didn't speak, just kept coming at her, the energy issuing from him like a river at spring thaw, rampaging. She bumped against the plaster-boarded wall as he closed in and pinned her there without laying a finger on her.

His scar stood bold on his cheek, intensifying his fearsome expression. He laid his palms against the wall on either side of her head and leaned his face to within inches of hers, his heated breath a slap on her mouth. She could barely swallow, but she made herself say, "I—I'm sorry I took off like that."

"Do you have any idea the trouble you've caused?" He snorted. "Do you even care?"

Trouble? She'd caused? For whom? Him? What kind of trouble? When he stood this close she couldn't reason, couldn't hold the old feelings at bay. Couldn't deny them. She blinked hard as a sudden heat crashed through her. "I...I was afraid."

"That's your excuse for everything."

He spat in disgust, his words hot sparks against her mouth, pulling her gaze to his mouth, stirring memories of those lips on hers, on her. She swallowed hard. He leaned impossibly closer.

"What about *my* fear?"

"Your...?" She lifted her gaze to his, and in his broiling emotion she saw it again, that fear she hadn't understood a moment ago, but she recognized it now: the fear one feels for something beloved and lost. Did he feel that about her? Had he been afraid for her? "You were afraid?"

"God, Laura—" His voice cracked with pain.

The agony in his tone rent the dike of self-protection she'd built around herself this past year, opening a vulnerable gash across her heart, and need as intense as the tides ripped through the gap, dragging her against him. The contact electrified her flesh from head to toe. She felt the whole length of him tense in response.

Yet he didn't pull way. Didn't reach for her, either. Just supported her without holding her. His chest began rising and falling quicker than before, as though he ached to set her away, but hadn't the strength or the desire to purposely touch her. She drew a ragged breath and lifted her arms, brought them swiftly around him and hugged his broad back. A long weighty sigh slipped through her lips.

A tortured groan sounded in his throat.

She raised her head and found him leaning back, his eyes closed, his face a grimace of internal agony. Her heart skipped a beat; her pulse danced higher. She curled her fingers into his hair and gently tugged.

He opened his eyes and she read confusion and desire and self-reproach in them. He shook his head. "No, Laura—"

Ignoring his protest, she offered her lips to him, motioning without word or gesture, something unspoken, something so personal between them their hungry spirits understood. Their lips touched, one tender feathering sweep, and need rushed in to deepen the contact, a connection too long denied, too fierce to be destroyed by time and distance, by the connivance of others.

Like one of the desert flowers in his garden opening to the sun, Laura opened to Jake, first her lips, then her heart, then her mind, as she welcomed his rejuvenating heat, matched his life-stirring passion touch for touch, tingle for tingle.

Jake groaned, a low, sensuous moan that sent shards of desire spiking through her. She traced every inch of his back, from shoulder to buttocks, again and again, and with each downward sweep of her hands, she pulled him closer, wanted to pull him into her, ached to feel him inside her, here and now.

He pinned her to the wall again, this time with his body, plunged deeper into her mouth with his tongue, and with bold hands stroked her hips, her thighs, her bottom, his touch ardent, fevered, needy.

"Oh, Jake..." she whispered.

He pulled away, as breathless as a terrified crime victim.

His chest heaved. He lurched back, held his hands up and away from her. "What the hell are we doing? What the hell am I?"

Also breathless, Laura stepped toward him, reached for him. "Jake—"

"No." He moved farther back, his expression reeking self-disgust. "I've been caught in your spider's web once too often today. No more."

"But I—"

"No." He cut her off, holding a palm toward her, a warning to keep her mouth shut. "I told you I'd take you wherever you wanted to go, so why did you run off?"

She heaved a sigh, still trying to catch her breath, to steady her pulse, her trembling knees. "What do want me to say? I already told you I was afraid. Whoever was driving that florist's van at the hospital came to kill me."

Jake jammed his fingers through his short, golden blond hair. "Did you get a look at his face? Do you even know if it was a man?"

"No."

"Then you don't know who was driving that van." He wasn't asking her; he was telling her. An accusation. "Or why they stole it and left it at the emergency entrance."

But she did know. In her heart. Exasperated, she glared at him. "Never mind."

"No. I'm tired of that game. I want some answers and I want them now. You can either come inside and give them to me, or you can hit the road for good."

Laura stared at him, his finger poised over the automatic garage door button. Anger stood on his face as fresh as it had been before their kiss. She sensed, however, that this anger wasn't about her leaving him at the hospital. This anger was old, twelve months old.

The self-preservation part of her wanted to "hit the road

for good.'' But she couldn't cut and run. Not this time.
Not after that kiss. She had to find out if Jake could love
and trust her, again. As much as he'd wanted her moments
ago, his passion had had nothing to do with love and trust,
but with anger and need—a need to prove something to
both of them. She could see that need lingering in his
narrowed eyes.

She started toward him. ''We should talk.''

Jake's eyes widened and he nodded, a glint of satisfaction in the corners of his mouth, as though he'd won some
important point in a game of wits. Laura wondered if he'd
feel the same an hour from now.

He gestured for her to precede him into the house. The
garage opened into a laundry room with a tiled floor and
gleaming white appliances. The faint homey odor of soap
and fabric softener filled her nostrils, but the pleasant scent
couldn't calm her anxiety at entering Jake's home for the
first time. A home without memories of her.

She waited for Jake to turn on the lights, then trailed
after him into a restaurant-sized kitchen where rust-colored
adobe tile and gleaming chrome dominated. The house had
been impressive outside, but inside it was incredible, huge,
expensive, masculine, inviting.

An eating bar with four rough-hewn stools appealed to
her weary limbs, her throbbing head. She trudged toward
them, her gaze surveying the rest of her surroundings. A
table and chairs similar to the bar stools divided the
kitchen from a massive sunken family room. Pale leather
couches, wearing Navajo throws, hugged either side of a
ceiling-high adobe fireplace. Clay pots and bronze artwork
occupied tables and corners with the ease of belonging that
she did not feel in Jake's home.

The windows were sheets of glass held in place by giant
unfinished beams, displaying the lights of the mingled

towns below as though the Milky Way had fallen to Earth and now twinkled up from a black velvet cloth.

This house spoke of wealth, the kind of wealth she'd never associated with the Wilders of Riverdell. Jake sure hadn't paid for all this from money saved on a cop's salary. She shrugged out of his coat, then placed it on the seat of one of the stools and edged her hip onto another. "Your new business must be a gold mine."

He looked at her oddly. "It's profitable."

He went straight to a cupboard, pulled out two chimney glasses. From the refrigerator, he gathered orange juice, ice cubes and a bottle of 7UP for a drink they'd shared a fondness for as far back as she could recall. He hadn't even asked if she wanted something. Just assumed.

It warmed her. She watched in silence as he settled the ingredients on the counter. Still reeling inwardly from their kiss, she couldn't stifle old images of Jake's possessive way with her, with her body. Jealousy reared inside her at the thought of other women enjoying his special touches, nurturing his wounded heart. How many had there been this past year? Was there one now? Someone special? Bile rose in her throat, twisted her stomach.

Jake watched Laura from beneath his lowered lids as he poured orange juice over the ice cubes. Half an hour ago, he'd decided he was better off with her gone. Out of his life permanently. Finally. And glad to be rid of her. But damn it all, what the hell had happened in the garage just now? He'd like to put it down to residual feelings, a few smoldering ashes that hadn't cooled in the past year. But he was scared to death it might be more. "How'd you get here?"

"Taxi."

"How did you know where I lived?"

"You're listed in the phone book." She tossed her head, making her shimmery hair sway across her shoulders.

He felt a jab of desire in his groin and pressed his lips together, went back to adding 7UP to both glasses. God, he was a Grade A jackass. He might still be willing to bed Laura, but he didn't love her anymore. Without trust, there was no love. And he didn't trust her...in or out of his sight. Everything she'd done reenforced that.

On the other hand, someone *had* blown up the Corvette. Someone *had* meant to kill her. Maybe her paranoia about the florist's van wasn't so far-fetched.

Then again, how the hell had she avoided being hurt worse than she was? The bomb hadn't been rigged to the ignition. Otherwise she'd have been behind the wheel when it blew. Had it been a time-activated bomb? He stirred the mixture and slid one of the drinks across the counter to her.

Laura thanked him, curling her fingers around the damp glass.

How would someone guarantee she'd be in the car at a given time? He studied her delicate hands and had an ugly thought. Had she learned to make a bomb in the past year? Would she go to that much trouble to convince him that someone was trying to kill her? The idea contradicted everything he'd known about this woman before she left Riverdell. But then, the woman he'd thought she was would never have run off with another man.

She was staring at him. "Where do you want to start?"

He took a sip of the tangy concoction, thinking he should add a shot or two of vodka to it. "Why don't you tell me who this 'he' is that you insist is trying to kill you?"

Laura lifted her brows slightly. If she knew *that* she'd have told him immediately. "I—"

"Is it Cullen?"

"Cullen?" She frowned at him, the suggestion so unexpected it disoriented her. She knew only one Cullen and she couldn't imagine Jake meant him. "Cullen Crocker?"

Something about her response seemed to throw him. Jake set down his glass and glanced away from her. "Look, if you want to call him, you can use that phone."

Why would she want to call Cullen Crocker? she wondered, her confusion growing. "Maybe my brains got rattled a little more than I thought—because you're not making a whole lot of sense. Why would I want to call someone you think might be trying to kill me?"

"I didn't mean to imply..." He blew out a breath, crossed to another cupboard and pulled out a bottle of vodka, then added a huge dollop to his glass. "I sh— would have called him earlier, but I don't remember the number."

"Well, neither do I."

His head jerked up and concern shone in his eyes. "Because of the concussion?"

"No. Because I haven't called him recently." She fingered her temple, knowing she'd be glad when the dull ache stopped completely, wishing the confusion would stop, too. "If you really want Cullen's phone number, you can probably get it from Riverdell information.

He cocked his head to one side and she'd have sworn his expression of befuddlement matched the one controlling her own features. Then he planted both palms flat on the counter and leaned toward her. "You know damned good and well that Cullen is not in Riverdell."

Her mouth dropped open. She shut it, then shook her head. "I left Riverdell a year ago. How would I know what Cullen Crocker was or was not doing?"

"Because you left with him."

She came off the stool as though pulled by an invisible rope. "I what?"

"You heard me."

Her hands landed on her hips. "I did no such thing, Jake Wilder."

He slapped the tile countertop, glowering at her. "Laura, I don't know what kind of game you're playing now, but I got the note."

Note? Did he mean the note she'd sent in the package of evidence? Had he had the evidence all along? Dared she hope? "What note?"

"The 'Dear Jake' letter you sent me on our wedding day." His voice low and menacing, he closed the distance between them and she felt his hot breath on her mouth again. Her pulse skipped. He said, "Nice of you to let me know you were eloping with another man."

"E-eloping?" Laura flinched, feeling as though he'd slugged her with a closed fist—something Jake would never do to any woman. Annoyance brought her inches closer to him. "Jake, I did *not* send you a note when I left. I didn't have time. And I certainly didn't elope—especially not with Cullen Crocker."

She couldn't believe this. Cullen? Oh, the lab assistant *was* gloriously handsome—in a dark, perfect sort of way that had never appealed to her. Besides, Izzy Dell, her best friend, was the one who'd set her cap for him.

She started to remind Jake of this, but the hurt in his eyes stopped her cold. In that moment, Laura realized the depth of pain he'd suffered from believing that she'd chosen a drop-dead gorgeous man over him, and she knew the scar from that wound cut a swath deeper and meaner than the one on his face.

He seemed to realize he was standing too close and took a step backward. Impotent rage gripped her. When she found the person responsible for ruining their lives—he or she would be lucky to make it to trial. "Cullen and I were friends, Jake. Period." She took a half step toward him. "I'm so sorry—"

"I don't want your pity," he interrupted her, halting her approach.

"We were friends." She shook her head. "That's all."

God, how Jake wanted to believe that. So much so, he hated himself for the weakness. He stared long and hard into her eyes. She didn't blink. Didn't back down. He'd swear she wasn't lying. But could he trust his instincts where Laura was concerned? Was she the unstable woman who'd kidnaped him this morning? Who'd run off from the hospital without so much as a note to ease his worry? Or was fear making her desperate?

He wished he knew. Wished he'd looked through her purse when he'd had the opportunity. But he hadn't had the guts.

Since she'd removed that wig and he'd realized who she was, his logic had been at the whim of his emotions, tugged this way and that. Damn. Had she left with Cullen or not? Had she sent him that note or not? If she hadn't...if she was telling the truth... "Then where is Cullen?"

She shrugged. "I thought he was still in Riverdell. Still working for Dell Pharmaceuticals."

"No, he left the same day and time as you. As far as I know, no one's heard from him since."

"No one?" She frowned. "Are you sure?"

He scrubbed his jaw. "I haven't asked about him, you know?"

"But we must," Laura insisted. "Right away."

"Why?" He scowled, his old jealousy of Cullen lingering like the foul odor of spilled whiskey in oak planking.

"Why?" She gaped at him. "The Crockers are tight-knit. If we'd run off as you thought, Cullen would have brought his 'new bride' home to their loving fold months ago. At the very least, he'd have contacted the family. In this day and age—even in a town the size of Riverdell—gossip would soon die. It certainly wouldn't result in permanent banishment."

Jake sank to the bar stool she'd abandoned. She was right. This made sense in ways he hadn't considered. If he hadn't been so hell-bent on hatred, he'd have realized it himself. Sooner. "Maybe he's turned up and Kim didn't want to tell me."

"I think we should call his brother Travis and ask him if Cullen has ever contacted the family."

He looked at her, their eyes locking for a long moment. Finally he nodded.

Hope took seed in Laura's heart. "Then you believe me?"

"Well, someone planted a bomb in that Corvette. Someone who was either after you or Sunny Devlin."

The mention of Sunny Devlin startled her. Then she recalled he'd gotten into the Corvette. Of course he'd checked the registration. Once a cop... "Why would anyone be after Sunny Devlin?"

He shrugged. "Private detectives get in all kinds of situations with all types of bad guys. Maybe she did."

"Private detectives?" Laura's eyes widened. "Sunny was a P.I.?"

"You didn't know?"

"No."

"I thought you'd hired her to find me."

"No."

"Then how did you come by her car?" He frowned, as though something had just occurred to him. "Did you say *was* a P.I.—as in past tense? Why isn't she one any longer?''

Laura swallowed hard as the memories of her burning beach house filled her head and tears stung her eyes. ''He killed her.''

Chapter Seven

"He killed her." The dull throb at Laura's temples mounted quickly as repugnant memories swam through her mind. She'd managed somehow the past two days to stifle the image of her burning beach house, the sickening stench of fire-ravaged wood, melting metal. And the god-awful horror of Sunny Devlin's fate. She shuddered.

The room spun. Laura reached for the counter to steady herself. Her hand collided with her drink. The glass skidded toward Jake. Its contents flew at Laura, ice cubes and all.

"Aw!" She gasped, lurching back as the cold liquid hit. It scattered her repulsive reverie, splattered her face and drenched her borrowed clothing, melding the fatigued fabric to her breasts, her tummy, her legs.

Jake leaped for the glass as it flew off the edge of the bar, hung airborne for a split second, then pitched for the floor. He bobbled it, bouncing it on his palms like a ball in a juggler's act, then he landed on the floor in a sprawled heap, catching the glass an inch before it struck the tile. "Whew!"

He gazed up at her, triumph on his face. Then he seemed to realize that 7UP and orange juice dripped from her nose, her chin, matted the worn scrubs she wore, flecked the tips of her pointed pumps. A smile tugged at his mouth and she knew he wanted to laugh.

Laura couldn't contain her own giggle; it ripped free, one high hysterical peel, then another and another, until Jake began to snicker, then chuckle, then guffaw. For two full minutes, their uncontrolled laughter echoed through his kitchen, as it had once echoed through his mother's, often, and long, long ago.

Holding her sides, Laura said, "Remember when we spilled the jar of popcorn?"

Jake chortled. "You thought the lid was on tight and pretended to throw it at me."

"And kernels flew across the room." Like two hundred BBs skittering into every pristine corner of Ruthanne Wilder's farm-sized kitchen. They'd been twelve, and Laura was so embarrassed she'd wanted the floor to open and pull her in; she'd wanted to cry. She wanted to cry now. In fact, that last giggle sounded more like a sob than laughter. She drew a ragged, sniffly breath, worried that if she gave in to the tears burning her eyes, she might never stop.

Jake's smile fell. He struggled to his feet, his expression sobering as if he'd just recalled where he was, who he was laughing with. The tension that had, for a brief moment disappeared, rose between them like a plate-glass wall.

Laura shivered, uncertain what she feared most from this man. His distance? Or his closeness? He made no move toward her after setting the glass on the bar. But his gaze rolled impertinently over her from head to toe, giving new life to the sensuous feelings roused during their encounter in the garage.

She ran her tongue over her mouth, tasting orange juice, and a teeny flavor that was all Jake. She swallowed hard, willing that thought away. But it refused to go, and she felt desire stirring inside her, answering the silent call in his darkening eyes.

She shivered again, aware for the first time that her wet top outlined her nipples, which stood hard and sensitive against the worn fabric, responding in equal doses to the cold and his gaze. She plucked at the fabric. "Where's your bathroom?"

"Down the hall," he croaked. "You'd better shower. I'll toss those scrubs in the wash."

A hot shower sounded wonderful to Laura's ragged spirit, her aching limbs. "I'll need something else to wear."

His gaze rolled over her again as intimately as any touch. He cleared his throat, slowly brought his eyes up to hers. "I don't know what I've got that will fit you."

His heated gaze reminded her that she hadn't so much as a stitch of underwear to call her own. A blush climbed her neck. Except for the contents of her purse, she had lost everything to her pursuer. She fought a growl of impotent rage, and made a mental note to keep one extra outfit, including bra and panties, in her shoulder bag from that point on...until her pursuer was arrested. "Anything dry will do. Sweats?"

Jake grinned wryly. "They're extra long, extra large and would probably fall off of you."

The blush reached her cheeks. "A T-shirt, then. Preferably something dark, with a high neckline."

A look of sheer discomfort twitched his eyebrows, as though he recalled the dozens of times she'd donned one of his T-shirts after their lovemaking. He jammed his hand through his hair and spun away from her. "The bathroom is in the master bedroom. This way."

She followed him down the hall and into a very stark, very masculine room where black and teal dominated. A king-sized bed faced the bare windows affording much the same view as the family room. She longed to climb into it, settle her weary body beneath the heavy comforter, nestle her thumping head on one of the dense pillows. Longed to share this bed with Jake, the way they'd shared his bed in Riverdell.

Their lovemaking had never been just sex. Each joining was a commitment, a sharing of their spirits, their souls, a baring of their deepest selves. She'd trusted him implicitly. He'd trusted her absolutely. That trust had been shattered. Without it, they would never connect again.

Still, she couldn't help yearn for the time when he'd carried her to this bed, laid her gently down and made slow, incredible love to her.

He strode past the bed without glancing at it. Leaden-legged, she followed him. The bathroom, decorated in adobe tile with black and teal Pueblo Indian designs, had a double-sized shower with one large, clear-glass door, and a tub set in an alcove surrounded by ceiling-high, adobe-encased windows.

There were two sinks, one at each end of a six-foot cabinet, but instead of mirrors above the counter as in most bathrooms, there were more bare windows. She wondered how he managed to shave without a mirror, but the proud thrust of his jaw told her not to ask.

She stared at the bright lights beyond and below the windows, silently cursing the thief who'd stolen their lives, the killer who'd made her bring this man to his emotional knees. Grief squeezed her heart at the depth of Jake's wounded ego. He apparently didn't care that the world could see him; he just couldn't bear to look at himself.

He said, "Shower or bath?"

Her gaze flicked to the shower, lingered momentarily on a damp washcloth tucked into the soap niche. Abandoned from Jake's morning shower? Her breath hitched. She glanced at the tub, which she guessed had been custom-made to his gigantic proportions, and realized she wanted to sink into a hot bath in the worst way, to wash all the stickiness from her hair and face, her body, all the ugliness from her mind. "Tub. I can keep my stitches dry that way."

"That's right." He turned on the water, then pulled a mammoth plush towel from the closet beside the shower and set it on the counter.

Before she could thank him, he was out the door. Her heart pounded as hard as the water spilling from the tap into the tub. He'd left the door ajar and she walked on mushy legs toward it.

It was one thing to have the anonymous world gazing at her, but she wasn't ready to face Jake at her most vulnerable. He was there, filling the doorway. He offered her a navy blue T-shirt. "I think this meets all your requirements."

One glance told her she'd never worn this T-shirt. It bore an LAPD logo. The only time he could have acquired it was after their thwarted wedding. She swallowed hard. "Thank you."

She closed the door, then slumped against it, holding the T-shirt to her face. It smelled of him. She breathed in the beloved scent and struggled to douse the firestorm of emotions burning to overwhelm her. Sunny. Jake. The woman at the motel. Jake. Uncle Murphy. Aunt May. Jake.

Tears blurred her vision, and she caught back a sobbing breath. She shut off the bathwater, turned off the lights and stripped off the offending clothes. Jake might not mind the world watching him, but she'd spent a year learning how to avoid that. This room left her too exposed, too vulnerable.

The night-lights offered enough illumination for her to see her way across the room. Bracing herself on either side of the tub, she stepped, one leg into the hot water, lowered her body gingerly and propped the ankle of the stitched calf on the rim. Steam rose around her as she ducked her head beneath the water, dousing her sticky hair and face. Sweet silence surrounded her, and the stinging tug of her stitches and all the other tiny scrapes and scratches eased. The afternoon's horrors vanished. But as she resurfaced and cool air touched her cheeks, all the misery and despair she'd bottled up the past two days broke free. Sobs climbed her throat, spilled out of her with chest-racking pain and echoed through the huge room like the cries of some pitiable creature lost and alone in the wilds.

JAKE STOOD RIVETED outside the bathroom door, drawn by Laura's presence. Hating himself for wanting her, unable to walk away, unable to control the yearning, he threw back his head and closed his eyes, fighting down a sob of anguish.

For half a second he thought he'd failed, that he'd actually cried out. Then he realized the sobs were coming from the other side of the door. Laura. Wailing with a pain that spoke to his own sad heart, which brimmed with tears. Unshed. Self-pity.

He winced at that admission. He'd mourned his misfortune for endless months now. Always concentrating on what she had done to him. How wronged he'd been by her. What did that say about him? What kind of man was he? If he'd loved Laura as he'd thought he did, he'd have trusted that she wouldn't have run off with another man.

He balled his hands into fists. And if she'd trusted him, she'd have gotten in touch with him within hours or days of the wedding fiasco. He blew out a heavy breath as it struck him that she had done exactly that, had tried reaching him through his mom. Ruthanne either hadn't wanted to tell him or hadn't remembered. *Dear God*. His throat tightened.

He reached for the doorknob.

The front bell rang, sending a jolt through him. He jerked around. Who the hell would that be at this hour?

The police?

The possibility jarred him. He should have called them. Called them off. Hoping they'd accept his apology and leave it at that, he hurried to the front door and peered through the peephole.

He grimaced. Damn. Don Bowman stood illuminated beneath the stoop light. He'd rather face the police tonight than his partner. Jake rolled his eyes, wondering how he could get rid of Don quickly, before he discovered what was going on. Who was soaking in his tub.

But Don shoved past Jake and into the house. "Your beeper's turned off. Your cell phone, also, and the one here is on the answering machine."

"Nice to see you, too." Jake shut the door and followed Don past the kitchen, past the sticky spill he'd yet to clean off the floor, and into the family room.

"This couldn't wait." Don dropped onto one of the sofas, his back to the view. "I've been leaving urgent messages for you everywhere."

"I've been...busy." Jake took the sofa opposite Don, silently willing Laura to prolong her bath. "Haven't checked my messages. Sorry."

"No problem."

"What's so urgent?"

"Got some more dope on that Bunny Jones-Sunny Devlin woman. It was her car that got blown up at the Days Inn."

Jake said nothing, just nodded, hoping Don would take this as encouragement to speed his story along to its conclusion.

"But that's just part of the strange story." Don leaned forward, propping his forearms on his thighs. "Found out this afternoon that Sunny Devlin died in a house fire in Malibu. Actually, the house exploded, gas leak. They identified her by dental records. The house was rented by a Cathy Lewiston."

Jake raised his eyebrows. Was this what Laura had started to tell him?

Don said, "The California police want this Cathy Lewiston for questioning, but she's disappeared. You wouldn't know where she is, would you?"

Jake scowled at him. "Why would I know?"

"Because it's damned likely that Bunny Jones is Cathy Lewiston and Cathy Lewiston's fingerprints match—"

"Mine." Laura stood in the kitchen, Jake's T-shirt skimming her knees, white cotton socks she'd confiscated from his dresser drawer on her feet, reaching high enough on her leg to hide her stitches, and a towel wrapped turban-style around her head.

Don's muddy-river eyes widened and he started up off the sofa. "Laura?"

Laura held herself stiff. Don rose to his full height, a mountain of a man. A frown furrowed his low forehead, crinkling his thick brows as he took in her outfit, shifted his gaze from Jake, to her and back to Jake. His feelings flashed across his sharp features: surprise, puzzlement, distress. At finding her here? Or at what he assumed was going on between Jake and her?

"What the hell is this?" he demanded from Jake.

Jake, who'd had his back to Laura, lurched to his feet and spun around. One glance at her and he understood

Don's question. His face went grim. "It's not what you…" He trailed off, swallowing hard. "Not what it seems."

Though if Don hadn't arrived when he had *that* might not be true, he thought, recalling how close he'd come to charging into the bathroom only minutes ago. His gaze softened as he studied her. Her face, devoid of makeup, was shiny. The only remnants of her upset, redness in her eyes and around her nose, were so slight he doubted Don noticed.

"In other words, Don—" Laura's chin shot up "—Jake isn't any happier about seeing me than you appear to be."

"No, I—" But even as he started the apology, Don seemed to realize they all knew he was lying. Giving up the pretense of manners, he dropped back to the sofa and asked Jake, "Is that true?"

"Is what true?" Jake snapped, suddenly oddly angry. Where the hell did Don get off treating him like some misbehaving kid? He wouldn't take that from anyone, not even his best friend. Especially not in his own home.

Don didn't heed his angry scowl. Few things intimidated Don, including Jake. "Are you as unhappy to see her as I am?"

"How I feel about *that,* is my business," Jake said, his voice a growling whisper.

Don pulled his lips into a flat line. His eyes gleamed dark and hard, shadowed with pity. As though to hide that from Jake, he turned his attention back to Laura. "So, what are you doing in Mesa?"

She squirmed beneath his cold stare. She'd never liked Don. As a kid he'd been sneaky, the kind of boy who did things for people only if there was profit of some sort in the deed for himself. She'd never fathomed how or why Jake and he had become fast friends.

"Well?"

He was waiting for an answer. She glanced at Jake, and realized he wasn't going to bail her out. But how much did she want Don to know? "I had some unresolved business."

This answer seemed to agitate Don. "Something that involved stealing Sunny Devlin's car?"

"I didn't steal it. She lent it to me."

Don snorted in disbelief. "She's dead."

"Yes." Laura blanched, the ugly memories rushing her anew. Her throat tightened. "I know."

Jake had had enough. "Quit badgering her, Don."

Don was on his feet again. "What is this, partner? She waltzes back into your life and you pick up where you left off?"

"That's not what's happening."

"Isn't it? If you've forgotten the hell she put you through, I haven't."

Laura retreated against the bar as though Don's words were fists striking out at her.

Jake saw the look on her face and wanted to hit Don. She's had enough torment for one day. "I think you'd better leave."

"I'm on your side, you know?"

"I know." Jake kept his voice level. He realized Don meant well. But he couldn't explain things to him now. "We'll talk about this tomorrow."

"Come on, man." Don hurried after Jake toward the front door. "Don't let her buffalo you."

"She's not doing that." But despite his protests, a niggling doubt ate at Jake.

Don stepped outside, then lowered his voice. "Do you at least want me to do some more checking up on her?"

"No."

"She *was* posing as Cathy Lewiston in Malibu. The

Devlin woman died in her house. The police are looking for her. And you want me to sit on this?''

"Yes, I do. She's not going to open up to me with you here.''

Don didn't like that, but he knew it was true. Finally he nodded. "Soon as you know something, call me.''

"Tomorrow.''

Don blew out a disgruntled breath. "Make it a.m., man.''

"I will.'' Jake shut the door and waited beside it until the taillights of Don's car were headed down the drive.

He found Laura curled on the sofa where Don had sat a few minutes earlier.

She jerked her head up. "I see he's still the same unpleasant—''

"He thinks he's protecting me,'' Jake cut her off. He had no patience left for the ongoing war between Laura and Don. Or for her reticence on the subject of Sunny Devlin. "It's time you told me what happened in Malibu.''

Laura hugged herself, her back to the glorious view that now seemed a shadowed reminder of another starry night—one with smoke blocking out the Milky Way. God, had it really been only days ago? "Yes. I need to tell you.''

Jake settled himself across from her, expectation in his eyes, in the way he leaned toward her, his hands on his firm thighs.

She blew out a ragged breath. Her heart felt heavy, a lump of icy granite in her chest. "I'd been in Malibu for three months.''

The words sounded flat to her, as though she had only heard this story and not lived it. But she knew if she allowed even a speck of emotion into her voice the dam would burst again, as it had in the bathroom. Then she'd never manage to tell him this.

She forced her gaze to his. "I was starting to get *that* feeling again—as though I were being watched. As though *he* were coming closer."

Laura swallowed hard, admitting to herself how very right she'd been about that sensation. And it hit her like a bolt; that same sense nagged her now. How much time did she have before he found her again? Tried to kill her again?

"Why don't you start with Cathy Lewiston," Jake suggested, as though he understood that the horrific outcome of the story made the telling of it difficult, painful, as though he sensed her thoughts were scaring her overmuch.

Gratitude cracked the icy crust around her heart, but still her distress lingered. Cathy Lewiston. The name she'd assumed for three months. Laura wondered if Jake would understand some of the things she'd had to do over the past year. If he realized she had associated with people he would arrest for the very services she'd procured from them. An awful thought clutched her heart. Had he looked in her purse? Found the half-dozen false identity cards in the secret compartment?

Deciding the only way to gain his trust was total honesty, she drew a bracing breath and said, "Cathy Lewiston came to life in Tijuana, in the back, back room of a local pottery stall, which is where Pedro Valdez does business."

"I take it Señor Valdez specializes in fake IDs?" Jake's voice held a wedge of disgust, reproval.

Heat brushed her cheeks. "I won't apologize for what I've been forced to do. It was the only way I could get a job. A place to live. A car. The only way to stay alive."

He said nothing. Neither did his look condemn; it was just stoic, a policeman's mask.

She cleared her throat. "I felt as though it was time to sell my car and move on."

"Why sell the car?" He frowned. "Why not just go?"

"I never keep a car when I move...in case he's somehow gotten onto it."

"Okay, so you were trying to sell your car."

"Yes, I placed an ad in one of those giveaways. As a practice I don't keep a For Sale sign in the window with a phone number because that would make it too easy to trace back to me." She heard herself rambling and couldn't stop.

But Jake was well versed in keeping a person on whatever subject he wanted discussed. "What does this have to do with Sunny Devlin?"

"She called about the car—said her parents' anniversary was coming up and if the car was as advertised, she might be interested. I arranged to meet her at a restaurant a few miles down the beach.

"Ironically, perhaps tragically, she looked a lot like the disguise I'd taken in California. Tall. Blond. Hair about the length of my wig."

Jake grimaced, and Laura felt the weight of guilt descend on her again. Sunny Devlin might still be alive if she'd been a brunette or if Laura had chosen a different disguise.

"Go on," Jake encouraged.

"She wanted to buy the car. I hadn't expected her to decide so quickly and hadn't brought the registration. She insisted on test-driving the Taurus to my house to get it. Said she had the money on her and that as good faith I could drive her new Corvette."

"What happened?"

"I gave her quick directions and told her she could follow me if she wanted. But out in the parking lot, she jumped into my Taurus and took off. I headed over to her Corvette and found it had a flat tire. By the time I got help changing it, I was running about half an hour behind her. I hadn't bothered to remove my house key from the ring. I arrived home to find the whole street blocked with fire trucks and gawkers. Neighbors I didn't know told me the woman who'd lived there had just gone inside moments before the explosion. I don't know what caused it.''

"According to Don—" Jake steadied his gaze on her "—a portable propane heater sitting in the living room had a jet leak.''

"And Sunny chain-smoked.'' Laura's hand went to her mouth as she recalled the woman lighting one cigarette after another in the half hour they'd talked at the restaurant. But it wasn't the only thing sending shock waves through her. "Dear God, Jake, I didn't have a portable heater.''

He reached out as if to touch her hair, then dropped his arm to the back of the sofa. "I guess you weren't supposed to be around to tell anyone that.''

"But how did he think I'd set off the explosion? I don't smoke.''

"The spark from a lamp would do the trick.''

"Sunny Devlin didn't have a chance.'' Tears burned Laura's eyes and she hugged herself tighter. "Even the Taurus was flattened.''

Jake grew silent, serious.

Something else Don had said struck Laura. "The California police want to question me. Dear God, Jake. They'll think *I* killed Sunny and stole her car. Just like Don does.''

She began to shiver.

Jake was beside her in an instant, pulling her into his arms as he'd done so many times after the loss of her aunt and uncle. She wanted to curl inside him and stay safe in his embrace forever. But he wasn't holding her the way he used to. He was rigid, as though the guard around his heart were as deep as a castle moat.

Jake felt Laura's heart pounding beneath his palm and wanted to stumble up and off of this sofa and run like hell. She felt too good nestled against his chest. Too perfect. Too vulnerable. Don's warning rang through his mind. Don was right. Jake was the vulnerable one. The one whose heart was still in shreds.

He leaned back and gazed down at Laura. Her lovely eyes brimmed with tears, and his pulse leaped uncontrollably. He didn't want to touch her, didn't want to ease her distress, and yet he could no more stop himself than he could stop the sun from rising in the morning. He brushed her tears away with the pad of his thumb. "No one's going to believe that you stole that great car just to blow it up."

She gave him a brave, lopsided smile, but her lower lip quivered. "I pray you're right."

Jake wanted the subject changed. Wanted his attention diverted to some less dangerous area than Laura's kissable lips. "Do you think Sunny was somehow connected to all this?"

Laura frowned. "How could she be?"

He blew out a breath. "I don't know. I just wonder if your meeting her was as innocent as it seemed. If all she really wanted was to buy your car."

She shoved away from him and sat straighter. "What are you saying?"

"Sunny Devlin was a P.I." He stifled the urge to pull Laura back into his arms. "Is it that much of a leap to think she could have been hired by someone to track you down?"

Laura's mouth dropped open. "You're suggesting that Sunny Devlin flattened her own tire?"

"Yes. I think she did."

"Why?"

"Probably wanted to snoop in your house."

"And I stupidly trusted her with my car. My keys."
Why? Why had she let her guard down with Sunny?

Laura's hand flew to her mouth. But of course. All this
time she'd been certain her pursuer was a man. Was she
wrong? Was *he* really *she*?

Chapter Eight

A bone-deep weariness settled over Laura. Could *he* be *she?* The possibility boggled her mind, jarringly altered her list of suspects. Her desperation to lay her hands on the evidence leaped. "Why don't we call Travis Crocker."

"It's 2 a.m.," Jake spoke softly. Their gazes met, and a connection as sharp as a zing of electricity passed between them. "Why don't we call it a night."

Laura sighed with resignation. "Okay."

A pang of yearning tugged at her heart, her spirit, tingled through the core of her. She wanted to crawl back into Jake's arms and stay there forever. But she knew his comforting gesture had only been an act of kindness. Something he'd do for any woman in distress. His generous heart was one of the reasons she'd fallen in love with him.

He cleared his throat. "You take my bed."

"No. I've imposed on you enough today." She stood and watched his eyes darken as they swept up her scantily clad body, knew that he knew all he'd have to do was reach beneath the T-shirt to touch her naked flesh and she'd belong to him again. At least for the moment...for the night. Could she settle for that? "I'll use the guest room."

"I don't have a guest room." He rose, averting his gaze with what seemed an effort, but not before she saw the lingering wariness in those teal depths. Emotions he could hide from others he'd never be able to hide from her. And yet, that familiarity held no guarantee they'd ever truly be close again.

He doused the family room light. "It's my home office. I'll take the couch in there. No, don't argue with me. You could be spending the night in the hospital."

She gave him a conceding smile. "And we'll call Cullen's brother in the morning?"

"Definitely."

"Good." Did this mean Jake was going to help her now? Or was she still on her own? The uneasy sense that she should leave grated her nerve endings as she approached the bedroom. But why? What did she fear? Her aching need to be with Jake? Or that the killer was closing in on her?

Those questions haunted her, and she slept fitfully until dawn, then finally fell into a deep, dreamless slumber. She awoke to find sun streaming through the unfettered windows. For several moments she felt disoriented. Too often this last year she'd awakened in a strange place, in a strange bed.

But this was no stranger's bed. It was Jake's bed. She hugged his oversized pillow, catching a hint of his aftershave. A thread of melancholy stitched her heart. If only this were Jake's and *her* bed.

But it wasn't and such foolish dreams would break her heart all over again. She lurched up. Her gaze snagged on a colorful array of shopping bags that sat on the opposite side of the bed. They hadn't been there last night. She scooted to her knees, gathered the nearest sack and peered inside. Jeans. She pulled them free. Her size. The remaining bags contained underwear, socks, a pale-yellow pull-over, a charcoal polo shirt, and sneakers.

All in the correct sizes.

How had he…? Her hand went to her mouth as memory dawned. The Christmas before the wedding Jake had wanted to buy her something special. But he hadn't wanted her guessing, so he'd insisted she give him a list of her sizes, including jewelry. His gift had been her engagement ring. Had he kept the list all this time?

As she'd kept his engagement ring?

She scooped her purse off the floor and delved into its secret compartment. A second later, she lifted the necklace free and gazed at the ring dangling from it, a small golden circle with a quarter-carat diamond mounting. It was the one piece of Jake the killer had not taken from her.

She clasped the chain around her neck, glad to have it back where it belonged. She'd placed it in her purse before meeting Jake yesterday. To wear it around him, even secretly, had seemed wrong somehow. But today, she wanted the cool metal next to her traitorous heart, a talisman against false hope, a reminder that it was not on her finger, that she was no longer Jake Wilder's betrothed.

For as encouraging as it was that he'd held on to something as personal as a list of her sizes, she'd come to a painful realization during the night about their previous relationship. Jake and she lacked the trust in each other essential to a lifelong commitment. Otherwise, their love would have been strong enough to withstand treachery from an outside force. It hadn't. Jake had readily believed she'd eloped with Cullen. She had readily believed Jake might be involved in the cover-up of her aunt's and uncle's murders. He should have known better. She should have known better.

What kind of marriage would they have had based on

so little faith? Her stomach pinched. And what about now? Could they trust each other enough to work together in order to bring a killer to justice? Or would Jake abandon her to her own devices?

She tugged the tags from the panties and slipped into them, but as she lifted Jake's T-shirt, she remembered how vulnerable she was in this room. Apprehension prickled her spine. Half expecting to find someone spying on her, she shot her gaze to the windows. Her eyes opened wider and a relieved laugh tripped from her as she saw why Jake had no curtains or blinds. This room appeared to sit two feet beyond the cliff edge.

Anyone wanting to snoop on Jake would need wings or some sort of high-powered telescope and a place to position it. His nearest neighbor's house hugged the next ridge, at least a quarter mile in the distance. Everything in between was sheer cliff walls and deep gully.

So much for protecting her modesty last night.

Grinning at herself, Laura began dressing, mindful of her stitches. She was glad to have clothes that fit, that felt as though they belonged to her, or that would belong to her as soon as she paid Jake for them. She tied the last shoelace, then tallied up the receipts. Her joy in the new clothes flattened. The cost exceeded the money left in her purse. How would she pay him back?

Now that she thought about it, when had he shopped for these clothes? What time was it? How late had she slept? She glanced at the clock radio on the bedside table, shocked to see it was nearly noon.

She pulled her brush from her purse, but without a mirror to consult, she couldn't determine how bad she looked, or how best to fix her hair. She settled for sweeping it off her face and securing it at her nape with a Scrunchie. Mascara and lipstick she applied by touch.

Almost as an afterthought, she realized her head no longer ached, not even one dull throb. She was lucky to be alive today, luckier still to have escaped with such minor injuries. Would she be so fortunate next time? Or was her luck running out?

Desperation nipped at her as surely as her pursuer nipped at her heels. Had Jake already called Travis Crocker? Already found out she was telling him the truth about Cullen? Would he finally help her locate the evidence…if it still existed? The thought that Kim Durant might have destroyed or disposed of it, accidently or on purpose, chilled her.

And what about Don? Jake had brushed off his questions last night, but Don was persistent. He wouldn't stand being kept in the dark for long. And once Jake related her story to him, he'd likely waste no time disclosing her whereabouts to the California police. Then Jake would insist she stick around and satisfy their curiosity. But would they believe a story that sounded as far-fetched as hers? Look at the trouble she'd had convincing Jake.

Worry hurried her into the hall. Jake's voice issued from a door directly across from her. She peered inside. This was obviously his home office, a space equally as large as the master bedroom, with the same wall-sized windows offering a view that seemed to extend into the next state.

He sat behind a mammoth desk, facing the breathtaking panorama, a phone to his ear. "Yes, Detective Healy. She showed up here last night."

He paused, presumably while the other man spoke. Laura's heart dipped to her toes. Police detective Healy?

Jake held his head high. "I know, I know, but better late than never."

Hearing only his end of the conversation, she couldn't tell whether Jake was with her or against her. She hated all the doubts, but that she could even wonder where his loyalties lay confirmed that they'd never trust each other enough for a lifelong commitment.

They'd be fortunate to make it through the next few days.

Laura's heart ached for them both.

"Thanks," Jake said, then hung up and spun his chair around until he faced his computer.

A scowl tugged his brows, puckered his scar. His jaw needed shaving. He wore the clothes he'd had on yesterday.

Sympathy fluttered through the butterflies in her stomach. How like him to put her needs before his own. Why must he think the full measure of a desirable man was a handsome face? What made a man sexy, in her opinion, came from within. And Jake could no more contain or hide his special assets than gift-wrap the moon. She grinned at him and gestured toward her new outfit. "Everything fits great. Thank you."

"You're welcome."

"I have some money—"

"I don't want your money." His expression darkened.

"I want to pay—"

"When you have a job again...."

She drew in a calming breath and nodded. For a moment neither said anything, then she pivoted, her gaze landing on the phone, her mind leaping to the investigation they wanted to make and the one that the police *were* making. "Is Detective Healy with the Malibu police?"

Jake stroked his bristled jaw. "No. He's one of the officers we ran into at the hospital last night."

Laura frowned at him. "Why were you talking to him about me?"

"Because when I got into my car and you weren't there, I thought—" He broke off.

His expression hardened to a pointed stare, and she realized he'd thought the person who'd stolen the florist's van had absconded with her. Heat climbed her cheeks. She'd been so frightened of that very thing she hadn't considered how her disappearance might affect Jake. She recalled his fury with her in the garage, his accusation that she didn't care about the worry she'd caused.

"I never meant—" she broke off, hearing how lame she sounded. Her only thought *had* been self-preservation. It was instinct these days. An instinct she heeded, perhaps irresponsibly at times, but always with haste. She felt bad that she'd caused him worry and disquieted that his worry might have caused her unwanted attention. "You set the police looking for me?"

"They did it as a professional courtesy. You have to be missing twenty-four hours before they conduct an official search."

She twisted her hands together. "Did they find the person who stole the florist's van?"

"No."

She blew out a frustrated breath and sank into the chair across from him. "How about Travis Crocker?"

"Haven't reached him yet, but I was about to try again." He lifted a mug that had been poised on a coaster near his computer. "If you want some coffee, there's a fresh pot in the kitchen."

"Are you hinting that you'd like a refill?"

"If you don't mind."

"Still like it black?"

"Yeah."

On her way to the kitchen Laura admired the wide-open, bright, almost porous feeling the house had, as though sunshine and light seeped through unseen cracks and crevices. The sense of being outdoors spoke of clever architecture. To own such a house, to furnish it as Jake had it furnished, would cost a small fortune. Did he own this house?

Her hand went to the spot on her chest where her engagement ring rested. Jake would never tell her how much the ring cost, but Ruthanne had mentioned one day that he was paying it off in four-hundred-dollar-a-month installments. It was why he'd moved back in with his mother six months before the wedding.

So, what had changed his financial situation in the past year? She freshened the coffee in Jake's mug and filled another for herself, plucked a banana from the bunch on the refrigerator and hooked it into her back pocket. Was his new business so successful he could afford this house, the furnishings, without burying himself in debt?

As soon as she entered his office, Jake hung up the receiver, but a metallic ringing echoed to her. He said, "Speaker phone."

Laura handed over his cup, set her own down, snatched up the banana, then reclaimed her chair. A man's voice sounded from the phone. "Hello?"

Although Jake recognized the voice, he asked for Travis Crocker.

"Speaking."

Jake could almost see Travis; Cullen's elder brother by four years, he shared the family trademark black hair and blue eyes, but his features lacked the perfect symmetry of Cullen's. Jake and Travis were school chums from as far back as kindergarten; in fact, he'd served as one of the ushers at the wedding. "Hi, Trav. It's Jake…Wilder."

"Oh, yeah?" He sounded surprised, leery. "You in town?"

He meant Riverdell. "No. I'm calling from home. I live in Arizona now."

"I heard. Kim told Izzy."

Jake nodded, glancing at Laura, who was taking tiny bites from the peeled banana. Izzy was Isabelle Dell, the kid sister of Payton Dell, CEO of Dell Pharmaceuticals. She'd been Laura's best friend, her bridesmaid, but the only outward sign that this conversation bothered her were the twin spots of color on her cheeks.

Jake frowned. "I want to ask you something, Trav, that might strike you as odd."

Travis was silent for a long moment, then with a cautious note in his voice, he said, "Go on."

"It's about Cullen."

"If this is about his running off with Laura, I don't want to get into it with you."

"No, no." But Jake wasn't sure how he should approach this. Should he tell Travis outright that he knew Laura hadn't run off with Cullen? If the Crockers hadn't heard from him, that was as good as telling them that he might be dead. He decided on a different tack.

"I got over that a long time ago. Cullen did me a favor running off with her." Jake saw Laura wince and felt bad he'd lied. But she seemed to realize the pointlessness of scaring Travis unnecessarily. "I know you were as shocked as I was."

"That's for sure." Travis chuckled ironically. "So, what do you want?"

"I wondered if you've heard from Cullen lately."

"Why?" The caution was back in his voice. "I mean, if you're over Laura and all, what do you care?"

Jake's stomach knotted. Over Laura? Yesterday he could have taken and passed a lie detector test on that very question. Today he'd flunk. "It's not for me. My mom.

She has Alzheimer's, fading in and out. Lately she's been asking about Laura. I thought it might ease her mind to see her."

"That's a shame, man. But I can't help you out. Cullen hasn't even called Ma. None of us has heard from him. We were all as shocked as you that he up and ran off like that—without a word to anyone. Not even Izzy. But what's stranger still is that he hasn't come home. Or called."

A shiver tracked Jake's spine. "Yeah, that is odd."

"I'll tell you something, Jake, I didn't want the folks to worry, but I even hired a private detective to try to find the little creep."

Cold settled at the base of Jake's spine. "A private detective?"

"More than one, in fact, but none of them sniffed out so much as a trail to follow. It's like Cullen and Laura fell off the edge of the earth."

"I'm sure they'll turn up eventually." But Jake feared Cullen would not be turning up alive. "Was one of those P.I.s you hired a woman in California by the name of Sunny Devlin?"

Travis paused again, too long to be considering. Either he'd hired her or he hadn't. The question didn't require deep consideration. "Nope. Name doesn't ring any bells."

Jake sensed he was holding something back, but what?

"Well, thanks for your time. If you should hear from Cullen, I'd appreciate a call."

He gave Travis his phone number and disconnected. Laura had finished the banana and was folding the peel with concentration. When she lifted her smoky eyes they glittered with unshed tears. "Maybe Cullen was killed for helping me."

"We don't know that for sure," Jake consoled.

"*I* know it for sure. My evidence will prove it to you."

He started to respond to that, but she cut him off. "Jake, I realize it's none of my business, but do you own this house?"

He frowned, taken aback. "Yes."

"How, I mean...where did you get the money?"

The sudden switch of subject befuddled him. He took a sip of his cooled coffee and then shrugged. "I happened to get in on the ground floor of what turned out to be a great investment."

She set the banana peel on an edge of his desk, her gaze sweeping over his computer, printer, scanner, fax machine, then back to him. "The stock market?"

He raked his hand through his hair. "No. It was a new cream that Dell developed last year."

Laura's smoke-gray eyes widened, darkened. "What sort of cream?"

"New Again. Surely you've heard of it. It's a cosmetic product."

"No. Cosmetics haven't been a priority for me this past year. What does it do?"

He shrugged. "Well, I'm no chemist, but basically, when applied to skin discolorations like age spots, birthmarks, even wrinkles, it makes them disappear for something like twelve hours. It's the only product of its kind that's sold over the counter."

Laura gaped at him in obvious horror.

The icy sensation at his spine spread, chilling the very blood in his veins. "What?"

"That's the cream Payton Dell stole from Uncle Murphy."

Chapter Nine

"You think Payton Dell killed your aunt and uncle for the New Again formula?" Skepticism arched Jake's eyebrows and puckered his scar. "You can't be serious."

"I don't know whether or not Payton killed my aunt and uncle. But he seems the most likely suspect, since he *did* steal the formula."

"How can you say that?"

"Because." Laura scooted toward the edge of her chair. "Uncle Murphy developed the cream for Aunt May. She had a port-wine birthmark on her neck and upper shoulder, similar to the one on my leg."

She stopped, choking at the mention of the star-shaped imperfection that adorned an intimate wedge of her inner thigh—which Jake had often stroked with affection. She saw his eyes darken and she glanced away.

Desire pooled in her lower belly, reached heated tendrils of longing through her blood. "Aunt May always wore scarves or high collars. Summers were awful for her. She worried obsessively that others would see her 'deformity,' often telling me she wished she could remove it. She insisted I felt the same about mine, even though I continually assured her otherwise."

"Poor May." Jake's hand went to his face, but he

dropped it quickly and looked away. "People can be cruel."

She nodded, certain that he'd felt the very scorn and cruelty her aunt had spent her days fearing. Laura's heart ached for him, but she wouldn't embarrass him by offering him sympathy. "I think she was harder on herself than anyone else could ever have been."

Jake faced her again. A slight lifting of his brow was the only acknowledgment he gave her gentle admonishment. He leaned back in his chair and crossed his long legs at the ankles, the relaxed posture pulling his jeans taut across his considerable male attributes.

Laura pulled her gaze away, but not before her pulse was leaping at the images his simple action fed into her mind. She sat straighter in her chair, chastising herself. If she couldn't keep her thoughts on the business at hand, she'd never be able to work with Jake.

He flexed his hands and her emotions skidded again at the memory of those hands on her naked flesh. She took a sip of coffee, letting the hot liquid give her composure.

Jake said, "Okay, so Murphy had reason to research a remedy for his wife's...blemish. He may have been working on something at the time of his death, but it was not New Again."

What would it take to make him believe? Roiling with frustration and pent-up emotions that she couldn't school, Laura wrenched out of the chair and strode to the window.

She stared out, oblivious to the breathtaking view. Her mind looked backward, back to the tiny lab her uncle had created in the basement of the Whittaker house in Riverdell.

It was cramped, every corner occupied with something or other necessary to his latest project. He'd built shelves on every wall, a huge counter in the center for his work space, installed an old refrigerator and a new sink, none of which he allowed Aunt May to clean.

His lab was his private domain, his responsibility. He kept it pristine, swabbing the sinks and vials with a disinfectant cleanser he'd developed. He claimed it was the best bacteria killer on the market, and that it saved him needless expenses by allowing him to recycle containers from project to project.

She pictured him now as he'd been that day, the day he'd told her about his discovery.

From the first time she'd laid eyes on him, until the day he died, he'd struck her as a man who controlled everything around him, from his weight—which she'd bet matched the national standard for his height and bone structure—to his environment.

As usual that day, his wavy red hair was oiled flat to his head, not one strand out of place. His eyebrows, ginger slashes, rose up his high forehead and excitement frolicked in his soft brown eyes. "I've found it, Laura. It's a miracle, this cream is. This stuff will eclipse your aunt's birthmark like it never existed. She's going to have the skin of a Venus."

She spun and faced Jake. "Uncle Murphy named his cream The Venus Masque. But I swear to you it was the exact same formula that Dell is calling 'New Again.' And if I can find my evidence, I can prove it."

Jake rose and came toward her. Emotions flickered across his face, as though he were having trouble coming to terms with this new twist in his reality. "I don't—"

The doorbell rang, interrupting him. Reflexively, he jerked toward the hallway, cursing under his breath at someone's bad timing. He glanced at her and shrugged. "I'll be right back."

Laura understood his frustration. Since their meeting

yesterday morning she'd thrown him one curve after another and expected him to accept them all. But he'd lived a different reality than hers this past year. He wouldn't capitulate because she told him to. Especially since she claimed so much of what he believed was false. *That* would throw anyone for a loop.

But eventually he would accept. If she could find the evidence. Her anxiousness returned with a vengeance. Maybe she should go and talk with his mother again. By herself. But remembering Ruthanne's Alzheimer's made the prospect distasteful. Heartbreaking. Not to mention that it might be a complete waste of time.

Voices neared, coming down the hall toward the office. A moment later, Jake entered, followed by Don and Susan.

Wearing leather slacks and jacket, his long hair caught at the nape with a leather thong, Don looked like something out of *Easy Rider,* a man on a mission, dark and dangerous.

Susan was a bit more voluptuous than she'd been last time Laura had seen her; her clothes dripped quality, and her left hand sported a wedding band with a hefty diamond setting. Apparently Don and she had married sometime during the year.

Some things, however, hadn't changed. Susan still wore her curly blond hair cut to chin length, and still preferred miniskirts, tight, low-cut tops and calf-high boots. Did she dress this way when she was protecting a client? Or did she leave the bodyguarding to Jake and Don?

Susan's bright blue eyes flashed like Bunsen burner flames as they landed on Laura. ''I couldn't believe it when Don told me you'd dropped back into Jake's life. You've got a ner—''

''Susan,'' Jake cut in. ''Laura was just telling me that

the original formula for New Again was developed by her uncle Murphy.''

"Stolen from my uncle," Laura amended.

"What?" Don laughed, a scoffing chuckle.

Laura stood at the window, her back to the view, her hands at her sides. She promised herself she wouldn't let Don Bowman get to her. Not today.

He dropped into the chair Jake had vacated earlier and steepled his thick fingers. A hint of distress churned in his muddy-river eyes as he bobbed his head. "Is that what's behind this nonsense about your uncle and aunt being murdered?"

"They *were* murdered," Laura fumed, curling her hands into fists, her nails biting the tender flesh of her palms.

"That's preposterous," Don shot back, but something odd, indefinable, flitted through his eyes. "Where do you get off questioning Jake's and my investigation?"

Even though he sounded furious, Laura would swear he was more discomfited than offended by her accusations of a botched case analysis. Why? "What's the matter, Don? Did you find something at the time of the investigation that you decided to sit on because you hate me?"

He laughed derisively and shook his head. "Now, that's precisely the reason you've never been at the top of my hit parade."

Susan's hands were on her hips, every line of her body taut, defensive. "Are you calling Don a dirty cop?"

"Name-calling isn't my style." Laura leveled a cool gaze toward the other woman. "All I want is justice for my aunt and uncle."

"It was an accident, Laura." Don's leather clothes swicked as he shifted in the chair.

Squirming like a man on a hot seat? Laura wondered, watching him.

Jake cleared his throat. "There wasn't any hint of foul play, Laura. If there had been, Don or I would have found it. We didn't."

"Then how did Dell get its hands on my uncle's formula? And why has someone been trying to kill me ever since I found out about it?"

"That's your story," Susan said. "I don't buy it."

"I don't care whether you do or not."

"Of course not." Susan's eyes swerved to Jake, pity bright in their blue depths as she silently questioned his judgment. "But we aren't all susceptible to your...tall tales."

"Sunny Devlin died in my house in Malibu. Someone thought they were killing me."

"I told them that," Jake said.

And still they did not believe? Why? Were they just protecting Jake? Or was there another reason? Had they also invested in New Again?

"We didn't come here to argue with Laura," Don said, turning toward the computer. "Did you get the e-mail from the Nelson twins this morning? They have that tour coming through town in two weeks."

As Jake and Susan joined Don at the computer, Laura pivoted toward the windows again. An unpleasant chill slithered across the pit of her stomach as her suspicions of Susan and Don soared. They were Jake's partners. The agency was named BMW. Bowman, Meade and Wilder, she supposed. That meant the newlywed Bowmans held a two-thirds ownership. They'd probably put up a third each of the original capital to get the agency off the ground. What size investment would that have taken?

Don had been a police officer in Riverdell; Susan, a receptionist at Dell. Neither had taken home hefty paychecks. Yet now, both wore enough jewelry to suggest deep pockets. Was the agency solely responsible for their newfound wealth? Or had their money also come from New Again?

This wasn't the first time she'd wondered whether or not Don had been involved in murdering her aunt and uncle. Until today, she hadn't wanted to believe it. She spun around and gazed at the three huddled around the computer. Had he and Susan been hunting for her all these months? Killed two innocent women in her stead? Bodyguards traveled. BMW was a worldwide company. Who kept track of where the agents were while they were supposed to be on assignment? Who did the books? Scheduled the appointments?

Laura turned back toward the window, hugging herself. If Don and Susan were the ones after her, they'd have no trouble keeping Jake in the dark. All they had to do was cover for each other.

"Why don't you get out of Jake's life for good?" Susan asked near her shoulder. Laura started, then lurched around. Susan spoke in a whisper, but her eyes roared with hatred. "I can't believe you'd think he still wanted you. Or that he'd bail you out of whatever trouble you've gotten yourself into."

"That's not why I came to him." Laura kept her own voice low.

"Oh, of course not," Susan hissed. "You drove all the way to Mesa in a stolen car just to make a pile of phony accusations."

Laura knew she should let the insults roll off her back, but her temper rose hot and furious inside her, spilling out. "Everything I've said is true and I have proof."

The men spun around at that.

"Then show it to us," Susan challenged.

Laura flushed. Horror slid through her. What was she

thinking? Why had she said anything about the evidence she'd sent Ruthanne? "I—I can't. Yet. But it does exist."

She glanced at Jake, saying a quick prayer that that was true.

Don rose from the chair, towering over her, reminding her how small she was. How easy it would be for him to break her in half. "Where'd you get this so-called evidence? And what is it?"

Laura's stomach flopped, the coffee and banana doing an unpleasant dance. She cursed her quick temper, fervently wishing she hadn't mentioned the proof. "It's obvious you don't believe me—so why should I tell you?"

Susan cocked her head to one side. "I'll bet Cullen and she dreamed up this scheme. Where *is* Cullen?"

Laura blanched.

"We don't know." Jake seemed to realize her distress and came to her rescue. There was something in the look he sent her that said he wanted to believe her. He glanced at his partners. "She didn't run off with Cullen."

"But the note…?" Don frowned.

Jake shrugged. "Cullen's family hasn't heard from him in over a year."

Don's frown deepened. Laura couldn't tell whether he was surprised or acting.

Susan gestured with her hands. "Did Laura tell you that?"

"No," Jake said. "Travis did."

"That's weird." She fell silent a moment, then glanced at Laura. "Where could he have gone?"

Jake answered, "The day he disappeared, he'd just finished analyzing a sample of Murphy's cream and comparing it with New Again."

Laura stiffened. She wished he'd kept that information

between the two of them, but she realized Jake trusted his partners, even if she had her doubts.

"And?" Susan asked. "What was the result?"

Laura lifted her chin. "The two creams were identical."

"You expect us to take *your* word for that?" Susan didn't want to believe, her mind obviously set to reject anything Laura said.

"Where'd you get a sample of your uncle's cream?" Don asked. Beneath his tan, his face seemed two shades paler. "Everything was destroyed in the explosion."

"She doesn't have any sample, Don." Susan shook her head, her eyes narrowing as she spun toward Laura accusingly. "I know what's going on here—the real reason you contacted Jake."

Laura's dander reared again. "Oh? What is that?"

Susan pointed her finger at Laura, its nail painted red with some sort of sparkling golden design. "You've filed a lawsuit."

"What?" Laura shook her head, at a loss to understand what Susan was talking about.

"A claim against Dell," she added. "Haven't you?"

Laura blinked and stepped back. All three of them were staring at her, expecting her to say it was true. Even Jake, she saw, feeling oddly disappointed in him.

He was scowling hard, his scar vivid. He swallowed as if he had a tennis ball stuck in his throat. "Laura?"

She shook her head. "No, I—"

"Forget it, sweetheart." Don took a step toward her. "We owe Payton Dell big-time for letting us invest in this product at its inception. We aren't going to help you do him dirty."

"I'm not suing Dell," Laura finally managed. But even as the words left her mouth, she realized she very well could. That to keep her from doing exactly that, someone was determined to kill her. Her knees turned liquid.

She fought the distress. She'd be damned if she'd fall apart in front of Don and Susan. Her determination seemed to clear her head, and she decided to push Susan further and see what happened. "I guess I *could* sue Payton, couldn't I?"

"You know damned well you could," Susan growled, her cheeks turning a bright red.

Jake broke in. "Ah, come on, Sue. Enough of this. It's not going to settle anything. Maybe we can all discuss it at another time…when cooler heads prevail?"

Don and Susan exchanged a look that suggested they both thought Jake had lost his senses. Don seemed ready to argue it out. He opened his mouth, then changed his mind and muttered, "The hell with it." He strode to his wife and caught her arm. "We've got to arrange a sitter for Sarah. The Texas oilman called, Jake. He decided to start his assault on the Vegas casinos tomorrow, instead of next month. We'll be out of town all week."

As they walked past Laura, Susan said to her in a muted aside, "Make sure you're gone by the time we return."

JAKE SAW HIS PARTNERS to the door, trying to pay attention to Don, who was telling him the particulars of the Vegas stint. Once they were gone, he returned to the office. Laura was standing with her back to him, facing the view, hugging herself as if she were terribly cold. He wanted to go to her. To apologize to her for Don's and Susan's rudeness. For his failure to stop them sooner.

But he was so confused.

How many times last year had Laura pleaded with him to reappraise the explosion of her aunt and uncle's house? More times than he could count, he admitted, feeling small now for dismissing her slant on the case as prejudicial. The truth was, he'd been insulted that she could even question whether he'd done a thorough investigation of the accident. Was that why he'd so readily disregarded her prattles about some discovery or other of Murphy Whittaker's being a motive for murder?

Cullen Crocker had not only listened to Laura, he'd tried to help her.

Jake grimaced, realizing that some of what had happened between Laura and him could be laid at his own doorstep. He did a mental run-through of the facts he'd gathered on the accident, but his memory was sketchy on important details. Had he missed something? Had someone blown up the Whittaker house to cover a double murder? He decided to try to keep an open mind, and discovered he had a sudden, urgent need to see that case file again.

He moved within inches of Laura, aching to touch her, to hold her, but knowing her trust had been shattered as completely as his own, he feared she might bolt. He kept his hands rigidly at his sides. "Tell me the rest of it, Laura."

She turned toward him, seeming startled to find him so close. Her smoky eyes searched his face. "Would you listen to me now any more than before? Or do you think I'm as bad as Susan suggests? That all I'm after is winning some lawsuit against Dell?"

"Are you?"

"No."

"Then tell me what happened. What made you suspicious?"

"I was head of product acquisitions. I ordered all the supplies needed to produce New Again in its developmental stage. It struck me as coincidental that I'd ordered exactly the same supplies for my uncle weeks before he died.''

''I see.'' Jake had to admit—he'd have been suspicious, too.

''How did you come by the evidence? As Don said, everything was destroyed in the accident.''

He watched her twist her hands together, run her tongue along her plump, kissable lips.

''It was the day before the wedding,'' she said. ''I was packing for our...honeymoon.''

The word seemed to catch on her breath and drop into the room like a rock, heavy with all the pain she and Jake had suffered, solid as the promise of all they might have had if only he'd listened to her pleas and set his ego and his pride aside.

She sighed. ''On my closet shelf I spotted the gift-wrapped package Aunt May gave me for my bridal shower. As you know, the shower was to have been held the night the house exploded.''

She stopped again, looking choked, ready to collapse. She drew a wobbly breath and unshed tears shone in her eyes. ''Of course there was no shower, but Izzy kept the gifts and gave them to me later, privately. I hadn't been able to bring myself to open the last thing Aunt May would ever give me.''

Laura trembled, swayed slightly. Jake caught her by her upper arms and pulled her to him. She didn't resist, but melded against him, still a perfect fit as only she had always been. His pulse kicked into high gear, desire singing through his veins.

He fought it as she laid her head on his chest. His heart thumped so fiercely it had to be thundering in her ear. For a long moment, he held her close, his hands splayed across her back, her heart beating sharply against his palms.

She leaned away from him, gazed up at him, her eyes free from tears now. Instead they held a smile, as though at some warm memory. "Aunt May had enclosed a note telling me not to open it until the day of the wedding. But at that moment, I just had to open it. The package contained a dozen sample bottles of Uncle Murphy's Venus Masque. I contacted Cullen immediately and he promised to get right to the analysis.

"I gave him one of the bottles."

She licked her lips again and Jake could barely keep from bending lower and taking possession of them.

She said, "He called me the morning of our wedding. He was excited. He insisted I meet him at Dell Labs. He wanted to show me the results of his tests. Jake, I swear, the two creams *were* identical."

"What did you do?"

"I was stunned. I drove home as if in a fog, the full implication hitting me only as I reached my apartment. The first thing I did was try to find you. I called everyone I could think of. Left messages with them all."

She drew a ragged breath. "Half an hour later the phone rang. I was sure it was you. But it wasn't."

His nerve endings jangled. "Tell me."

"The person on the phone told me they knew what I'd been doing at the lab and I was going to die like my aunt and uncle."

Jake's breath left his lungs in a whoosh. "Did you recognize the voice?"

She shook her head, her sable hair shifting like silk across her shoulders. "I don't even know whether it was male or female."

"Cullen must have gotten a similar call."

She shivered in Jake's arms. "Maybe he didn't take it as seriously as I did."

Jake needed all his willpower to keep from surrendering to his desire to comfort Laura with his whole body. She was too vulnerable. He was too susceptible to her vulnerability. Dear God, he wanted to quell her anguish in the fire of his passion, wanted to bury himself deep inside her again and again until they were both too exhausted to think, to question, to fear.

With a supreme struggle, he reined in his needs, but his voice rang with pent-up hunger even in his own ears. "Who did you speak with when you tried reaching me before the wedding?"

She shuddered, and he supposed she'd gone over the list in her mind thousands of times.

She moved out of his embrace. "Your mom. Your cousin Kim. Izzy."

He ached to pull her back, his body cooling where hers had touched it.

Her breath puffed from her. "Travis. Ralph—"

"Chief Russell?" Jake's eyes widened. "My boss?"

She nodded, then continued. "And Don and Susan."

"That's it?" he asked, incredulity in his voice.

"I didn't talk to Payton, but one of the others might have."

"Just those seven people?" She didn't answer, didn't need to. Of course if there was someone else she would have told him. Jake felt like an anvil had landed on his chest. Was he really supposed to believe one of his family or friends had destroyed his wedding? His life? Had killed Laura's aunt and uncle and two other people? Had tried killing Laura over and over again?

His blood ran cold at the thought.

And yet, could he afford to dismiss the possibility out of hand? Again? No, not after the last attempt on Laura's life.

She was clasping her hands so tightly in front of her that her knuckles were white. "What are we going to do?"

It was a challenge more than a question. She was asking if he was with her or if she was on her own. He cocked his head to one side and rubbed his whiskered jaw. "I'm going to shave, shower and dress."

Her shoulders sagged, disappointment and frustration issuing from her like a powerful perfume.

With the pad of his thumb, he brushed her quivering lower lip, aching to kiss it. He gave her a wry grin, instead. "Then I guess we should go to Riverdell and look for that evidence."

Chapter Ten

Jake stood in his shower, cold water beating down on him, washing away the raging desire he found harder and harder to control. As his ardor cooled, he made no move to adjust the tap, just stood there lost in thought. The icy droplets pelted his flesh, as relentless and stinging as Laura's implied accusation about his friends and family. If she was right, this all revolved around New Again.

The person who'd benefited most from that was undoubtedly Payton Dell. But Jake didn't believe the man capable of murder, not even of hiring someone to kill Laura. Air whistled through Jake's pursed lips. His years in law enforcement had taught him few killers looked the part, but damn it, he knew Payton. Knew him well. If not Payton…who?

He shivered, uncertain whether his goose bumps were from the cold water or his chilling thoughts. He bumped the tap to warm, lathered his washcloth and began scrubbing his flesh with a fury. If not Payton…who? he asked himself again.

His partner and oldest friend? He couldn't believe it. Admittedly, Don had his faults—unmitigated selfishness, for one—but that didn't make him evil, or a murderer. He sure as hell wasn't stupid. If he was behind this, he'd never flaunt his open hostility toward Laura and risk suspicion falling on him—should something happen to her.

Susan was too smart for that, too. Besides, he'd bet the Texan's Vegas winnings that Don and Susan didn't believe anyone was after Laura. They seemed convinced Jake was an idiot to believe a word out of her mouth.

God, that glorious mouth. Laura's image flashed into his mind, bringing memories of last night's kiss. He'd been so relieved to see her, so furious with her, so completely out of control he'd nearly taken her then and there. She'd nearly let him. He swallowed hard, recalling. Passion threatened anew. He tamped it down with a muted curse.

He had to keep focused. Had to find the bad apple in this barrel. If it wasn't Payton, or Susan, or Don...who? Izzy, Payton's kid sister? That made little sense. She'd been dating Cullen, and she seemed as heartbroken as Jake when they assumed Laura had left town with Cullen. Izzy's motives seemed divided. On the one hand, she'd become even richer than before. On the other, she'd lost her best friend and lover.

Maybe Jake wanted Izzy to be guilty. Maybe he just wanted the person least close to him to be responsible for the hell he'd been living.

He shut off the water and stepped from the shower, jerking a towel from the bar. Travis? He couldn't imagine a Crocker killing one of their own. Besides, what had Travis gained by Cullen's absence and the success of New Again? Jake dried and dressed. Who else had Laura mentioned? His cousin Kim? That was laughable. The most vicious thing she was capable of was keeping the gossip about Laura and Cullen alive.

He ran a comb through his wet hair. Splashed on after-shave, wincing as it stung his cheeks. The scent filled the room. He'd changed brands after Laura left. Never wanted anything to remind him of her as the Old Spice had.

Now he couldn't get her out of his mind and he'd associate *this* scent with her after she was gone, only because he'd worn it while she was here. Hell, how had he been sucked into returning to Riverdell? Again, Laura's face filled his mind. She'd looked so forlorn. He'd been unable to resist the impulse to help her at any cost to himself.

"Damn it." Were Don and Susan right? Was he the world's biggest fool? What had he gotten himself into? Distaste lodged in his mouth. He didn't want to step foot in Riverdell. Didn't want to face any of the men he'd worked with…who'd laughed behind his back when Laura ran out on him.

He tossed his dirty clothes into the hamper and dropped the lid with a thump. The only man on the force he wouldn't mind seeing was his former chief, Ralph Russell. Another of Laura's suspects. He started toward the kitchen, drawn by the aroma of fried bacon. Ralph had run the least corrupt department Jake had ever seen. Not to mention he'd been Murphy Whittaker's best friend. That left his mom. At this, Jake did laugh.

Laura glanced up, a quizzical frown furrowing her lovely brow as she stirred eggs in a frying pan at his stove. He sobered, caught by how natural she looked here. His chest filled, then seemed to freeze, leaving him unable to exhale. He didn't want memories of Laura infusing every corner of his mind, visions of her in every corner of his house. He'd thrived here because there were no reminders of her.

Ever after this, his sanctuary would be tainted by her presence, her essence.

Would the memories be melancholy or painful? It depended on what they discovered in Riverdell. He swallowed over the lump in his throat. Would the trip be a wild-goose chase? Or would they find Laura's evidence among his mother's belongings? Doubt reached icy fingers around his heart. What if it wasn't there? What the hell would he do then? Was this innocent-looking woman going to make a fool of him twice in twelve months?

The possibility dampened his palms, grabbed his chest.

"I've made scrambled eggs." Laura smiled at him. "Jake, I'm so relieved that you've agreed to go to Riverdell with me."

He nodded, his mouth too dry for him to speak. *Just don't make me sorry, Laura.*

Laura discerned his unspoken warning as though he'd shouted it at her. She pressed her lips flat, her hand reflexively tightening on the frying pan handle. The last thing she wanted was to let him down. But his doubts mirrored her own. If the evidence wasn't among Ruthanne's belongings, he would never trust her again.

Forget that she'd had no control over where the sample jars might have been put. Without them, there was only her word that any of this had actually happened as she claimed. A man with Jake's law enforcement background could conjure a number of counterscenarios for Cullen's disappearance, Sunny Devlin's murder and that of the woman at the motel.

Laura knew none of those concepts would shed favorable light on her. She scooped the eggs onto plates, layering the largest portion onto the one she meant for him. She doubted she could choke down a single bite now. "When do you want to go?"

"I've got to call Kim."

"Why?" The knot in her stomach doubled.

"I told you—she's the one who packed up the house and arranged storage."

"Of course. I'd forgotten." Laura took the stool next to his. She lifted her fork and poked at the fluffy egg mixture. Contemplating facing Kim, and all the other Riverdellites who thought the worst of her, destroyed her appetite.

But Jake attacked his breakfast with the same gusto he'd shown since hitting his teens. A wistful smile swept through her at the memory of Ruthanne standing in the Wilder kitchen—amid a sea of grocery bags—laughingly complaining that it would be cheaper if she bought the Shop-rite until Jake was grown and paying for his own meals. "The boy's as bad as his papa's old Chrysler—a regular fuel guzzler."

It seemed he still burned calories like mad, Laura thought, recalling last night's passion in his garage, recalling the feel of Jake's leanly muscled body pressed against her. A flush swept her, and she strove for something else to concentrate on. "Did you sell your mom's house or keep it?"

His fork stopped halfway to his mouth. "Sold it."

The discomfited look that stole across his face twitched her nerves. "Who bought it?"

He finished chewing, swallowed, took a sip of coffee, then dug the fork into the last of his eggs—all without meeting her gaze. "Ralph Russell."

Laura's pulse leaped. One of their suspects had been living in Ruthanne's house? Dear God, what if the skin cream had never made it into storage? What if it was left in the house? Laura shoved her plate aside. "How long has he lived there?"

"Since escrow closed." Jake swabbed his plate with a last wedge of toast. "About nine months."

Her hopes hit the floor.

He finished the toast, reached for his coffee cup again

and stood. "If you're not going to eat, we can call Kim now."

"Are you going to mention me or tell her why you're coming to Riverdell?"

He frowned, obviously still unconvinced that his cousin might be involved in something as heinous as murder. "I won't tell her anything worth repeating."

"You call, then." She gathered the plates. "I'll clean up here."

"DELL PHARMACEUTICALS," Kim Durant answered in that falsetto voice that had annoyed him since they were kids. Why Payton had hired her as the receptionist, of all things, baffled Jake. He'd think the first impression Payton would want customers to have of DP would be something melodious. Harmonious.

"Hello, Kimmie." Jake settled down at his desk and leaned back in his chair. He could almost see her, tucking a lock of her auburn hair behind her ear, her deep-set hazel eyes heavily veiled in the latest makeup craze.

"Jake?" There was a note of expectancy in her tone. "Is Aunt Ruthanne worse?"

"About the same." He suspected this news disappointed his cousin. Not that Kim didn't truly love Ruthanne; she just loved gossip more, and sources outside of Riverdell were far and few between. "I wanted to make sure you were going to be around tomorrow."

"Well, yes, I am. Why?"

"I'm coming to town."

He heard her draw in a sharp breath. "My goodness—this is unexpected. What changed your mind?"

Her curiosity oozed through the phone line. Jake raked his hand through his hair and shifted uncomfortably in his chair. He'd told Kim months ago that he'd never step foot in Riverdell again. Damn. She'd jump on this news like a cub reporter gathering her first big scoop. Seeking to cool her ardor, he said the first thing that popped into his mind. "Business."

"Really? Payton doesn't have any meetings with bigwigs scheduled. So, who's visiting this one-horse town who needs a bodyguard?"

Laura's image filled his mind. How much she needed someone to guard her luscious body worried the hell out of him, wore on his nerves, shortened his temper. "*Personal* business."

"Oh, I see. Well, in that case, the guest room is ready and waiting," she said, a bouncing, eager note in her voice.

"I won't be there that long."

"Oh." She sounded disappointed. "I was hoping to get some of the gang together and give you a real welcome home."

"Riverdell isn't my home anymore, Kim. I won't be back after this trip."

"I see." She was quiet a moment. "Well, then just why are you coming?"

As Jake had expected, "personal" didn't register on Kim's brain as being "none of *her* business." He'd thought long and hard about what to tell her, realizing it had to be something believable—something to do with his mother's belongings. "I want to make arrangements to dispose of Mom's things. Close out the storage unit."

"I don't understand—I thought you said she wasn't any worse."

"She's not, but let's face it—she won't be getting any better."

"Well, that's pretty brutal."

"It's realistic."

"Well, forgive me for finding it just too sad." There was a catch in her voice now that cut straight to his heart and roused the anger he felt at losing his mother bit by bit to the ravages of the disease she'd developed.

But it wasn't his cousin's fault. "I'm sorry, Kim. Didn't mean to bark. I just hate this, you know?"

"Yeah. Me, too," she said on a sigh. "Well, look, if this is too painful for you, Jake, I could empty the storage unit."

"No." The word snapped out of him, sounding a bit quick, as though he had something to hide. He strove to soften his tone. "Er, I appreciate the offer, Kimmie. But there might be one or two things I'd like to keep."

"Well, sure, silly," she said. "Just tell me what they are and I'll ship them to you."

He frowned, his brows coming together with such force a jab of pain poked his forehead. Dear God, one day soon he would have to empty that storage unit for real. Dispose of all the items that had constituted his parents' lives, his childhood. His throat closed as if grabbed by a giant fist. "That's just it—I may not want anything. But I have to look."

"Oh. Well, sure."

She giggled, a nervous tittering that grated on his ragged nerves.

"Well, I've got the key. I'll either be home or here."

"I'll call when I hit town."

As she stacked the dishes in the dishwasher, Laura considered the problem of the missing skin cream. They had to find it. Nothing else would restore Jake's trust in her. His love for her. He'd been a part of her life for as long as she could remember. Losing him had felt like losing her parents all over again. It had opened the wound in her heart and left an ache as deep and mean as some viral strain, rendering her vulnerable in ways she detested.

That could change tomorrow—*if* they found her evidence. Just thinking that she might have a future filled with friends and family—instead of the bleak one she'd envisioned these past twelve months—roused her anxiety. Her hands trembled and her skin prickled. She doubted she could get through the next twenty-four hours on hope alone.

If only somewhere in her befogged brain Ruthanne knew where she'd put the sample bottles.

Laura closed the dishwasher with a thump. And if Ruthanne did know, could she tell them? Just how "good" was she on her good days? Perhaps they should visit her today. If Ruthanne could tell them what she'd done with the sample jars, they'd have a starting point.

Better that than a blind search. Thinking of all the furnishings and knickknacks Ruthanne had in her home, Laura imagined a storage unit filled to the rafters. It would take forever to go through all the boxes. And it might be a waste of time if the jars were still in the house now occupied by Chief Russell.

She headed for Jake's office. Strange that she should feel so disquieted. Anxious with anticipation, yes. The hair on her arms standing up, no. She rammed to a stop. She knew this sensation. This gut-crawling premonition. It came whenever her pursuer neared.

Jake! If the killer had seen her with him at the hospital, he would know to look for her here. Laura hastened down the hall again, realizing as she neared the office that Jake was still on the phone. She slowed as she heard him tell Kim that he was coming to Riverdell to get into his mother's storage unit. She froze. He'd promised he wouldn't mention that. Promised he wouldn't mention her. Had he broken both promises?

Disappointment wedged its way into her heart, but she understood he would continue to betray her until he truly believed her. If the sense of foreboding she felt was any indication, she doubted his trust would come soon enough. She tamped down her resentment, bit back the sting of tears behind her eyes and shrugged off her hurt feelings. She didn't have time for the luxury of self-pity.

Jake settled the receiver on its cradle as she stepped through the doorway. For half a second, she watched him staring thoughtfully at the phone and wondered what had caused the sadness searing his face.

She moved closer to him. "I think we need to leave as soon as possible."

He shifted toward her, his features rearranging themselves into a concerned expression. Frowning, he stood. "What's the rush?"

She buffed her arms, rubbing down the gooseflesh. How did she describe this sense of impending doom without sounding hysterical? "It's just a feeling...."

Once, that would have been enough for Jake; once, he had trusted her hunches. She held herself rigid. What would it take to make him heed her instincts now?

He cut across the distance between them and caught her gently by both upper arms. "Are you okay?"

He searched her face, his gaze intense and probing, the scar giving him the look of a menacing inquisitor. But such kindness issued from him, caring so palpable it could only come from deep within and then only if it was genuine. This Jake believed in her. This Jake owned her soul.

All her misgivings about him fled. She wanted to fold herself against his beloved body, huddle in his embrace like a small child escaping from the world and its evils.

But they weren't children. The passion brewing in his darkening teal eyes was pure adult male...and it thrummed a chord deep within her woman's body.

She gathered a shaky breath and reached up to stroke his cheek, feathering her fingers across the scar. He flinched, but she whispered, "No. Please, let me...."

He hesitated, then swallowed hard and nodded. His grip tightened on her arms. She knew him well enough to know he feared her revulsion and the humiliation and pain that would follow if she recoiled in disgust. But nothing about Jake disgusted her. And as she traced the uneven skin from the ridge of his cheekbone to his jaw, she reassured him with a tender smile. "It isn't deep, is it?"

"No. I was lucky. No muscle damage. It's just ugly."

She cupped his face in both hands. "I'll admit it's given you a dangerous visage, but ugly? No, Jake. Ugliness comes from within, and by that measure you're the most handsome man I've ever met."

His eyebrows lifted slightly, then dipped low. He shook his head and laughed softly. "You never did have good taste in men."

She trailed a fingertip down to his mouth, her tongue sliding out to lick her dry lips. "My taste in men is singular and A-one."

He groaned and pulled her against him, his arms slipping around her waist. She buried her hands in his hair as his mouth claimed hers. The instant their lips touched heat poured through Laura, spilling life into every corner of her being, this man's touch as essential to her as electricity to a lightbulb. But this wasn't the urgent, anger-driven kiss of last night. This was two wounded hearts testing, discerning, relearning.

Her body melted against his with all the ease of fitted pieces in a jigsaw puzzle, natural and right, both complementing the other, both incomplete without the other. Joy hummed through her veins, numbed her mind.

She wanted nothing more than to be swept away on these delicious sensations, nothing more than to savor every ounce of Jake's sweet love, nothing more than to be one with him, to feel him inside her, to have all that should have been theirs....

If not for a murderer.

The thought swept through her like an Arctic tide, shattering the crest of desire she rode and bathing her with renewed foreboding.

"No, we can't..." She gasped the words on a ragged breath, struggling against the embrace she'd ached so long to enjoy.

Jake blinked, confusion and suspicion written on his ardor-flushed face, heady in his gruff response, "Why not?"

"I told you we have to get out of here. Now."

He stepped back, shaking himself as though he were shaking off his feelings for her—the way a wet dog shook water from his fur. She expected anger from him—hurt, even. Anything but the disappointment and distrust etching the tight line of his mouth. "Why?"

She cast him a silent plea for understanding. "I don't know how to explain it. Call it woman's intuition."

He dug his hand through his hair. "Call *what* woman's intuition?"

"This awful feeling I have that my pursuer is closing in on me. On us." Her smoky eyes turned the color of charcoal with fear and her hands trembled.

The last of Jake's frustrated passion fled as he realized she was terrified. He wanted to pull her back into his arms, reassure her that he'd keep her safe. But at the moment, she needed solid reason, not well-meaning promises. "Your hunches are seldom wrong, Laura, and I'm not dismissing this one, but...I don't think the person after you would try something as blatant as coming to my house to kill us. That's not his M.O. So far every attempt on your life has been made to look like an accident—which shows our murderer is a patient person. He's not going to panic now."

She twisted her hands together. "Tell that to this awful feeling in the pit of my stomach."

"Okay." He nodded, and smiled wryly, hoping to ease her distress. "Our flight isn't for two more hours, but it won't hurt to go to the airport a little early. Get your things and meet me in the garage."

"You don't have to ask me twice." Her grin was all the thanks he needed. She hurried into the hall.

Minutes later, they were backing out of his garage. The sun shone golden in a sky as blue and wide as the Pacific, reminding him of the day he'd found this hilltop, had stood staring out at its see-forever view. For the first time in months he'd been able to breathe and set aside his disappointment, his heartache. He'd bought the house immediately—without a second thought to its access: a winding, single-lane road with several sheer drop-offs on either side.

"I didn't realize on the taxi ride up here last night how treacherous your driveway is," Laura said, her gaze craned over the edge.

"That's why I own this four-wheel baby." He patted the steering wheel as though the Cherokee were a person he admired.

"It must be pretty dicey when it snows or there's ice." She glanced questioningly at him.

The concern in her smoky eyes spread warmth through his chest, but he was instantly dismayed. Having Laura near felt too normal, too comfortable. Once this was over and she walked back out of his life, would his private aerie still hold the heartache at bay? "There's a cot in the downtown office for those nights the weather misbehaves. It's not—"

His car phone interrupted. He snatched it up. "Jake Wilder."

"Oh, good." Relief rang through the vaguely familiar female voice, followed by a heavy sigh. "This is Mrs. Thatcher at Sunshine Vista Estates."

The tremor in her voice pricked his nerves. "Is something wrong, Mrs. Thatcher?"

"Well, dear me, yes, I'm afraid so."

"What?" Disquiet chattered through him. He hadn't expected his mother to suddenly worsen. Had helping Laura set the killer after Ruthanne?

He asked tightly, "Has something happened to my mother?"

Laura's eyes were huge, the fear in his heart mirrored on her lovely face.

Mrs. Thatcher hesitated. "Then...she's not with you?"

"Of course she's not with me."

"Oh, dear me. We—er, I had so hoped she'd come to your house."

"Come to my—" He shook his head as what the woman was trying to tell him sank in. "She's missing?"

Laura gasped, her hand flying to her mouth.

Mrs. Thatcher said, "Dear me, yes, it seems she is."

"I'll be right there." He dropped the phone on the seat, then grasped the steering wheel with both hands and accelerated. The wheels keened as he rounded a curve.

"Jake, I know you're scared—I am, too." Laura pressed her body against the seat as though braced for a crash. "But if you don't slow down you're going to drive off the bluff."

He shook himself, easing up on the gas. Damn. He stepped on the brake. "Sorry, I didn't mean—"

The pedal slammed flat against the floorboard. Jake's heart jumped three beats. Dear God, no! "Hang on, Laura! The brakes are gone!"

Chapter Eleven

"Hold on!"

Jake's command stole Laura's breath. She grasped her armrest and jammed her feet to the floorboard as though that would help, as though the Cherokee had a backup brake on the passenger side.

The car accelerated, plunging past thirty to forty in the blink of an eye. Her stomach dropped to her toes. Her heart galloped. A scream climbed her throat, but she didn't cry out. She'd survived the horrors perpetrated on her this past year by keeping silent and disappearing. But she couldn't run from this.

"There's a pull-off halfway down the drive. If I can get the car to slow before then—" He broke off, jerking the steering wheel left, then right.

She slammed against the door. Pain punched her shoulder. Panic bloomed inside her like a poisonous plant digging tainted thorns through her skull. She was used to worrying about herself. About her own survival. But this terror threatened Jake. And she knew without seeing a shred of evidence that she had brought this on him by seeking refuge in his house.

A metallic screech rent her thoughts. Widened her eyes. The Cherokee skidded sidelong against a concrete-hard wall of sand. She blinked and the wall vanished, giving way to sheer cliff again. Fear soured her tongue.

The Cherokee's rear end skidded toward the drop-off. Laura swallowed a yelp. Her muscles were so tensed they ached. Jake turned into the skid. The vehicle bounded back onto the road. Sweat beaded his face. His knuckles were white on the steering wheel. His gaze riveted the road. The speedometer read fifty and climbing.

She forced her gaze from the drop-off to the twisting black ribbon they traveled at breakneck speed. It looked like one of those tubed water slides—except this seemed like a never-ending slide into hell. Cacti loomed every few feet, their arms raised as though they were waving. Waving goodbye? Was this the end?

"It's just around the next bend," Jake said. "I'm going to hit the emergency brake."

The next curve fell away and she saw it, a turnout on the opposite side of the road, wide enough for two cars, and beyond it solid-rock embankment. Instead of being relieved, she grew more frightened. Knowing this vehicle came equipped with dual airbags did nothing to calm her.

A crash was inevitable.

Jake yanked on the brake. She felt the rear tires lock. The car bucked. She was jerked back in her seat. The seat belt cut into her shoulder.

He yelled, "Come on, compression. Kick in. That's it— that's it."

Her eyes steadied on the dropping speedometer gage. Forty. Thirty-five. Thirty. She braced for the crash, her feet all but implanted in the floorboard now.

But Jake still had the Cherokee on the road. Why?

She felt it then; the sharp grade had lessened, the descent suddenly half as steep as moments before.

He drove past the turnout. "We aren't out of the woods

yet, but I think we can make it to the bottom without further harm.''

Laura's chest heaved once, then twice, then again, as though she had bucketsful of air trapped in her lungs. Seconds later, he pulled onto a long flat section of shoulder. The car bumped over tumbleweed and thick sand and gradually rolled to a stop.

He turned off the motor, dipped his head back against the headrest, let out a huge breath of his own, then turned toward her. His eyebrows flickered and concern threaded his expression. ''Are you okay?''

''I—I—'' But she couldn't get out the words of reassurance. She felt chilled, bloodless. Inside she began to quiver, a gentle quaking that started in mini shock waves, building and building until her hands trembled, her body shook. She hugged herself.

Jake unhooked his seat belt and scooted over to her, unhooked her seat belt and scooped her close. ''Hey, hey, it's okay. We're safe.''

Oh, how she wanted to believe that, but she knew they were safe only for the moment. The killer would try again. And again. Until he finally succeeded. She buried her head against Jake's chest, heard the steady, comforting beat of his heart and welcomed his solace. This time she wasn't alone. This time she wouldn't run. This time she would stand and face her pursuer head-on.

Jake cupped the side of her head in one hand, his other splayed against her back. Little by little, her heartbeat steadied beneath his touch, and the tremors racking her body eased until they disappeared altogether. She drew a breath, leaned back and lifted her gaze to his.

With the back of her hand, she brushed a strand of hair from her forehead. ''This was no accident, Jake.''

''I know.'' He wanted to turn the Cherokee around, race

back up the bluff to his house and give it a thorough going-over. He wanted to find out where and how the perp had gotten into his garage. Then call the local gendarmes and have the place dusted for fingerprints—though he doubted the killer had been careless enough to leave any.

"Are you still sure he or she is patient?" Laura asked. "Isn't it possible that this person has grown frustrated by all the failed attempts on my life?"

"If he or she were impatient, we wouldn't have been alive this morning to make the drive down the bluff."

She considered a moment. "I guess you're right. What now?"

Jake flicked her chin gently and gave her a tight smile. "As much as I'd like to hold you like this all day, we have to get to Sunshine Vista and find Mom."

Laura nodded and sat straighter. "How do we do that with a sabotaged car?"

"My mechanic is just down the road, and if we take it slow we won't have a problem."

GARCIA'S GARAGE STARTED life as a mom-and-pop gas station and grocery store in the forties. The buildings had been remodeled somewhere along the way and now held three huge work bays and an office. No one had bothered painting the outside in years and the weathered exterior looked dismally gray against the desert backdrop.

Jake pulled up to the bay closest to the office and emerged from the Cherokee. Laura didn't wait for him to open her door, but climbed out, too.

"Hector," Jake greeted the approaching mechanic.

Hector Garcia was a wiry, middle-aged Latino with mid-night-black hair and warm brown skin. Despite a limp and features far removed from classically handsome, he possessed a confident air that Jake had seen draw many an inviting female glance.

Hector had big hands—with grease embedded in every crease and under the nails—which he was wiping on his grimy coveralls as his coffee-colored eyes swept the damaged Cherokee. He shook his head and gazed at Jake. "What the hell…? Somebody sideswipe you?"

"Brakes gave out," Jake answered.

"No way, Jake-man. I check those out myself."

"Well, I want you to check them again…and don't be surprised at what you find, *amigo.*"

Hector's ebony eyebrows shot up. His wicked grin showed off strong, white teeth. "You piss somebody off, Jake-man?"

Jake flashed a wry smile of his own. "Yeah, maybe."

"You shouldn't be running around with other men's women. Learn from Hector's mistakes." The mechanic nodded toward his bum leg. "Some men no like you mess with their lady."

From the moment they'd met, Hector assumed Jake had gotten his scar in combat with some jealous lover. Flattered that the charismatic man thought him an equal player in the game of love, Jake hadn't bothered correcting the misconception. "Yeah, but Maria ended up marrying you instead of your brother, didn't she?"

"A woman with hot passions like a chili pepper—theys worth the troubles." He winked at Jake. "Good thing Mateo such a lousy shooter."

Jake bit back a laugh at the startled look on Laura's face. Her eyes were as huge as the hubcaps nailed over Hector's office door.

Hector's gleaming smile flashed again as his gaze drifted over her. "This one has the fire, too, no?"

Laura's cheeks pinkened, and Jake grinned at her. "Yes."

Hector nodded. "She the reason for this?"

"Could be." Jake's smile fell and his gut clenched. Hector's troubles had been resolved without anyone dying. Would Laura and his? He pulled his wallet from his back pocket. "If you find somebody tampered with the brakes, will you keep it to yourself?"

"Hector no tell nobody nothin'." He shook one beefy hand at Jake. "No. *No dinero.* We settle later. You need the loaner?"

"If you don't mind."

"*No problema.* Mateo! Get Rubia's keys for Jakeman."

Laura's eyes widened again as Hector's brother, the one who'd shot him, came scrambling out of one of the bays and ran into the office.

"Thanks." Jake patted Hector's shoulder.

Hector laughed. "Just keep Rubia away from the jealous *hombres.*"

RUBIA, THE LOANER CAR, was a ruby red 1975 Impala, its front dipped low to the pavement and its rear pitched saucily toward the heavens like some teenaged girl bending over to touch her toes—all gleam and polish and tight body. Inside, tucked and rolled, crushed-velvet, bloodred upholstery covered the seats and door panels. A fringe of navy blue, hanging yarn balls circled the velvet headliner.

Laura, still puzzling over the dynamics that made up some families, burst out laughing. "Is this what they call 'hiding in plain sight'?"

She settled onto the passenger seat, her gaze locked with Jake's as he shut the door. He grinned at her. "It's not the most inconspicuous vehicle we could choose, but time isn't on our side and it is reliable."

He strode to the driver's side and got in. "Hector treats this car better than Maria, and believe me, he treats that woman like a queen."

Rubia smelled as if it were imbued with little vanilla-scented air freshener trees. Laura reached for the seat belt, but found none. If the seat had been vinyl she might have slid off onto the floorboard, but the velvet hugged her new jeans like Velcro.

Jake started the engine. The mufflers roared like a disturbed lion and the huge speakers, occupying the space normally reserved for the back seat, flared louder, booming out a Freddy Fender classic. Laura threw her hands over her ears. Jake punched the off button on the radio.

They looked at each other and laughed again. The humor slid all the way to the core of her, chasing off the last of her shock over their harrowing ride down the bluff.

As they gained the main road, Laura's gaze flicked across the unfamiliar instruments on the dashboard. "I saw cars like this in L.A. They had those hydraulics that pumped the rear end up and down to the beat of their boom boxes."

"Rubia can shake her bootie, too. But I think we'll skip that this ride." Jake raised the darkened windows, closing out the cool breeze that stole the warmth from the sunny day. His face sobered, all humor gone.

She knew he was thinking about Ruthanne. Laura had suppressed her own worry for nearly an hour, but as they roared along in the noisy car, it returned with a rush that stole her breath. Had the poor woman just wandered off on her own? Or had someone lured her away from the senior complex?

God help her, Laura didn't want to think the worst. But

fear railed at her as loud and fierce as the uncapped mufflers. If they were right about someone tampering with the
Cherokee's brakes, then Ruthanne might be in the hands
of a killer. She shuddered.

The Garcias crossed her mind again. Mateo and Hector
had apparently found a way to live with the fallout from
their shared love of Maria. "Family" had many definitions
in these modern times—mom, dad and 2.5 kids seemed
the exception rather than the rule.

The families she'd known in Riverdell varied from the
close-knit Crocker clan to her own odd household. How
would the Crockers deal with the loss of Cullen…if, as
Jake and she suspected, he was dead?

And what about herself? Raised by an aunt and uncle
poorly suited to parenting, she'd sought and found a sur-
rogate mother in Ruthanne Wilder. She loved Jake's mom
as much as he did. If something happened to her… She
gulped. *If I've brought something or someone evil down
on Ruthanne, how could Jake and I find a way to live with
the fallout of that?*

Her stomach felt heavy, a cold brick against her heart.
She tried telling herself that Ruthanne had merely wandered off and would be found by the time they reached
the senior complex. But as they sped down one road then
another, she feared the killer had somehow guessed Jake's
mom might know where the face cream was.

The thought raised goose bumps on every inch of her.
She rubbed her arms, but the raw worry gnawed at her the
rest of the ride.

Jake pulled into the parking lot of the Sunshine Vista
Estates and swore. "What the hell is going on?"

Unlike yesterday, the parking lot was jam-packed. Jake
frowned as he maneuvered through row upon row of
spaces. "I've never seen it this crowded."

"That car over there is leaving," Laura told him, spotting glowing backup taillights at the end of the lane. But when they reached the vacated spot, "compact" was painted on the curbing of the short narrow slot. Definitely not the space for a zaftig lady like Rubia. She needed room to stretch her shiny hood and wide tail. They settled for parking her on the street and hurried to the complex.

"I would have thought the cops would be here by now," Jake said, commenting on the absence of any police vehicles.

"Maybe they've come and gone and are looking for Ruthanne already."

"God, I hope you're right."

People, milling about and visiting in small groups, crammed the entrance hall and huge foyer. It reminded Laura of the audience at Riverdell's Vale Theater enjoying intermission during the special showing of *Gone With the Wind* the year she'd turned thirteen.

Jake clasped her hand and hurried through the crowd to the reception desk. "Where can we find Emily Thatcher?"

They were told she awaited their arrival in her office, and a moment later, they were ushered into a room as sterile as any research lab. The decor ran to chrome and blue Naugahyde, without a single personal touch.

Mrs. Thatcher sat behind an uncluttered desk beneath a window with a view to the front entrance. Her once-brown hair had prematurely grayed and now resembled striped nutmeg. She wore it in an unflattering little bun at the crown of her head, pulled off her face so severely that her eyes—a flat blue, with straight, thick lashes and thicker eyebrows—seemed to bulge.

Jake went toward her. "What's going on? Where's my mother?"

"Oh, dear me. I'd hoped your delay meant you'd found her."

A bony woman, the manager of Sunshine Vista Estates had the voice of a twenty-year-old and the face of someone in her sixties. Laura guessed she was thirty-five and old before her time. She pointed to the two chairs pulled up to her desk.

"Please, sit down."

"I don't want to sit down," Jake said. "Just tell me what happened. Have you notified the police?"

"Goodness, no. Dear me, the police…"

The woman started up in her chair, then dropped back with a plop. She seemed shaken to the point of not knowing proper procedure. How, Laura wondered, had she been promoted to the manager's position of a senior housing complex? Didn't anyone monitor this place?

Mrs. Thatcher sighed. "I so hoped you'd found her."

"I want the police called now," Jake said.

She flinched as though he'd slapped her, but she quit whining and reached for the phone. "Certainly. Certainly."

Laura sank into the chair nearest the wall and Jake paced. As she listened to Mrs. Thatcher explaining the situation to the person on the other end of the line, Laura realized from the answers the woman gave that she was being asked the same questions that would be asked about a missing child. What had Ruthanne Wilder been wearing? When was the last time someone saw her? A knot formed in Laura's throat. With her failing mind, Ruthanne *was* as vulnerable as any toddler.

Laura exchanged an anxious glance with Jake. Was he also worried about the encroaching night? It would be getting dark soon. And cold. What if they didn't find her? What if she hadn't taken warm clothes, didn't find a warm place to stay? Laura's throat constricted and her eyes burned.

Mrs. Thatcher replaced the receiver. "They've dispatched a car, which should arrive at any moment."

"Now," Jake said, clearly trying not to fume, "tell me how this happened."

"Of course."

Emily Thatcher's plain eyes steadied on Jake. Laura detected a glint of resentment in them—as though Jake's barely suppressed anger at her were misdirected. The woman folded her hands on her pristine desk, appearing in control of herself and the situation.

Her words, however, exposed her cracked composure. "We are hosting a bake sale and craft fair today. That's why all the people are here. They've been coming and going all day. Mr. Jarvis, the activity coordinator, is in charge of these special events. This is really his responsibility. Not mine. But he called in sick. That new strain of flu."

She lifted her chin indignantly. "Fool man. Should have gotten his flu shot. Can't say I didn't warn him. Anyhow, he didn't dare come in. Couldn't have him exposing everyone. So, well, I ask you, what else could I do? I told him I'd man the cash table."

Jake hit the desk with his open hand. "I don't give a damn about Mr. Jarvis. Get to the part about my mother."

"Of course." Her face went white. "I saw Mrs. Wilder when she came to buy some chocolate donuts. She said they were your favorite and she couldn't cook them without a stove in her room." She offered him a weak smile. "Well, I sold them to her and then she went on, walking around the lunch room, and, dear me, I was just so busy, of course, I lost track of her."

"When did you realize she was missing?" Jake's raised voice cut through the tension in the room like a buzz saw.

"Oh," Mrs. Thatcher chirped, twin dots of bright pink standing out on her hollow cheeks. "Well, we were serving all the residents lunch in their rooms today, you know, since we were using the lunch room tables for the special event."

"Get to the point." Jake dug his hand through his hair. His face muscles were so taut his scar looked raised and angry and as fresh as the fear in his eyes. "Please."

"Certainly." Ice layered the word. "She wasn't in her room when her lunch tray was delivered. I wasn't alarmed—what with all the visitors. Mrs. Wilder was excited about that, you see. She's very social most days. Loves talking to anyone who will listen. So, of course, I figured she was around somewhere." She shifted her gaze to Laura, as though seeking the sympathy and understanding she wasn't getting from Jake.

She wouldn't find any here, either, Laura thought, wanting to strangle the incompetent woman. "Did you look for her?"

"Not personally. I was in charge of the cash, after all. But I set Muriel to the task." Muriel, she explained, was her secretary. "She spent the next hour checking through the crowd and was eventually told by one of the aides that Mrs. Wilder had had visitors today."

"Visitors?" Jake said. "Who?"

"All I know is that it was a man and a woman."

Laura's pulse skipped. "Did she leave with them?"

Mrs. Thatcher twisted her hands together again. "Well, dear me, of course I checked on that, but I'm afraid no one signed her out and that is the only way she can *officially* leave the premises."

"Did she or didn't she leave with these people?" Jake pushed.

"Dear me, how should I know? It would certainly be against all of our policies."

Laura saw a police car pull up in front of the building.

Jake smacked the desk again. "But it could have happened?"

Mrs. Thatcher cringed. "Of course it *could* have happened. We're not running a prison here, Mr. Wilder. We only lock the outside doors at night. Conceivably your mother could have walked out, but that just hadn't been a concern before today."

"She has Alzheimer's! It *should* have been a concern!"

"Alzheimer's?" Mrs. Thatcher unclenched her hands and an unpleasant spark lightened her dull eyes. "This is the first I've heard of that."

"You didn't know?" Jake oozed disbelief. "That's your excuse?"

"It's not an excuse. I cannot be held accountable for something I knew nothing about." Emily Thatcher squared her shoulders and met his glare with one of her own. Confidence returned to her scrawny frame. This was a woman more concerned about her own welfare than the welfare of someone who'd been left in her charge. And she'd just discovered an argument against her inept handling of a bad situation, a buffer between herself and a pink slip. "Mrs. Wilder should have been in the twenty-four-hour-care wing. But I must warn you that the board will have to review the matter and they may not be willing to allow her to continue on here in any manner, under the circumstances."

Jake planted his palms on her desk and leaned to within an inch of her. His eyes narrowed, his expression hard. "If you think I'd entrust my mother's care to this slipshod establishment for one more night, you're sadly mistaken. As soon as she's found, I'll make other accommodations for her.''

Before she could respond, the police interrupted, a man and woman both in uniform. Laura stood to one side as Jake and Emily Thatcher gave them the necessary information about Ruthanne. Laura felt helpless and impotent and scared. Her stomach seemed awash in acid. She wanted to rush them on their search, go searching herself. But within minutes, they had set the hunt in full swing.

The ensuing hours brought increased anxiety and no sign of Ruthanne. As darkness fell, the officer in charge suggested Jake and Laura go home; he promised he'd call the minute there was something to report.

''I'm not going anywhere until my mother is found.'' Jake's face was set as hard as his mind.

Laura wasn't sure she wanted to go back to Jake's house, either. Not if someone *had* tampered with his brakes. But Jake was dead on his feet. He needed to eat, to rest. And he would flat refuse to do that in a motel or restaurant. She knew him well enough to know that he wouldn't tolerate any more strangers this day.

''Please, Jake.'' She touched his arm. He glanced down at her, and the hurt in his eyes, the fear, twisted around her own frightened heart. ''You're exhausted. You need to eat something. Get some sleep. Then we'll come back.''

''No, I—'' The fight seemed to rush out of him and for half a second she feared he'd collapse on her. But all he did was nod. He turned to the police officer. ''Okay. But I'll be back by midnight.''

Jake was silent on the ride home. But he clutched her hand on the drive up the bluff, a silent reassurance that he was there for her, an unspoken proclamation that he needed her to be there for him.

He parked Rubia in front of the house and shut off the engine, but made no move to exit the car, or to release her.

Laura glanced at the light glowing from somewhere within his huge home, then squeezed his hand. "Come on, you eatin' machine, let's see if there's something besides eggs to feed you."

He acquiesced.

But halfway to the door, he caught her arm and pulled her to a stop. Alarm scurried through her. "What is it?"

"The door. I locked it when we left."

Now it stood ajar.

Chapter Twelve

Jake pressed the keys into Laura's hand and whispered, "Go back and get in the car. If I'm not out in two minutes or if something—anything—happens, take off. Get the police."

"No, Jake, I'm not letting you go in there alone. Come with me," she pleaded, her voice as muted as his. "Let's just leave. We can call the police together—let them go into the house and make sure it's safe."

"No. I've had to stand by and let others take charge of the search for my mom, but I'll be damned if I can't handle an intruder. I'm a cop, for God's sake, Laura." His voice was a growl, but he hadn't meant to take his frustration out on her. She'd been the only thing, the only one, who'd made the last few hours bearable.

"I want you out of harm's way." He wanted this danger behind them. He wanted them safe to examine the lingering feelings between them, to see if there was a chance to regain the trust and love they'd once shared. He smoothed his knuckles along her cheek. "Please, get in the car."

Laura nuzzled his hand and released a quavery breath. "Be careful?"

"I promise."

She squeezed his arm and started back toward Rubia.

He waited until she rounded the front end of the car, then he moved stealthily through the shadows toward the open door. He had a gun in the secret compartment inside his entry closet—if he could get to it...

Cautiously, he inched the door inward, his nerves alert, his muscles poised to stem off any sudden attacks. None came. He slipped through the narrow opening. The foyer lay in darkness, but he wondered at the light in the family room. He didn't remember leaving one on. He slipped gingerly to the closet and caught hold of the knob.

A noise from the kitchen riveted through his nerve endings. He froze. His pulse tripped loud inside his head. He strained to identify the noise. It came again. A clink, clink... No, that was nuts—but it sounded like ice cubes hitting a glass. He listened again and came to the same conclusion. Was his intruder so comfortable he was fixing himself a drink? The possibility doubled Jake's fury.

He eased the closet door open and ducked inside. A moment later he had the loaded gun. He cocked it, held it in both hands, the barrel pointed toward the ceiling, and emerged from the closet. The noise in the kitchen had stopped. He noticed an unfamiliar scent in the air. Something feral, spicy. Like a man's cologne.

Dog-tired, jackal-hungry and coyote-rabid that his mother was missing, Jake felt like storming into the next room and blowing off the intruder's head. Damn the consequences. The compulsion slivered through him like shards of glass. A wayward thought of Laura filled his mind, stole the energy from the urge to lash out and inflict pain on someone. He'd promised Laura that he'd be careful. And he'd never broken a promise to her.

He forced himself to calm detachment, to act like the cop he was. With slow, deliberate steps, he crept toward the family room with his senses honed like radar. Someone spoke. Jake's heart stopped. He stood stock-still, trying to figure out his opponent's position. The voice sounded again, and he realized the person hadn't spoken to him.

His heart skipped and thumped. He frowned and listened harder. But all he heard were voices. He couldn't make out what was being said—only that there was more than one person, carrying on a quiet conversation. And one of them sounded like a woman. What the hell?

He rounded the corner and stepped to where he could see a man and woman sitting on the sofa that faced the kitchen area. Each held a glass filled with dark liquid and ice cubes. He leveled the gun at them. "Freeze."

Two startled people jerked toward him. The woman let out a squeak of alarm, sloshing her drink on her clothes.

She was petite, curvaceous, Laura's age—with natural white blond hair cut like a cap around her triangular face, and jade-green eyes generously layered with mascara. Her slacks, sweater, and windbreaker had a retro-seventies flavor, and were all in varying shades of green, a favorite color Jake recalled. "Izzy?"

"Put the gun away, buddy."

The man sitting on the sofa next to Isabelle Dell started to rise, holding out his glass like an ineffective and tiny shield. Travis Crocker. He wore a letterman's jacket, in the purple and white that were Riverdell high-school's colors.

His ebony hair was swept off his forehead, a dark frame for his arresting features.

Travis's aqua eyes steadied on the gun. He pointed to the couch opposite him. "She let us in."

"She?" Jake kept the gun leveled at them. He'd known these people since childhood, but after the day he'd had, all friendships were null and void. Trust would have to be earned anew.

Movement brought his gaze to the second sofa. Someone rose into view, her back to Jake. A woman's age-spotted hand lifted to her mussed gray hair, fingers plucking at the tightly permed do. He knew this head, this hand, the colorful pantsuit he'd given her last Christmas, that he'd heard described again and again all afternoon and evening—that he feared he'd have to identify when her remains were found.

But he made no move toward her. The shock of finding her here after all the hours of searching, of fearing the worst, of stifling one atrocious image after another, stole his senses.

His chest felt too small for his lungs, his heart. He couldn't breathe, couldn't move. He stood transfixed as a statue, uncertain if he was seeing this woman or if he wanted to see her so badly he'd made her up. "Mom?"

Ruthanne Wilder shifted toward him and her eyes opened wide. "Jacob Jerome Wilder, put that nasty pistol away. You might need it for your work, but I won't stand for you flashing it around the house when we have company, J.J."

J.J. His mother's pet name for him finally penetrated his paralyzed brain. He lowered the hammer of the gun and thumbed on the safety.

Izzy rolled her eyes, her hand on her ample bosom. Travis emitted a noisy sigh and his chest heaved as though he hadn't breathed in the last few minutes. He sank back to the sofa beside Izzy and took a huge gulp of his drink.

Jake put the gun into the back waistband of his pants and hurried to his mother. He reached for her tentatively, grazed his fingers down the sides of her face, then laid his big hands on her tiny shoulders with the care he would give a frail, antique China doll. He knew it was ridiculous, but he worried she'd collapse at his very touch. She seemed solid enough, however, and physically unmarred.

He studied her eyes, the teal so like his own, and saw recognition there, a gift usually absent these days. The tension that had encased him since Mrs. Thatcher's call shattered, and relief ebbed through him like an incoming tide.

"Thank you, God," he whispered, and folded her into his arms, thrilled to have her safe. At last.

"J.J., I can't breathe." She squirmed, pushing her hands against his chest. "You forget your own strength."

He laughed and released her. "You are okay, aren't you?"

"Now that I can breathe, I'm just dandy."

Jake had to admit she looked none the worse for her misspent afternoon and evening.

"*She's* fine," Travis said. "But I'm not so sure about you. What's going on? You really had me worried for a minute there, buddy."

"*I* had *you*—?" Jake couldn't believe his ears. His fury returned, sweeping his body with the power and heat of a hot breeze blowing up the bluff. "We've been frantic about my mother for hours. The police are out in force looking for her. How dared you take her away from Sunshine Vista?"

Travis's mouth dropped open. He glanced questioningly at Izzy. She shrugged, then shifted toward Jake. "What are you talking about? What is Sunshine Vista?"

"Her home."

Izzy shook her head as though he were speaking in tongues. She swept her free hand about the room. "I thought *this* was her home."

"You thought—" He stopped, feeling as confused as she looked. Had he jumped to some erroneous conclusions? He narrowed his gaze. "Are you saying you didn't bring her here?"

Travis interjected, "I told you she was here when we got here. She let us in."

The energy fizzled from Jake's temper, and he dropped to the sofa opposite Izzy and Travis. All the questions he'd planned to ask them would now have to be answered by his mother. But would she be capable? He ignored the pain in his lower back, caused by the ill-positioned gun. All he felt was the anxiety churning his gut. "Then what are you doing here?"

Travis took a swallow of his drink, as though whatever was in it might give him fortitude. He lowered the glass and held it between both hands. "We came to talk to you about Cullen."

Jake's relaxing nerves tensed again. Did they have news of Cullen? Or did they expect him to give them news? Either way, they could have called from home instead of flying to Arizona. Fear slithered through him. Were they really here because they were after Laura? Laura! Dear God, he had to warn her. But how?

THE MOON HUNG LOW over Laura's head, bathing the land with a soft light. She could see the face of her watch clearly. Four minutes had gone by since Jake had left her standing here, her stomach awash with nerves. Had someone overpowered him? Worry blocked the chill night air from penetrating her clothing.

She paced the length of the house, half expecting to see a car tucked alongside the garage. But the only thing parked there was a rusted wheelbarrow. Where was the intruder's car? Parked in the garage?

The thought hurried her back to the front of the house. Still no Jake. She glanced at the open door, then at Rubia,

torn with indecision. If she started the noisy car it would
alert an intruder to her presence. That might get Jake
killed.

She shuddered. Her pursuer wouldn't hesitate to eliminate Jake. He may have tried once already today. He may
even have taken Ruthanne. Her throat clenched at the
thought.

She needed to know what was going on. She ran to the
house, slipped inside and gingerly shut the door. She expected utter quietude, but voices floated to her from the
family room. Her pulse skittered. She identified Jake immediately, but who was he talking to?

Her heart gave a sudden leap of hope as she heard a
woman's voice rise in a scolding tone. Ruthanne? She listened harder. Dear God, it was.

A joyous cry climbed her throat. She smashed her fist
against her open mouth just in time. She had no idea what
the situation was. They might be in trouble. She stole a
little closer, then ducked into the hall that led to the bedroom and office. A third voice reached her.

A chill skittered up her spine. Her palms dampened.
Another woman. She strained to identify this new voice
and a jolt of recognition shot through her. Izzy! She'd
know those whiskey-throated tones anywhere. God, how
she'd longed this past year to call Riverdell and hear Izzy
say, "Hello." A friendly voice in a world without friends.

But it hadn't always been that way.

Laura leaned against the wall and closed her eyes, recalling the day they'd become friends. Real friends.
They'd been in the ninth grade—and the town was abuzz
with the news of a plane crash in Honolulu. Izzy's parents
had gone down with the 259 other hapless souls.

Laura had been the only one of her classmates who'd
really understood what being an orphan meant. She knew

exactly how Izzy felt. The sole difference between their losses was that Izzy hadn't been wrenched from the only home she'd ever known. Her brother, Payton, ten years older, returned from college, took over the family business and the guardianship of his teenaged sister.

Laura opened her eyes. Throughout the ensuing years, the friendship had blossomed and grown into something wonderful; they had been as close as sisters, sharing their secret hopes, their deepest disappointments.

But this past year had torn Laura away from everything and everyone she'd ever trusted, made her doubt all that she'd ever taken for fact. A year ago, she'd have trusted Izzy with her life. Would that have been a mistake?

Travis Crocker's voice snatched the thought away. What was he doing here with Izzy? She heard him ask Jake something; the only word she caught was "Cullen." Wanting to hear more, she took a step toward the family room.

Approaching footsteps froze her in her tracks. She swung around and darted down the hall into Jake's office.

"I FORGOT TO SHUT the front door," Jake told his guests, hurrying into the foyer. He had to warn Laura to stay outside until he could get rid of Izzy and Travis. "Wouldn't want any critters crawling in from the desert."

The front door was closed. Jake's heart dipped to his toes. Had Laura shut it to muffle the sound of the Impala's noisy engine when she'd left? Please, God, let that be the case. Gingerly, he yanked the door open. Rubia still hugged the curb, looking in the moonlight like a lady of the evening willing and ready to party.

He pivoted to find Travis right behind him, eyeing his actions with suspicion. "Have you heard from Laura and Cullen? Is that why you called the other night?"

Jake pushed the door shut with his heel. Damn. Laura

must have come inside. She had to be in the office or his bedroom. He prayed she'd stay there until he could get rid of these two.

"Jake, have you heard from my brother?"

Jake's nerves felt as tight as newly strung barbed wire. He glanced at his mother, hoping to God that she wouldn't mention seeing Laura yesterday. That she wouldn't call him a liar. "No. I told you the other night that I hadn't seen or heard from either of them. Didn't you believe me?"

Travis's handsome face crumpled. "Oh, I don't know. I'm just damned scared that something awful has happened to Cullen."

Izzy sidled up to Travis and snaked her arm around his waist. The gesture was more than friend to friend. It was intimate. Familiar. Sometime in the past year these two had gotten close. Was that the reason Travis wanted Cullen found? Did he want to tell his brother that he'd moved in on his woman while he'd been gone? Or were they after Laura?

Izzy sighed. "I was afraid this would be a wild-goose chase. Let's go back to our motel."

Travis nodded resignedly. "Okay, hon. Call the cab."

LAURA PRESSED HER BODY to the wall just inside Jake's office. Her heart thudded against her chest. She held her breath. A minute passed. Then another. No footsteps sounded in the hall. She blew out air and shoved away from the wall, shaking the tension from her arms.

Moonlight filtered through the windows, bathing the room in a dusky light. She crept over to Jake's desk, sank into his thick leather chair and stared at the telephone.

She wanted to call the police.

But she didn't want to have to spend hours explaining

why she'd summoned them, if it wasn't necessary. The thought that that might somehow put the Malibu police onto her chilled the blood in her veins. Until she and Jake found the face cream, she had no proof that any of her claims were true. She could be slapped into jail on a first-degree-murder charge. Or two.

But what were Travis and Izzy doing here? Did they suspect from the phone call the other night that Jake had a line on Cullen and her? Had they come looking for information about Cullen? Or were they looking for her?

The threads of fear and confusion that tangled inside Laura now twined with pity for them all. Izzy had been in love with Cullen Crocker for years. Her heart must also have been broken by that awful, lying note. Unless...

Unless Izzy was behind this.

Laura could barely stomach the notion. But she couldn't dismiss it. Izzy had motive, means and opportunity. Laura wanted to scream. She hated not knowing. Hated suspecting everyone she'd once trusted. Hated wondering whether Izzy and Travis were friends or foes.

But the fact that they were in Jake's house, with his missing mother, didn't bode well for their innocence. And Laura would not risk Jake's and Ruthanne's lives on speculation. She reached for the phone.

There was no dial tone. Fear crashed in on her. Had someone cut the lines?

"Hello?"

A man's voice leaped out of the receiver and landed against her ear like a gunshot. Laura flinched so hard she dropped the phone. The line wasn't dead. Someone had called at the same time she'd picked up the phone. Shaking, she retrieved the phone and gathered her breath, but before she could answer, the voice came again.

"That you, Jake-man?"

"No, it's Laura."

"Laura?" A second voice sounded in her ear. This time it was Izzy's.

Laura's heart dropped to her toes, dragging her stomach along for the ride.

Izzy had to be on the extension in the kitchen.

Panicked, Laura disconnected too quickly to hear Hector ask, "Laura, you the hot tamale with Jake-man today?"

Chapter Thirteen

Jake couldn't hear what Izzy was saying, but he watched her face pale and clench. What the hell was going on? She'd wanted to call a cab for Travis and herself. That shouldn't have caused her to look like she'd spoken with a ghost. She held the phone out to him. "Someone's on the line. They're asking for 'Jake-man.'"

Hector. Jake felt himself grow pale. He didn't want to accept this call in front of his unwelcome guests. But he had to know about the brakes.

He took the phone from Izzy. "Jake Wilder."

"*Amigo,* you gots the *señoritas* in the blender. *¿Sí?*"

Jake didn't know what the hell Hector was talking about, and he hadn't the patience to figure it out. He mumbled in the affirmative and turned away from Izzy. "What did you find?"

"The brakes?" Hector said.

"Yes. Was it what we thought?"

"HELLO, LAURA." Izzy flipped on the office lights. "Why are you hiding here in the dark? Afraid to face your old friends."

Laura gulped hard, shaking off the unreasonable fright. It wasn't as though she were alone in the house with these people. She rose from Jake's chair and shoved a lock of wayward hair from her forehead. "*Should* I be afraid of you, Izzy?"

Izzy laughed, a throaty "Ha" that held no mirth. Her gaze was as hard and cold as green glass. "Last year at this time I wanted to scratch out your eyes. But I've had twelve months to get over it. How's Cullen?"

"More to the point—*where* is Cullen?" Travis stepped into the room, crossed to Izzy and laid a hand on her neck. The possessive gesture cleared up any questions Laura had about just how "over it" Izzy was.

Still, her spine went rigid. Where the hell was Jake when she needed him? And how exactly was she supposed to answer Travis's and Izzy's questions? *Gee, I don't know, but Jake and I think Cullen might be dead—that maybe you and Izzy murdered him.* She hugged herself. "I haven't seen him."

"And you expect us to believe that?" Izzy's hands were on her hips.

Laura started to defend herself, to tell Izzy she didn't care what she believed, but it struck her suddenly that she did care. She cared right to her core. "I didn't run off with Cullen."

"What—?" Travis shook his head. "Oh, please. The whole town saw the note you lef—"

"Laura." Jake appeared in the doorway, as tall and shining as any knight. Relief and gratitude swirled through her. He motioned for her to come to him. "Why don't you take Mom to my room and tuck her in. She's had a long day. I've got to call the police and tell them she's been found."

Laura hurried to the doorway. "How is she?"

"She seems fine, but I haven't had a chance to question her yet."

Laura nodded and escaped.

"Hey, what about my questions?" Travis released Izzy and started after Laura. He gave every appearance of a spoiled child who thought his concerns more important than any other.

Jake blocked the doorway. "Let me call off the police and then we can talk. I'll answer your questions and you can answer some of mine. Meanwhile, why don't you help yourselves to another drink."

The standoff lasted a full minute, both men unwilling to back down.

Izzy touched Travis's shoulder. "It's your call, Trav."

"Okay." He retreated a step. "One more drink. Call the cab, Iz."

He turned back to Jake, and shook his finger. "Laura better tell us what she knows."

LAURA FOUND RUTHANNE sitting alone in the family room. Against the rough-hewn beams, the huge windows, the floor-to-ceiling fireplace and the oversized furnishings, she seemed smaller than she was, a lost and lonely dwarf in a giant's castle.

Laura wanted to run over and sweep her into a bear hug. But what if that startled her, frightened her? "Ruthanne?"

She was surprised when the older woman's head came up and her eyes widened with dismay.

"Laura!"

"Hello."

Ruthanne's gaze narrowed with suspicion. "Does J.J. know you're here?"

"Yes." Laura noticed Ruthanne's gray curls were still flattened against her head, as though no one had washed her hair for a week. Could patient neglect be added to the grievances against Emily Thatcher?

"I can't believe he let you into his house—after you ran off with—with that other man." She pointed to Travis as he entered the room and gathered up his glass. "*His* kid brother."

That startled everyone. Jake claimed his mother was worn out, but she seemed to know where she was, who she was and who was with her. And from the scorn in her voice when she mentioned Cullen, she even seemed to remember that Laura had left Jake at the altar.

If Ruthanne was this coherent, would she remember what she'd done with the face cream? The possibility excited Laura. But she couldn't, wouldn't, bring it up in front of Izzy and Travis. "Jake said I should help you get settled down for the night in his room."

"I'm not tired and I won't be shuffled off to bed like some child. I'm just as curious to hear what you've got to say for yourself as these two are." She gestured toward the kitchen. "Fix me whatever you're having, Isabelle. I'm as thirsty as a marathon runner."

Jake arrived several minutes later to find them all sitting in the family room, drinks in hand. He gave Laura a bewildered glance. "I thought you were putting her to bed."

Laura shrugged. "She's not tired."

He eyed his mother's drink with alarm. "What is she drinking?"

Ruthanne bristled. "Wipe that policeman's scowl off your face, J.J. A little whiskey and water isn't going to kill me."

But Laura could see he feared it would. She rose and crossed to him. "Want me to fix you one? You look like you could use a shot of something potent."

"No. Not now."

As Laura slipped onto one of the bar stools, Jake strode to the sitting area. Once again, Izzy and Travis sat across from Ruthanne, but they were eyeing Laura with disdain at her choice of seats. Probably wondering why she was distancing herself from them. Either that, or they knew why she was.

Jake sank down beside his mother, landing so close to her that he rustled her shiny sweat suit and caught the scent of her clothes—not the sweet, dried-outdoors smell of his childhood, not the fabric-softener smell of his own clothes, but an antiseptic, bought-by-the-gross, detergent scent. This odor defined the residents of Sunshine Vista Estates; even the perfume he got for her every few months couldn't purge the institutional tang.

A familiar resentment knotted his gut. Why did growing old reduce so many to commune dwellers? Snatching their individualities? Their personalities? He detested that nature could level the strong, detested that it had forced him into putting his own mother into such an establishment.

It had seemed the best thing to do when Mel Van Sheets, her doctor in Riverdell, diagnosed the Alzheimer's. Jake had considered having her live with him. Knew it would require twenty-four-hour care due to his work—which often took him away for weeks or months. But he'd feared she'd be too lonely—isolated as this house was. Besides, he was terrified she'd wander outside and step off the bluff.

He couldn't risk that. In the end he'd decided she'd like it better somewhere with arranged activities and daily access to others her age. No more. Tomorrow he would start interviewing home health-care agencies.

"Are you zoning out on us again, Jake?" Travis's question held impatience.

Jake shook off his dark thoughts and glanced at Travis. He didn't want to deal with these two people tonight.

"J.J." Ruthanne tugged his shirtsleeve. "What is Laura doing in your house after what she did to you?"

The question startled Jake. He turned his full attention to his mother. Intelligence registered in her eyes. Shock rippled through him. This past year, Ruthanne's inherent forgetfulness had grown so that it was a rare day that she had her wits about her this strongly. Hope that she could answer his questions flared inside him.

The hell with Travis and Izzy. Right now it was more important to find out whether the person after Laura had had anything to do with his mother leaving Sunshine Vista Estates this afternoon. "Mom, who brought you here?"

She made a face, obviously wondering why he'd switched the subject. "Well, I don't know the man's name."

"The man?"

"The taxi driver."

Disbelief lifted his brows. "You came by cab?"

She gave him a tolerant smile and patted his hand. "J.J., I'm an adult and perfectly capable of getting around on my own."

Before Jake could respond, Travis set his drink on the coffee table with a thunk. "What has this got to do with why Laura is in your house?"

"Yes," Izzy added. "Why the heck are we talking about this again? Who cares how your mother got here?"

"I do." Jake ground the words between his clenched teeth.

Izzy rolled her eyes and sank back against the cushions of the sofa. Travis reached for his glass again.

Jake gathered a calming breath. "Did you have some visitors at the complex today?"

"Are you accusing us again of kidnapping your mother?" Izzy's face beamed an unattractive red.

Travis jumped right in. "We never—"

"Shut up both of you. I didn't invite you here and I'm barely tolerating you as it is."

"But you said you'd answer my questions," Travis whined.

"I don't care what I said! *This* is more important to *me!*"

"Well, I've got a mother, too, you know." Travis tossed his head like a bull that was one snort away from attacking. "And she's losing sleep wondering why her son doesn't call."

"Then maybe if you'll quit interrupting we could find out something that would help us all," Jake retorted.

Ruthanne ignored the melee, smiling as though recalling some pleasant memory. "There was a special event today—a craft fair with baked goods. I bought you some chocolate donuts."

"I heard," Jake said, grappling with his temper.

She glanced at the couple across from her. "J.J.'s awfully fond of chocolate donuts."

Jake lost the struggle with his patience. Someone had tried to kill Laura and him earlier today. That same someone might well have gone after his mother as a warning to them. Or as a lesson in how vulnerable she was. "I don't want to talk about donuts."

Ruthanne patted his hand again. "They're in the kitchen, J.J."

Jake tried gently to move her back onto the subject. "Then you didn't have any visitors?"

She frowned, her scruffy brows bobbing down, then immediately arching. "Oh, you know, now that you mention it, I believe I did."

"Who?" Jake said quicker than he'd meant. He knew he should proceed slowly, but he feared if he didn't get the question answered immediately his mother's mental clarity would snap and the information would slip into that never-never land she occupied most days lately. "Who were they?"

"They?" she said vaguely.

"You do!" Izzy yipped. "You think it was us!"

"I think we've talked this visitor of your mother's to death," Travis said, his tone clipped with ire. "Could we, please, move on to Cullen?"

"I'm warning you two for the last time." Jake glared at them both, his nerves as raw as open wounds. "Keep quiet or you can wait for your cab outside."

He gazed at his mother and his nerves tightened. She could be seconds away from checking out on him. It usually happened without warning. "Mom, do you recall the man and woman who came to see you at the senior complex today?"

He heard Izzy draw a sharp breath and tossed her a dark scowl. She blinked and clamped her lips shut, but fury rose from her like a bad smell.

"Man and woman?" Ruthanne repeated, her tone as vague as the dullness that was creeping through her eyes. "Well, now, I don't think there was a woman...was there?"

Jake's heart skipped anxiously. "A man, then?"

Travis set his glass down again. "Can't this wait? Our taxi will be here soon and—"

Jake rounded on him, fury surging through his veins. Travis might hold his own in a brawl with Jake, but they both knew he'd never win. He closed his mouth, but anger mottled his handsome face.

Ruthanne took a big swallow from her glass. "The man, oh, sure...a friend of yours, J.J."

Friend? Someone she knew? Hope and fear collided inside Jake. If the man was someone his mother knew, then it could very well be Laura's pursuer. "What friend of mine?"

"You know." She snapped her fingers. "Oh, what's his name?"

Jake plowed a hand through his hair. He glared at the glass she held. Was it her illness or the alcohol that was muddling her thoughts? He reined in the urge to yank the drink from her and toss the contents in the sink. "You'll have to give me a hint, Mom."

"Oh, darn it all." She clicked her tongue and her expression darkened, as though she hated herself for not being able to tell him this simple thing. "I can't remember his name...and I was so sure I knew it."

Jake recognized the signs of her illness, edginess and agitation, in the trembling of her hands, the tenseness of her posture. He gathered her free hand in both of his. "Forget his name for now. Maybe you could tell me, instead, what he looked like."

This seemed to calm her. She nodded and grew thoughtful. "Hmm. Well, I'm not positive, mind, but I think he looked, well...maybe like him."

She pointed at Travis.

"Cullen?" Izzy said, scooting close to the edge of the sofa.

"Was it?" Travis barked.

Jake scowled at him again. This time Travis ignored him. "Was it my brother?"

Total dismay controlled Ruthanne's features. She seemed not to have heard any of their questions. She blinked five times, then she shook herself and steadied her gaze on Izzy. "On second thought, maybe he looked like her."

"Like me?" Izzy's green eyes opened as wide as a

mountain meadow. "Are you saying it was Payton? That's impossible. He's in New York on business."

"Besides," Travis added, "Cullen has black hair. Payton's blond. Why isn't this woman under a doctor's care?"

"She's much worse than Kim told me." Izzy set her drink down on the coffee table, oblivious to the water ring forming even as she withdrew her delicate hand and wiped it on her green slacks.

"I told you two to shut up and I meant it." Jake started to rise, intending to toss these uninvited guests out on their collective butts. "I won't have you confusing her."

"No one's confusing me," Ruthanne protested, pulling him back into his seat. "I know exactly what the man looked like."

"Then tell us," Travis insisted.

She took another drink. "Tell you what?"

"Dear God." Travis sighed disgustedly.

Jake blew out a frustrated breath. He'd dealt with his mother's memory lapses too often this past year. And every time he felt the same impotent rage at its unfairness. But he knew she might have already told them all she could. Knew they might never learn if Laura's pursuer had visited her at the senior complex today. He jammed his hand through his hair again, inadvertently gazing at the duo across from him.

Izzy and Travis wore twin expressions of disgust. Travis mumbled, "Next thing you know she'll say her visitor looked like Laura."

"Laura?" Ruthanne twisted around and glared at Laura. "He didn't look like her."

Jake offered Laura an apologetic smile. He hated that his mother's attitude was hurting her, but he knew she understood his quest to find out who was behind Ruthanne's disappearing act. And right now, her hostility toward Laura was the only sign that Ruthanne clung to some shred of reality.

He squeezed her hand, deciding to give it one more shot. Laura's life depended on it. Hell, maybe his own and Ruthanne's did, too. "Mom, take a deep breath and imagine that you're seeing the man again—as you saw him earlier today."

"Oh, sort of like the association game Doc Van Sheets uses. I like that game." Ruthanne closed her eyes and scrunched her face.

Jake kept his voice monotone. "Imagine you're at the craft and bake sale again. Do you see it?"

"Yes…all the lovely items for sale…all the people. Like a big party."

"Yes, yes, concentrate on the people…visiting with one another…with you…someone familiar approaches…a man. Picture him again in your mind. Can you see him?"

"Yes…I think so."

"Okay. Good. Can you describe him?"

She opened her eyes and gave a groan. "Oh, the image vanished."

"Don't fret, Mom." Jake stuffed his disappointment and frustration and tried a different tack. "Maybe you can still remember. How about his hair color? Or was he bald? Tall? Short? Medium? Fat? Thin?"

"Good grief," Travis muttered, tossing back the last of his drink.

"J.J., is this really important?" Ruthanne laughed self-consciously. "Of course not. Anyway, there were just so many people at the craft fair…I—"

She broke off. "Wait, I do recall something. He was from Riverdell. Guess that's why it's so strange that I can't remember his name. Because I used to know it. Oh, well."

She snapped her fingers again, dismissing the whole subject.

With that, Jake knew he ought to give it up, but he couldn't resist one more question. "Did he tell you to come here?"

"Oh, no, dear. I don't think so. I wanted to bring you the donuts...while they were still fresh."

That much he conceded could be true. She could have gotten it into her head to bring him the donuts and even called a taxi. Hell, she might even have remembered his address. But there was one thing that could not be explained by sudden recall, because he didn't keep any hidden keys outdoors. "Mom, how did you get into the house?"

"Why, the door was open. I thought surely you were home with the door open."

A car horn sounded outside.

"Damn it, that's our taxi." Izzy lurched to her feet, bristling with annoyance. "And Travis didn't get to ask any of his questions."

"I'd say it worked out the way Jake and Laura planned." Hostility seeped from Travis like a bitter fog as he set his glass on the table beside Izzy's and stood. He poked a finger in the air separating himself from Jake. "But don't think this is over."

Jake was still trying to process the fact that his door wasn't locked when his mother arrived at the house. He waved a dismissive hand at Travis. "I fear you're right, Crocker. There's more going on here than meets the eye."

Travis froze. "You do know something about Cullen. For God's sake tell me."

"If I learn anything that you don't already know, I'll get in touch with you."

Travis stepped toe to toe with Jake, the difference in

their sizes apparently no longer concerning him in his fury. "Oh, don't worry. You haven't seen the last of me. I'll be back."

Jake straightened to his full height, squaring his shoulders. He didn't blame Travis for worrying about his brother—he even understood his anger—but he'd had all he was going to take of his insolence. "I'm not the enemy here. So back off and get out of my house. We'll talk again when we're both in better moods. I'll be here. I'm not going anywhere."

Out of the corner of his eye, Jake saw shock capture Laura's face. She froze, her glass halfway to her mouth. Damn, he'd promised her they'd leave for Riverdell immediately. It was the first promise he'd ever made her that he'd have to break. He wasn't going anywhere until he'd moved his mom out of Sunshine Vista Estates and had her ensconced here.

"We're going," Travis grumbled, leading Izzy toward the foyer. "But we will be back."

"You gonna be here, too, Laura?" Izzy asked as they came alongside the bar.

"I don't know," she murmured, her voice hoarse with emotion.

Izzy eyed her with cruel speculation. "Travis and I deserve to know whatever you can tell us about Cullen."

"I've told you all I know."

One of Izzy's blond brows lifted. "And I think you're holding out on us. If you change your mind, we're staying at the Days Inn on Main Street."

Jake watched the blood drain out of Laura's face, and he figured she was thinking the same thing he was. It seemed mighty coincidental that these two people were staying at the same motel where Sunny Devlin's car had been blown up.

He wondered anew whether they were sincerely looking for Cullen, or if they had come to see him only to get a bead on Laura. Just how long had they been alone with his mother? Had she told them anything about Laura's missing face cream? And if she had, why had they insisted on sticking around to confront Laura about Cullen?

Because the best offense is a good defense?

As Jake followed them to the foyer, Ruthanne caught up with him and tugged his sleeve. "J.J., aren't you going to make Laura leave, too?"

Jake's gaze locked with Laura's and he offered her a silent apology, a look that said they would talk as soon as they were alone.

But Laura understood better than he realized.

She'd spent the last twelve months relying on herself, surviving by her wits, by any means at hand. In the past two days, she'd selfishly involved Jake, reveled in the sharing of her fears, begun to count on his help in her search for the missing evidence, in her quest to unmask a murderer.

But she'd thrust him into a dangerous game and placed Ruthanne's life on the line, as well.

She finished her drink and slipped off the stool. Now he couldn't go with her to Riverdell. Ruthanne had to come first. But the journey couldn't be postponed. Laura cringed at the thought of returning alone. But fear wouldn't stop her. She'd get the key to the storage unit from Kim and search for The Venus Masque herself. Even though it might be the last thing she ever did.

The need to move swept through her. Laura gathered the drink glasses off the coffee table. Noting the faint stains left by Travis's and Izzy's glasses, she wiped the sleek oak surface with a dish towel, again and again. The cloth left flecks of fiber, but all her scrubbing didn't diminish the ugly circular blots.

Why had they been so careless? It was almost as if they'd wanted to deface his furniture, pay him back in some spiteful way for his reticence about Cullen. She could see where they'd resent *her*—if they truly thought she'd run off with Cullen last year and was keeping his whereabouts secret.

But what had Jake ever done to either of them? Until today, he'd treated them both with deference and friendship. But all bets flew out the window when his mom vanished. Not even their death-defying plunge down the bluff that morning had scared Jake the way Ruthanne's disappearance had.

His relief at finding her here, unharmed and under suspicious circumstances, reduced the cordial manner he reserved for company to plain old-fashioned rudeness.

Any sympathy he might feel for the Crocker family counted for nil. Ruthanne came first. She suspected Travis would put his own mother above any concern Jake might have if circumstances were reversed. Especially when a killer was on their tail.

And *he* was near. She could almost smell him. She hugged herself as Jake and Ruthanne strode toward her. The old urgency prickled her skin like a heat rash, and Laura knew she would have to leave here. First thing in the morning.

Before someone else died.

Chapter Fourteen

Jake hated sleeping on his office sofa. It was too short, too narrow and too hard. Only the view offered pleasure—stars that looked close enough to grasp. But he could no more grasp them than he could silence the uneasiness that crowded his thoughts.

Ten minutes after Travis and Izzy left, he'd finally convinced his mother that Laura wouldn't break his heart all over again. But would she? What if he acted on his need for her? Gave in to the ache he struggled with even now?

Damn, he wanted her.

Her image filled his mind, teased his senses, throbbed through his veins. And he knew what scared him. He wanted more than sex—he wanted Laura. He wanted to feel her, to inhale her scent, to touch her hair, to press his flesh to hers, to bury himself inside her. He wanted her secrets, her dreams. He wanted to know if they matched his own...the way they used to. He wanted her to want him.

And he wasn't sure she did.

He socked his pillow and rolled over. His feet shot out of the covers. Oh, she needed him—to help find the evidence and end the hell she'd been living. But any ally would suit her purposes. As much as he'd like to think she'd chosen him because she'd never stopped loving him, the truth was, she'd sent his mother that face cream. What quicker way to find it than through him?

He swore, shifted around once more and landed on the floor with a loud thump. His long legs tangled in the blanket and sheet. Cursing, he struggled out of the bedding and stood. Although, he'd made the noise of a clumsy burglar, neither his mother nor Laura emerged from his bedroom to investigate.

He bunched the covers onto the sofa, flipped on a light, then blinked as his eyes adjusted. He took a long melancholy look around his office. Tomorrow, he'd dismantle it. Tomorrow, he'd see about getting it renovated into a suite for his mother. Ruthanne living here would require a real adjustment—he thought, tugging jeans on over his otherwise naked body—but he wouldn't put her back in a private facility until he exhausted all other avenues.

Until her illness left him no other choice.

The fear that that day would arrive too quickly sent him heading to the kitchen for a shot of whiskey. He decided to check the locks once more on the way. He padded down the hall and into the foyer, where he quickly tested the door. Finding nothing amiss, he moved toward the kitchen, and froze.

Laura stood near the family room window, her shape outlined by the gentle moonlight swathing her. His heart caught at the sight of her, and his loins tightened even before he realized she wore only his T-shirt again. It stopped midthigh on her long, slender, creamy-looking legs. His mouth watered. His throat closed. His need grew.

"Couldn't sleep?" he asked in a voice too full of desire.

She wheeled around slowly, as though she'd been expecting him. "Your mother snores."

He grinned. "Dad complained about the same thing."

Their gazes met and held for ten heartbeats. Then Laura's eyes slid from his face. "Still sleep in the nude, huh?"

He frowned. He'd put on his jeans. But as his hand collided with his fly, he realized he hadn't bothered with the buttons. Grinning sheepishly, he fastened the middle one. "Guess Mom will be the end of that. I've decided to move her in here."

"Yes, I think that might be best...for now." They both knew it was a temporary solution, but she was glad for Ruthanne. "When I grow old, I want a son like you."

"Just like me?" He hadn't meant to ask that and hated himself for spilling his guts like a fool.

Oh, yes, Jake, Laura thought, *exactly like you—half a dozen babies, just like you.* But she wouldn't say that to him. It would raise his hopes, both their hopes. And she realized now how cruel that would be. If he believed in her again, in them again, and something happened to her before she unmasked the killer, Jake would feel that she'd abandoned him. For a second time. She could spare him that. She would spare him that. "A son just like you would eat me out of house and home. Are you hungry? Want me to fix you something?"

She started past him, but he gripped her arm. "I came out here for a shot of whiskey—to help me sleep. But I think this would do the trick better."

He pulled her against him, simultaneously lowering his mouth to hers. Although her mind screamed "Don't do it," her body melded to his as though it had once been part of him, fitting perfectly curve for curve, plane for plane, lip for lip. The stars she'd been studying moments ago seemed to have crawled inside her head. They swayed; they danced; they burst in bright sparklers, spraying across her awareness, scorching her resolve like so many twinkling illusions, burning her from the inside out.

She gave in to the shower of desire raining through her, and her arms climbed his naked chest, circled his strong neck, her hands twining his thick hair. She felt starved, her body as bereft of love as another's might be of food.

He pulled back, but not away, gazing down at her with desire-glazed eyes. His breath came short and fast. He cupped her face in both hands, groaned her name. Then deepened the kiss. Her heart swelled and her hunger bloomed, seeping hot and moist through her.

His big hands grazed her back, the touch known, welcomed, missed. Little sighs of pleasure floated from her again and again. Then his hands were under the cloth, pressed to her flesh, exploring, renewing, awakening.

He ground his hips to hers, and she lifted one leg around his thigh as she massaged his naked back. Her fingers found their way to his waistband, and despite her promise not to hurt him again, she knew she couldn't stop the inevitable finish of this encounter.

Nor did she want to.

"J.J., what are you...?" Ruthanne's voice rang out as the light flared on. Her sharp, indrawn breath sounded a second quicker than Jake and Laura could leap apart.

Laura's face burned with embarrassment at being caught like teenagers.

"Mom." Jake's voice was hoarse.

Ruthanne's expression held outrage. "I thought you said Laura wasn't here as your girlfriend? But the moment I turn my back you're sucking out her tonsils."

"I, we—" Jake bit his cheeks, obviously trying not to laugh. He strode to his mother, caught her gently by the shoulders and moved her back toward the hall. "It's okay."

"No. It's not. You're falling for her again. Mark my words, J.J., once burned, twice learned. She'll only hurt you."

It was so much what Laura feared she would do she blanched. If even Ruthanne, in her confused state, knew that Laura could hurt Jake, then Laura would have to stop all future sexual encounters before they started. No matter what it took. She felt suddenly numb, her spirits battered by Ruthanne's hostility and her soul empty without Jake's love.

Ruthanne couldn't help her attitude. But a killer was responsible for Laura's broken heart.

Jake returned a few minutes later. She could see he was ready to pick up where they'd left off. In truth, so was she. But she determined not to let him see that. "I think we'd better settle for whiskey as a nightcap."

"Mom won't get up again." He reached for her.

She sidestepped him, shaking her head. "Just the same, I'd rather not risk it."

"Okay." Hurt flitted through his eyes so swiftly she couldn't swear she'd seen it. He moved to the cupboard and took down the half-empty bottle of Jack Daniels, then set two glasses on the counter beside it. "One or two fingers?"

Her gaze dropped to his hands, to his strong, tapered fingers. She'd rather have them on her, in her, than measuring the height of whiskey in a jelly glass. "One."

She slipped back onto the bar stool and he joined her, sitting two stools away as though he needed the distance. His jeans, she noticed, were buttoned properly now. She reached for her drink; the glass was cool against her palm, the liquid hot going down. "Did you speak with Hector tonight?"

"Yes." His expression was grim. "Someone messed with the brakes."

The tiny sip of whiskey she'd taken landed in her stomach like a dollop of acid and she shuddered. She'd known in her heart that whoever was pursuing her was responsible for the failed brakes. But having it confirmed, somehow made it even more horrifying. "How did he or she manage to sabotage your Cherokee? By breaking in here?"

"As soon as the sun is up, you and I are going to figure that out. Then I'll beef up my security."

She tossed back the last of her drink, wincing at its bite. She had to get away from Jake before she succumbed to his magnetic draw and threw away all her resolves to save him from herself. "First thing in the morning, then."

But the first thing Jake did in the morning was call Riverdell. At the grogginess in Mel Van Sheets's voice, Jake said, "Sorry to call you so early."

"No problem, Jake."

The doctor's baritone rumbled into his ear like water crashing through a tin pipe.

"Is Ruthanne worse?"

"About the same, I'd say. But she is one of two reasons I'm calling."

"Oh?"

"I'm taking her out of Sunshine Vista Estates and moving her into my house." He explained the events of the day before as they pertained to his decision. "But I haven't a clue how to find a good home health-care agency."

Mel rattled off some suggestions, pausing while Jake jotted them down. Then, sounding more awake, the frogginess gone from his voice, he said, "Now, what's that second thing, son?"

"This one's more touchy, Doc. It will require your complete discretion."

"Say, now, I reckon we both know I can keep a secret or two. So, what's up, son? I confess you've whetted my appetite."

Jake could almost see Mel stroking his thin, gray mustache. Or had it silvered by now? He leaned back in his desk chair and reached for his coffee. "Have you had any John Does during the past twelve months?"

Mel Van Sheets had been the county doctor and medical examiner in and around Riverdell since before Jake was born. He'd never married, but treated the whole town as though he were its patriarchal head: Father Wisdom, Daddy Comfort—the Know-all, Cure-all Wizard of Riverdell.

Not a giant, as that title implied, but a man of average height and stocky build, with kind blue eyes and medium-brown hair, now turned completely gray.

"A John Doe, huh?" The doctor cleared his throat. "That's an odd question from someone no longer on the RPD. You thinking of ditching that bodyguard business of yours and coming back home? Somebody's gotta fill Ralph Russell's shoes when he retires next month and you'd do the office proud."

"I appreciate the vote of confidence, but I'm not moving back to Riverdell any time soon."

"That's a pity. You're missed around here."

"Thanks. So, what about the J.D.s? Anything you can tell me?"

"I've had three, as a matter of fact. One found beside the tracks east of town, one at the dump and one near Handley's farm. All badly decomposed by the time I got my hands in them."

"But you did the usual, right?"

"Autopsies R me," he joked, chuckling.

"Any of them murdered?" Jake held his breath.

"Well, now, like I said, wasn't much left but bones when they were found, but I wrote up two of them as suspicious. One had a smashed skull. But whether or not he was murdered would be hard to prove. Drifters meet with a wide manner of woes."

"I see."

"So, spill. Why is a bodyguard in Arizona so curious about the deaths of three vagrants in eastern Washington?"

Jake hesitated. What he was about to say would likely surprise this good-spirited old man. "I have reason to believe one of them might be Cullen Crocker."

"What!" Mel shouted. He'd delivered nearly every citizen in Riverdell and took personal offense whenever God called one of them home without first consulting him. "But he and Laura— Lordy, son, I'm sorry, that was insensitive as hell. But—"

"It's okay, Doc. I felt the same way as you the first time I faced this gruesome possibility. But I ran into Laura this week and she definitely did not leave Riverdell with Cullen."

"But the note…?"

"Forged." Jake could see he was going to have to offer Mel a little more information in order to circumvent his disbelief. "No one in the Crocker family has heard from Cullen for a year."

"A whole year?" Mel whistled. "Well, now, that's plain old mystifyin'. Why wasn't I told? I usually know all the gossip in town before it hits the grapevine, but this is a new one on me. His ma was in last week, but not a peep out of her about Cullen."

Jake suspected Cullen's mother had had enough speculation, sympathy and pity thrust on her after the wedding fiasco to last her a lifetime. He knew he had.

At length, Mel said, "If what you're saying is true, then we could be looking at murder."

"Yes."

"Don't take offense, son, but other than you, why would anyone want to kill that nice young man?"

"That's a long, nasty little story that I'd prefer to tell you some other time."

"All right, but can you tell me why you're coming to me instead of Chief Russell?"

Jake's gut clenched. Ralph Russell wielded a power in Riverdell that lent itself to both sides of the law. As far as he knew, Ralph had always landed on the honest side. But he had access to paperwork that could turn a murder into an accident, he'd been Murphy Whittaker's best friend, he would have known about the face cream and Laura had talked to him the day of the wedding. Ralph was one of the original investors in New Again. All of which gave him motive, means and opportunity.

Jake couldn't rule him out as a suspect, or put Laura in further jeopardy by alerting Ralph to any investigation he, Jake, initiated. But he wouldn't smear his good name without proof. "I've got my reasons, which I'd rather not go into today. But I'll explain it all to you once the matter is cleared up. Okay?"

"Okay." Mel paused, then said, "Would this have anything to do with your partners visiting Chief Russell?"

The question startled Jake. When had Don and Susan been to Riverdell? "When was that, Doc?"

"Last night."

"Impossible. Susan and Don are in Las Vegas."

"Well, then my eyesight is going downhill faster than tumbling rock. Could have sworn I saw them going into Ralph's house around suppertime yesterday. Must of been their clones, then." Doc chuckled again.

But Jake didn't find any humor in this. What the hell were Susan and Don doing in Riverdell? Why had they lied about going to Vegas? His nerves jangled at the possibilities. The awful, ugly implications. "Look, Doc, don't mention this phone call to anyone, no matter who. And please keep secret, too, what you're doing on my behalf."

"Sure. Guess I'll need to finagle a copy of Cullen's dental records from Peterson."

"And if there's no match, this call never happened, okay?"

"Sure. But what if there is a match?"

Jake had no doubt there would be. "I guess that depends on whether or not the match is your J.D. with the smashed skull."

LAURA STOOD in the doorway, watching the morning sun play across Jake's golden hair as he cradled the telephone. She wanted to sear this image into her brain to carry with her through the treacherous days ahead.

She'd decided not to tell him, but she was leaving for Riverdell today. He would worry and probably insist she wait until he could come with her. But her urgency to locate the bottles of Venus Masque grew by the minute, as though she were running out of time. Her skin prickled at the possibility. She couldn't put it off. Not even for Ruthanne.

And Jake couldn't put Ruthanne's needs off. Not even for her.

She stepped into the office, catching his attention and his wide smile. Her heart tripped warmly and she couldn't stop herself from beaming at him. "Your mom is still asleep. Maybe we should check for the break-in before she awakens."

It didn't take them long to find what they sought. Jake

squatted, gripping the side door into the garage in both hands, peering at the keyhole. "Someone jimmied their way in here, all right. But if we weren't looking, we wouldn't have noticed."

Laura shivered at the idea that *he* had actually been in the house. "Why bother with the brakes at all? Wouldn't murdering us in our beds have been simpler?"

"Yes and no." Jake shrugged, rising to his full height. "More risky with the two of us here. He or she wouldn't know the layout of the house."

"Why not? House plans are easy enough to get hold of."

"You watch too much TV." He shut the door and double-bolted it. "But if you were right, then your pursuer would have had to plan this for some time. I don't think I was in the mix until you came here after Sunny Devlin's death. I think he or she followed me home from the hospital."

Laura nodded. That made more sense. "But how could anyone trust we'd go off the bluff?"

"Chances were better than average." Jake started past Rubia, who hogged the garage like a whale in a swimming pool, and into the laundry room. "And even if we hadn't died—we'd be more accessible to attack laid up in a hospital bed."

A chill settled at the base of Laura's spine. She hurried after him. "But the police would have found out the brake line was cut."

"Not if the Cherokee was smashed enough."

A vision of the sheer drop-offs along the bluff filled Laura's mind. "And it would have been."

Jake doused the garage light and pulled the door shut behind them. "Besides, I think he or she hoped people would think I killed us both in a jealous rage."

"Why?" But she knew why. "The note?"

He nodded. "The whole of Riverdell seems to know about it. And most would probably claim I had it in me to do just that."

"But you don't."

He winced and she realized she had no idea how he'd reacted when he'd read that vile note. Whatever had happened, he'd left Riverdell for good immediately after. With every fiber of her being, she longed to slip into Jake's arms, to annul the hurt and humiliation he'd suffered at the hands of an evil killer. But she dared not even touch him.

He needed her to be strong, to resist her selfish desires. She wouldn't risk hurting him again. Not even to assure him that they would win, because she knew they'd have to be faster and smarter than her pursuer. And right now, he was two steps ahead of them.

"Are you going to talk to the police about the brakes and the break-in?"

"I'll call a friend on the force and have him come by when he's off duty. I don't want Mom upset, but we need this on the record." He shut the door and locked it. "I've got to make some phone calls."

"I'll check on your mom, then."

Ruthanne was awake and dressed when Laura entered the room. Her hair was damp and she was sitting on the bed, slipping her feet into flats that matched the predominate turquoise of her sweat suit. Laura braced for a fresh onslaught of contempt and suspicion. But Ruthanne's face lit with warmth as though she'd just spied a beloved friend. "Laura, dear, how nice. I was hoping I'd know someone here."

Laura's heart caught. Where did she think she was? "Ruthanne, this is Jake's house. This is his bedroom."

"Well, I know that. Didn't I bring a change of clothes? A gal likes fresh undies every day, you know."

Laura bit back a smile. "I don't think you planned on spending the night."

"Oh, of course. I remember now."

But she didn't look as though she did.

She said, "It's a good thing J.J. and you are getting married soon. This house needs a woman's touch. Why, he hasn't gotten the mirrors hung in the bathroom, and these windows could sure use some nice curtains. Can't leave that sort of thing to the menfolk."

Laura didn't know whether to be pleased or dismayed at Ruthanne's confusion over time and place. But she was grateful the hostility had vanished. So, did it really matter that she didn't recall Jake hadn't built this house until after the aborted wedding?

Ruthanne made a face. "I took a shower, but I can't fix my hair without a mirror. Don't know how he shaves. Everybody needs mirrors. Do you suppose you could help me with my hair?"

"Of course." Laura plucked her brush from her purse and crossed to Ruthanne. Gently she swept the bristles through the damp curls, feeling like a mother to the woman who'd always been like a mother to her. The sadness in her heart deepened.

"That feels good." Ruthanne sighed, but she rubbed her hands together and grimaced. "Old age is the pits. Turns a pond into a pile of sand. J.J. hasn't got any hand lotion and my skin is as dry as that desert outside those windows."

"I think I have some in my purse." Laura finished Ruthanne's hair, then gave her a nod of approval, assuring the older woman that she looked fine now.

A forgotten memory surfaced and arrested Laura's hunt

for the hand lotion. A few years ago, Ruthanne had offered her much the same approval of her appearance—on prom night. Although it hadn't started out that way.

Aunt May had insisted on making Laura's dress and fixing her hair. She'd beamed with pride at the finished product. Laura hadn't wanted to hurt her aunt's feelings, but the gaily colored, multiruffled dress would have better suited a clown than the football captain's date. A disastrous home perm added insult to injury.

She'd been in tears before Jake had driven her a block. Instead of continuing on to the high school, he'd taken her to his house. Ruthanne's sympathy had opened the floodgates of her tears. But this woman had saved the night. She loaned Laura a simple black dress and brushed her hair into a chic French roll. Jake's eyes had bugged out at the transformation.

Laura grinned now, remembering. "Let's see if I can find that hand lotion."

"Oh." Ruthanne sighed. "I hope it's some of that good stuff you sent me last time."

Laura froze. Her hand in her purse still gripped the hairbrush. The hard plastic handle bit into her palm. Had she heard what she thought she'd heard? Her breath snagged. "What are you talking about?"

"You know, the stuff in the little green bottle."

Uncle Murphy's Venus Masque had been in little green plastic bottles. Laura's heart thunked. Her pulse stumbled, then began racing. "Where is that hand lotion, Ruthanne?"

"Where? I thought you had some."

No! Don't let her forget. Not now. Laura took a steadying breath. Somehow she found the small tube of Vaseline Intensive Care she carried in her purse. She offered it to

Ruthanne, whose expression fell when she saw that it wasn't the "good stuff."

"Sorry, this is all I have with me." Laura popped the lid and squeezed a little of the lotion into the other woman's upturned palm. "Ruthanne, do you have some of the hand lotion I sent you?"

She glanced up, but kept rubbing her hands together. "Not here."

"Where?"

"Oh." She nodded, seeming to understand the "where" question this time. "In my nightstand. But I'm running out. I was hoping you'd bring me more."

Laura's ribs seemed to contract like a fist around her chest. "Your nightstand at Sunshine Vista Estates?"

"Yes. Next to the bed. In the top drawer." Ruthanne's eyes were narrowed and she spoke the words slowly, pointedly, as though Laura didn't comprehend the concept of a nightstand. "In the little green bottle."

Chapter Fifteen

Laura hurried to Jake's office. He leaned on his desk, phone to his ear, a lock of hair across his forehead, papers spread around him as though he'd been taking copious notes. With a grim expression he cradled the phone, then glanced up, spotting her in the doorway.

He blinked, distress flitting through his teal eyes. As though she'd asked him for an explanation, he said, "The remodeling is going to take longer than I thought. And none of the home health-care agencies can send anyone until tomorrow."

"She's remembered!" Laura shouted.

He frowned, total confusion wiping the dour expression from his face. "What?"

Laura forced herself to speak slowly. "Your mother has some of Uncle Murphy's cream in her nightstand at Sunshine Vista Estates."

His eyes grew huge and he lurched out of his chair. "Are you sure?"

She gripped the door frame on both sides, the oak solid, fortifying. "I won't be sure until I see it for myself. Can we go now?"

"Well, sure, but I can't leave Mom alone."

"Can't she come with us? I know she'd like a change

of clothing. We could pack her things and start the paperwork to get her moved out of there." Anticipation motored
through Laura like cars around a racetrack, fast, careering,
one emotion pulling ahead, then another. For the first time
since this deadly contest began, winning seemed guaran-
teed. *If* they could avoid unforeseen mishaps. Could they?
"Besides, if Ruthanne stashed The Venus Masque somewhere other than the nightstand..."

"Okay, I already called Mrs. Thatcher and told her I'd
be there sometime today. Might as well be this morning.
Have to pick up the Cherokee now anyway. Hector has
the brake line replaced."

A shiver went through Laura. She'd been so excited
about the face cream she'd momentarily forgotten the
killer lurked nearby. Had he planned another deadly surprise for them? The likelihood made her blood run cold.
She had to get away from Jake and Ruthanne. Today. It
was her only hope of keeping them safe.

"WHEN DID YOU GET this snazzy car?" Ruthanne exclaimed over Rubia. "It's very pretty, but can't be much
good for catching criminals."

Jake frowned. Today his mom thought he was still a
cop. On so many levels she seemed her old self, but she
wasn't. Would never be again. She glanced around from
her perch on the wide bench seat between Laura and him.

He reached for the key. "This car belongs to my mechanic, Mom. We're going to pick up my wagon on the
way to Sunshine Vista."

He started the engine and Ruthanne let out a squeal.
"Ooh, it's noisy."

Precisely the reason, Jake mused, that he wanted the use
of his own wheels. The less attention the group attracted,
the better. Laura was edgy enough already. So much so,

he'd decided not to mention the John Doe in Riverdell with the smashed skull...until after Mel Van Sheets ran his tests.

He backed the car out of the garage and lowered the door. Not wanting to upset Laura further didn't explain why he hadn't told her about Doc's seeing Don and Susan at Chief Russell's house. But Jake had confirmed it only a moment before Laura showed up at the office shouting her news about the face cream.

That had wrenched his thoughts away from his partners for a while. Now, however, he could think of nothing else, and his mind chewed their deceit like a termite on new wood, burrowing holes into the very foundation of his trust. Disappointment soured his stomach. His partners had lied to him. The wealthy Texas oilman hadn't moved up his plans for his trip to Vegas. He was still at home in Houston.

What was so important they'd risked their partnership, his friendship, by lying? Jake gripped the steering wheel so hard his knuckles ached. Why were Susan and Don in Riverdell? Why had they visited Ralph Russell? Suspicions sped through his brain faster than the cacti whipping by the windows on either side of the car. How could they do this? They knew trust was an issue with him.

"My goodness, you've got a pretty view, J.J."

Ruthanne's awestruck voice penetrated his dark thoughts. He smiled at her, but the chill inside him rivaled the breeze sweeping up the bluff and across the Impala. Facing the possibility that his partners could be murderers was proving the toughest thing he'd done since accepting Laura's betrayal last year. These past two days his beliefs had taken a 180-degree spin.

It now appeared Laura deserved his trust and Don and Susan did not. He steered the car onto the main road. He didn't want to believe Susan and Don capable of murder, but yesterday he hadn't thought they'd lie to him, either. Whatever else remained murky, one thing stood out crystal clear: somehow, the Bowmans were involved in this mess all the way up to their necks.

HECTOR GARCIA RUBBED his neck with his grease-smeared hand. He trudged slowly around Rubia, inspecting her like a jeweler looking for flaws in a diamond.

"You takes *buen* care of *mi* Rubia, Jake-man. No jealous *hombres* shoots your legs for Señorita Hot Tamale." He winked at Laura and her cheeks burned.

Ruthanne leaned toward her, looking alarmed. "Why is that mechanic talking about someone shooting my J.J.? Is he on a case?"

Laura's heart dipped to her toes. Ruthanne didn't need unnecessary worry. God knows how her ailing mind might process fear. "Jake's not on any case. His only concern is you."

The unconvinced look on Ruthanne's face gave Laura pause. Although Jake had quit the police force, as long as Laura remained in his company she invited as violent an enemy as any he'd ever encountered on the streets of L.A. Every minute held danger for him and his mother, and even Ruthanne sensed it. As the thought took hold of Laura, the hair on her neck rose. Was her pursuer here? Watching them? Waiting to pounce?

She glanced the length of Hector's establishment. Cars in varying stages of repair were parked from one end to the other, several with the hoods up and mechanics in attendance. Garcia family resemblance dominated the busy overall-clad workers.

Although no one appeared out of place, Laura's internal antennae bleeped through her head like blips on a radar screen. She lurched around, this way and that. She saw nothing, no one looking back. But the sensation lingered, grew. "Jake...?"

His head came around at the urgency in her voice. But fearing she might frighten Ruthanne, she could only communicate her anxiety to him with a look. He nodded, and turned back to Hector. "Where's the brake line?"

"Hector, he fixes *bien* good the brakes line."

"Where is the damaged one?" he asked again, impatience in each word.

"In the trunks." Hector pointed a grimy finger toward the Cherokee.

"How much do I owe you, *amigo?*"

Jake settled his account as Laura helped Ruthanne into the front seat of the Cherokee, then climbed in back. Jake and she hadn't discussed the killer following them, but the sensation settled over her like a blanket of nettles. She couldn't say anything to Jake. Didn't want to alarm Ruthanne. But as their gazes collided in the rearview mirror, she saw that he understood.

He drove a circuitous route to the Sunshine Vista Estates. Fortunately, Ruthanne seemed not to notice. She chattered on about the dirty mechanic, who had the odd limp and the sexiest smile she'd seen since Jake's dad.

The senior complex looked as it had the first day Laura visited, the parking lot more empty than full. Today it would have accommodated a dozen Rubias. Jake eased the Cherokee into a spot near the front of the building.

The sensation that someone was watching struck Laura again and she jerked around. Imagination? Or intuition? The other cars in the lot seemed empty. Goose bumps lifted across her limbs. She bit down the urge to run for the front door. Always before when she'd felt this foreboding, she'd had the protection of a disguise. This time the killer wouldn't mistake someone else for her.

With every step, she feared a bullet would hit her in the back. But they made it through the front entrance unscathed. Still the feeling persisted. Warily, Laura eyed two elderly women residents in the entrance hall. Were they who they appeared to be? Or had her killer taken to using disguises even as she had shunned them? Her throat squeezed.

Her gaze swept the rest of the room. Yesterday this area had seemed as small and crowded as a movie theater. She hadn't noticed how grand it was. How large. How many huge plants someone could hide behind. The sensation that they should hurry pricked at her brain, shivered her spine.

Jake whispered, "Hope we don't run into Mrs. Thatcher."

Or anyone else, Laura thought, recalling the person who'd shown up at Saguaro County General in the guise of a florist's deliverer. She forced herself to slow to Ruthanne's choppier gait. Her impatience to lay her hands on her uncle's cream gnawed at her already frayed nerves. Ruthanne continued to chatter, but her conversation couldn't penetrate the hum of apprehension zinging through Laura's ears.

She rounded the corner too quickly, nearly knocking a wizened-faced, white-haired couple to the floor. The woman huffed at the rudeness of young people, and her husband scowled at Laura's apology. "Just slow down. This ain't a racecourse, you know."

But slowing her impatience proved impossible. Her stomach was a tangle of knots by the time they arrived at Ruthanne's door. Laura bounded inside first, took three steps and froze. Her breath punched out on a loud gasp at the sight before her. All Ruthanne's treasured photographs lay in a broken heap in the center of the floor. Drawers gaped. The bedspread and drapes brought from the Riverdell house hung in shreds. The Christmas cactus sprawled from one end of the rug to the other, limbs severed, blooms crushed, the favorite planter broken into small pieces.

Shaking with horror, Laura stumbled to the nightstand. But her heart lay on the floor among Ruthanne's destroyed possessions. She knew before she reached it that the drawer would be empty. It was.

Impotent rage swelled inside her, stung her eyes. But what had she expected? She'd let her hopes climb, anticipated the joy of a gift she would never be given. She knew better. This year had taught her many lessons about hope. None of them good.

Jake swore. "What the hell...?"

"What is it, dear?" Ruthanne's view of the room was blocked by Jake's body.

He spun around and caught his mother by both upper arms and scooted her back out into the hallway. Over his shoulder, he told Laura, "We'll notify Mrs. Thatcher. Meanwhile, don't touch anything."

AT MRS. THATCHER'S request, the police arrived without sirens. Sirens usually meant ambulances; ambulances at a senior complex usually meant disaster. The residents of Sunshine Vista Estates would be upset enough at the presence of police officers two days in a row. No sense contributing calamity to the mayhem.

Mrs. Thatcher did not appreciate Jake's attempt to take control of the situation—reminding him with an imperious air, which Laura found inane under the circumstances—that she was in charge. But her bluster wilted beneath his fury. Even she realized the security in the senior complex needed a severe overhaul.

Police came, inspected Ruthanne's rooms, questioned staff and residents and took copious notes for their report. Morning crept into afternoon; much, Laura mused, as whoever had broken into Ruthanne's room crept farther and farther away with Uncle Murphy's cream. Even if the police found evidence that led to an arrest, it would not bring back the one thing she needed most.

Laura gazed around the dining room of Sunshine Vista Estates. Ruthanne and she occupied a corner table. Despite the commotion the police caused, routine proceeded as normally as possible. Lunch had been served two hours ago and now kitchen staff busied themselves setting up the room for dinner.

From where they sat, Laura could see Jake in the doorway, talking to the last remaining police officer. She felt no compunction to join them, not even for an update on the investigation.

She'd passed the hours in a numbed state, tending to Ruthanne—who seemed not to understand that all the excitement centered on her room—and keeping out of the way of the police. But if Ruthanne felt no violation, Laura did. It was as if *her* possessions had been pawed and destroyed. As if *her* privacy had been invaded.

A dirty, unwashed sensation climbed inside her, dominated her. She wanted to scream, to hurt the one responsible, to make him or her suffer as long and hard as he or she had made Jake and her suffer. But the only way to do that now was to find the missing evidence. And the last chance had disappeared with the little green bottle in Ruthanne's nightstand.

Or had it?

The thought struck her with such fury it stiffened her

spine. Why hadn't it occurred to her to ask earlier? "Ruthanne?"

Jake's mother was watching the women arranging the place settings with a disapproving air. For years she'd held the reputation for setting the prettiest table in all of Riverdell. She jerked around and blinked a second. "Yes?"

If Laura had learned nothing else this past year, she'd learned that nothing in life stayed the same. Change was so inevitable one had to relish the treasured times with each passing second. She didn't want ever to feel the longing she saw in Ruthanne's eyes now. And yet, she knew she had. "Where did you get the little green bottle with the good hand cream in it?"

Ruthanne gave a startled laugh and shook her head in disbelief. "Goodness, and they say I'm forgetful. Don't you remember sending it to me, dear?"

Laura drew a taut breath, recalling the difficulty Jake had had last night making Ruthanne understand his questions. She schooled her impatience, taking encouragement where she found it. At least Ruthanne remembered where she'd gotten the cream originally. She ran her tongue across her parched lips. "I know that I sent it to you, but what I was asking was whether or not you brought that box with you when you moved to Mesa."

"Oh, well, let's see, now." She frowned and grew quiet, her eyebrows pinched low on her forehead. "The box was in that lovely silver-and-gold paper, right?"

"Right." Hope skittered inside Laura. The wedding paper she'd wrapped the box of plastic containers in had had silver-and-gold bridal bouquets on it. "What did you do with the box?"

"Hmm. Well, at first I didn't do anything with it." She looked puzzled. "Why was that?"

Laura flinched. If Ruthanne recalled she'd left Jake at

the altar her animosity would return. If she became as hostile to Laura as she'd been last night, that would be the last she'd get out of her on this or any other subject. "I don't know."

"Well, I did finally open it. Opened all the wedding presents." Her expression darkened. She turned cool eyes on Laura. "All the wedding presents…"

Her heart clutched. But Ruthanne said nothing more; her attention was back on the place settings at the nearby tables.

Laura prompted, "When you opened the package, what did you do with it?"

"What?" She glanced at Laura again. "Oh, well, the labels said 'Venus Masque,' but I'd never heard of that. I wasn't sure what I should do with the bottles since I didn't know what was in them. Finally, I just opened one and sniffed it. Smelled kind of like lavender. So, I dipped my hand into the cream and it felt delicious on my skin."

She looked at her hand. "You know, I swear it eclipsed these ugly freckles on the back of my hands. Hand cream you gave me this morning doesn't do that. Look."

She held her hand up for Laura; age spots stood like polka dots on her pale flesh. Laura nodded. "It is special cream."

"Don't have to tell me that." She rubbed her hands together again as though the dryness irritated her.

"Would you like some more hand lotion?"

Her eyes widened and she smiled. "Oh, that would be nice. I've got some in my nightstand. Some of the good stuff. Could you get me that, dear?"

Laura drew a shaky breath as Jake strode up to the table, toting a suitcase. He arrived in time to hear his mother's request. Laura gazed at him, unable to conceal the sadness she felt. She didn't know what to say to Ruthanne. She didn't want to try to tell her about the break-in again. It was better to let her bask in her oblivion.

Jake said, "You used up the last of that cream yesterday, Mom."

"Oh?" She looked unconvinced.

"Yes." He hoisted the suitcase. "I've got your clothes packed. We can go home now."

"Are you sure about the cream, J.J.? In the little green bottle? The one shaped like a cold-cream container?"

"I'm sure." He helped her to her feet.

"Well, if you say so, but I could've sworn Kimmie just sent me that bottle."

"What?" The word choked out of Laura. "Kim Durant?"

"Yes. She is my niece, you know. She sends me little care packages every once in a while. Almost always one of those little bottles is included."

Laura and Jake exchanged an excited glance and for the first time in hours Laura felt her hope surge with newfound life. "We've got to call Kim. Now."

Jake agreed. "Come on, we'll use Mrs. Thatcher's office."

But Mrs. Thatcher had gone for the day, leaving her secretary in charge. Muriel was a study in opposites with her boss: whereas Mrs. Thatcher was a dried-up beanpole, antagonistic and unobliging, her secretary was a fresh young sprout, gregarious and accommodating.

"That's weird," she said, rifling through her file drawer. "I can't find Mrs. Wilder's file." She shuffled through the folders again. "Oh, here it is. Someone moved it." She opened the folder and read. "Yes, Mrs. Wilder is absolutely right. A K. Durant from Riverdell in Washington State periodically sends her a package. Toiletries usually. Cologne, toothpaste, Chap Stick, hand lotion."

Jake noted the hope in Laura's eyes with dismay. She was more vulnerable than she realized. He wanted to pull her close and tell her it would be all right. But what if the missing bottle from his mother's nightstand was the last of the bottles? He had to talk to Kimmie. Alone. "May I use Mrs. Thatcher's phone?"

Muriel hesitated, puckering her plump lips. "Gee, I don't…"

"I'll put it on my charge card," he assured her.

Muriel shook her head. "I don't have the key to her office, but I don't see the harm in letting you use my phone as long as you're putting it on your card."

She rose and Jake sat down, checking the time. "Kim should be at work."

But instead of his cousin's falsetto voice, a man's deep bass rumbled through the line. "Dell Pharmaceuticals."

Jake didn't recognize the man. "Is Kim there?"

"Nope. She called in sick yesterday with that bug half the plant's been passing around."

Jake thanked the man and rang off, then immediately punched in the combination of numbers needed to reach Kim at home. But all he got was the answering machine. Frustration tripped through him as his gaze connected with Laura's. He shook his head.

"Kim, are you there? If so, pick up." Nothing. "As soon as you get this message call me. It's urgent." He left his home and cell phone numbers and hung up.

Laura wrung her hands. He recognized the anxiety issuing from her. The same emotion heated his blood. "Apparently, Kim has some flu bug. I got her answering machine. She's likely in bed. Not well enough to answer the phone."

"So all we can do is wait?" Laura looked as though that was not something she intended to do.

"For now," he said, trying to assure her, but a squiggle of alarm zipped across his gut at the lift of her jaw and the calculating gleam in her eyes. He understood that she'd sat still for too many hours without direction or purpose. Now she had both. Worry spilled through him.

They thanked Muriel and left. Laura settled Ruthanne on the front seat of the Cherokee while Jake put her luggage in the trunk. Laura met him on the driver's side of the car. "Jake, I'm not going with you."

"What?" He'd feared this. He reached for her shoulders and grasped them gently. She felt fragile to his touch, tiny and defenseless. Every protective instinct he had surged forward. "I don't want you out of my sight."

She traced a hand down his scar and he felt the love vibrate through her. Could he really be that lucky? Could she really not mind how ugly he looked? She smiled. "Every minute I'm with you and your mom, your lives are in danger."

"Let me worry about that."

"No." She flung an arm toward the senior complex. "This wouldn't have happened if not for me."

"No one was hurt. Only possessions. And Mom isn't aware of it, so really the harm is minimal."

"The harm is deep and irreparable. I can't wait around for the next shoe to drop. I have to get the jump on whoever's been after me. And I finally have a chance. I'm going to Riverdell."

"No!" Alarm leaped through Jake. "You can't go alone."

She laughed. "Two days ago, you couldn't wait for me to go alone. Two days ago, I didn't think I could go alone. But now, I know I can. I can't afford to put it off. If any of Uncle Murphy's cream still exists, I have to get it before anyone figures out Kim might have access to it."

"Wait a few days...until I can come with you."

"The risk is too great. Even Kim may be in danger."

"All the more reason I should come with you."

"But you can't. Not now."

She was right. He couldn't leave Ruthanne at Sunshine Vista Estates and he couldn't take her with them. He had to get her settled somewhere safe. "There must be something I can do."

"If you think of anything, I'll be at the airport. I'm going in to call a cab."

Jake had never felt so torn in his life. There had to be something he could do to help both the women he loved. For the life of him, he couldn't think what. He cupped Laura's head in his hands and kissed her long and hard. "I don't want to let you go."

"I don't want to leave. But I have to."

Jake realized it would do no good to insist she come home with him. She wouldn't. She'd always been as stubborn as Handley's mule when her mind was set. He pulled her against him. Sometime in this last year she'd learned self-reliance. He'd thought he'd miss the needy girl he'd grown up loving. He realized this new, mature version of Laura had more to offer. Which meant they both had all the more to lose.

Grimly, he opened his arms and stepped back. He took three one-hundred-dollar bills from his wallet and pressed them into her palm. For your ticket and whatever."

"I'll pay you back."

He nodded. "Have you got your stun gun?"

She patted her purse and gave him a wry smile. "Right here."

"They won't let you on the plane with it unless you've stowed it inside your luggage in a hard case. You'll have to sign for it, too."

"Okay. I should be able to pick up a small suitcase and a gun case in a pawnshop on the way to the airport." She touched his face once again, a look of abject regret in her smoky eyes, then she pivoted and hurried into the senior center.

Feeling as desolate as he had the day she'd left him at the church in Riverdell, Jake climbed into the Cherokee, telling himself this was not the same thing. They would work this out; they would get together again. No matter how many times he repeated it, he didn't believe it.

Ruthanne said, "Why isn't Laura coming with us?"

Jake pulled into traffic. "She has something to do."

His mother tsked. "Did you two have a lovers' spat?"

"No, Mom." But he felt as though they had. The cell phone rang, jolting his unsteady pulse as though he'd touched an exposed wire. He grasped it. "Jake Wilder."

"Been trying to reach you for a while, son."

It was Dr. Mel Van Sheets, he realized, hitting the brake as the light turned red. "Ran into a complication here." That was all the explanation Jake offered him. The light changed and Jake drove on, aware that every mile took him farther from Laura. "What can I do for you, Doc?"

Ruthanne glanced around at that. "Is that Mel?"

Jake winced at his slip. "Yes, Mom. Mom says hi."

"Then you're not alone?" Mel said.

"No." Jake's patience thinned. "What's up?"

"Got the results you inquired about." Mel's voice was reedy, angry.

Jake's breath tangled in his throat. Ruthanne was staring at him as if she had heard and understood both sides of the conversation. As impossible as he knew that was, it rattled him nonetheless. "And?"

"Sad to report you were right about Cullen Crocker."

"How right?"

"He was the John Doe with the smashed skull."

"Damn, damn, damn." In his heart he'd known Cullen was dead, but having it confirmed spread a layer of ice through his gut…and quadrupled his fear for Laura. Why the hell had he let her out of his sight? He pulled an illegal U-turn and headed back to Sunshine Vista Estates.

"I think we'd better bring Chief Russell on board with this, Jake." Doc intruded on his dark worry. "You gonna do the honors or should I?"

Jake cut in front of a slow-moving car and received a blast of the other driver's horn. "I'd appreciate it if you'd take care of that. Ralph will want to talk to me and I have to handle another matter first. By the time he catches up with me, I should be free to answer all his questions." No matter what Jake's suspicions about Ralph might be, the lawman could no longer be left out of the case.

Doc said, "I'll be calling him soon as I hang up, then."

Jake rang off and immediately dialed another number. He had a lot to do and a short time in which to do it.

This conversation was briefer than the last and had Ruthanne staring at him in disbelief. He dropped the phone on the seat between them and careered into the parking lot of the senior center on two wheels. He parked in the loading zone and raced into the building. But he was too late.

Laura had gone.

Chapter Sixteen

Jake unhooked his seat belt and stood, vacating his seat in the tail section of the 727. Aiming for a casualness he didn't feel and couldn't effect with his bulk and his scarred countenance, he strode the length of the plane, searching for Laura. But he reached the pilot door without spotting a single woman with sable hair.

Panic nipped him. He quickly cruised the aisle all the way to the tail of the plane again, drawing unwanted glances, but no sign of Laura. Distress spread another layer of ice across his gelid heart. She had to be on this flight. It was the only one to Spokane since he'd left her at the senior center. Striving to curb his worry, he checked the rest room signs. All read Vacant. He retraced the aisle, slower this time, studying each individual. Something caught his eye. A flash of color. He pulled up short, wondering why. Then it hit him. The woman in the window seat two rows ahead had on a coat the same color as the one he'd bought Laura.

Staring at the gray-haired, bespeckled matron bent over a magazine, he moved forward. She wore not only Laura's coat—he saw—but her jeans and shoes, as well. The tightness in his chest eased.

"Excuse me." He tapped the shoulder of the swarthy-skinned businessman sitting next to her.

The guy looked up from the open briefcase on the empty seat between himself and Laura. Annoyance pinched his mouth, but as he caught sight of Jake towering over him, he flinched.

Jake held no illusions about his own expression. He scowled, purposefully puckering his scar. He wasn't above using his unpleasant resemblance to a stereotypical movie mobster if and when it suited his ends. He kept his voice even, his tone polite but firm. "Look, pal, could you be convinced to trade seats with me?"

"Well, I, er, ah…"

Red tinged the guy's complexion. He seemed to struggle with his pride, as though he wanted to tell Jake to go to hell, but couldn't decide if it would be a life-threatening mistake.

"The plane is hardly full. Why do you want my seat?"

The woman's hands tensed on her magazine, and she peered sideways up at him. Her eyes were a startling blue. But they were Laura's eyes nonetheless. Jake winked at her.

Then he addressed the distressed businessman and gestured toward Laura. "My mother has Alzheimer's and sometimes she gets angry for no good reason and starts spitting."

"Ye, Gods!" The man gawked at Laura in disgust. Grabbing the excuse to save his ego, he gathered his briefcase and jacket and scrambled up and out into the aisle. "Thanks for the warning."

Jake directed the man to the seat he'd been assigned at the rear of the plane, then eased himself into the one beside Laura. She continued staring at the magazine.

Jake studied her. The wig hugged her head like a knit

cap of ashen curls and the rhinestone-encrusted eyeglasses kept sliding to the tip of her nose. She wore no makeup and the colored contact lenses were the turquoise of a California swimming pool. "I think I liked you better as a blonde."

"Keep your voice down." She ground out the words through clenched teeth, her gaze riveted to the magazine. "What are you doing here? You're going to blow my disguise."

"And a fine disguise it is, too," he said on a laugh, but he lowered his voice to match the tone she'd used. "What made you think of it?"

She turned a page in the magazine. "What better way to exit a senior center than dressed as one of its denizens?"

"Ah...clever."

"Thanks. But your being here makes it worthless. If whoever's after me is watching you to find me, you've just given me away."

Chagrined, Jake glanced around quickly. He probably should have used more caution, but he'd been so damned anxious to find her. So damned glad to find her. No one seemed to be paying them the least attention. He shifted back to her. She was frowning so hard it had to hurt.

He shoved his hand through his hair. He'd imagined their reunion in quite different terms. A little hug. A little kiss. A little hand-holding. Never had he thought she'd be annoyed. Not after their emotionally charged farewell. Maybe she needed reminding. He leaned closer to her, tracing his fingertip across the back of her hand. He was rewarded with her sharply drawn breath.

He whispered, "Are you saying you're sorry to see me?"

She bit the corners of her cheeks in an obvious effort to suppress a grin. She said, "Where is Ruthanne?"

"She's with a friend." He shifted in his seat again, realizing there wasn't enough room for legs as long as his. "She'll be fine until I get back."

"You haven't told me what you're doing on this flight."

"I'll explain in a minute." He leaned away from her. The flight attendants were approaching with the drink cart. Jake asked Laura, "Want something?"

They ordered Cokes, his in a can, hers in a plastic cup with ice, and accepted packets of peanuts. Jake opened the pull tab on the pop can and downed the nuts, keeping silent until the cart had moved on and he wouldn't be overheard. "I called Doc Van Sheets today."

"About Ruthanne?" Laura took a sip of her Coke.

"Yes, but also about Cullen."

She angled toward him, frowning. "Cullen?"

Jake felt as though he were conversing with Granny Clampett. As serious as the situation was, he couldn't stifle a smirk. Laura's disguise roused an old memory of a Halloween party they'd attended their junior year of high school.

They'd double-dated, the four of them dressing like The Beverly Hillbillies. Don and Susan had gone as Jethro and Elly May. Laura and he had gone as Jed and Granny. His mother made their costumes. They'd been certain they'd win the first place prize, but they'd been bested by none other than Cullen Crocker. He'd dressed up as Elvis, the resemblance striking, uncanny—and now he was just as dead as The King.

The sobering thought wiped all amusement from Jake. He reiterated his conversation with Mel and his request that the doctor, in his role as coroner, check Cullen's dental records against those of the three John Does found in the county during the past year. "Doc called me back right after I left you at Sunshine Vista Estates. One of the bodies was Cullen. He died of a smashed skull.''

Laura drew a sharp breath. Since learning no one in the Crocker family had heard from Cullen for a whole year, she'd lived with the likelihood that he'd been murdered. Still, it was a shock. Guilt fell heavily across her heart. "He was a friend. He died because he helped me."

She reached for her drink, and washed down the sick feeling with a swallow of cold liquid. The poor Crocker family. This would be devastating for them. At length, she asked, "How did Travis and Izzy take the news?"

Jake's eyes narrowed. "When I went by their motel to tell them, they weren't there. They checked out last night."

"What? But they said—" She broke off. What did it matter that they'd sworn they'd be back to see Jake for answers? Obviously they'd had their answers all along. "My God, Jake, they must have broken into your mother's after they left your house last night."

"Unless, whoever broke in did it yesterday while the craft bazaar was in full swing." He grimaced, hating his altered perspective on his partners. "I'm not sure the perpetrators weren't Susan and Don."

"Don and Susan?" She gaped at him over the top of the glittery glasses, her eyes brimming with surprise. "But they're in Las Vegas."

Jake shook his head. "Maybe not. Doc swore he saw them last night at Chief Russell's house."

Laura's complexion turned the color of her wig. "Your mother's house? God, Jake, what if the remaining sample jars are there?"

"More than likely they're at Kimmie's." If any remained, he thought grimly. At least there were apparently more than had been in Laura's possession. He drank his soda. "She's the one who's been mailing them to Mom."

"I guess that makes sense." Laura chewed the honeyed nuts provided by the airlines. "I suppose we can eliminate Kim from our list of suspects, too. She wouldn't have any reason to kill me if she's had the cream in her possession all this time. Did she ever return your call?"

"No. And I left another message before I caught the plane."

Laura swirled her Coke, the ice cubes clunking the side of the plastic cup. "Seems no one is where they're supposed to be."

Jake contemplated the remaining names on their suspect list: Izzy, Travis, Don, Susan, Ralph Russell, Payton Dell. "Wonder if Payton actually went to New York like Izzy claimed. Maybe he came to Mesa with his sister and Travis."

Laura sat straighter. "They could all have been at the senior complex yesterday. That might explain your mom's confusion about the man she saw from Riverdell."

Jake had to agree the idea had merit. But maybe they were giving his mother too much credit. She might just have been confused. They couldn't know.

"And Payton collects cars," Laura said. "He can take apart about any model ever made and put it back together again. Cutting a brake line would be nothing to him."

"And he was a demolitions expert in the army," Jake added thoughtfully, then scowled. "But, so was Don. And he and Susan were at my house the night before the brakes failed."

He looked like he'd swallowed something bitter.

Laura sighed. "But neither of them went near the garage."

"Not that we saw. And a locked door presents only a minor challenge to people with our backgrounds." Jake realized Laura had, in fact, no reason to trust him. He knew enough about the mechanics of a car to fiddle with the brakes, he could pick a lock with the best of them and New Again had not only saved his bacon, it had plopped him right into Ms. Luxury's lap.

As though she'd been thinking the same thing, she pushed the eyeglasses up the bridge of her nose and said, "Given those criteria, I ought to reconsider my suspicions of you."

Jake swallowed hard. "Maybe you should."

Laura drank some of her Coke. "What about Ralph Russell? You said he was one of the original investors in New Again. He spent a lot of time at our house. He had to know about Uncle Murphy's Venus Masque."

"It's possible."

Laura nodded. "I recall he started his career with the bomb squad in one of the major cities. He'd know how to blow up a house and make it look accidental. And as chief of police, he'd have access to the case file."

"And," Jake finished for her, "could *edit* the findings to suit any outcome he wanted."

"Yes."

Jake didn't like it. He didn't want to suspect his former boss, the most honest cop he'd ever known, of being corrupt. But could he trust his instincts about people? Susan's and Don's behavior had shaken his belief in his own judgments. "Travis's background could have provided him with the skills exhibited by your pursuer. He worked in a fireworks factory for a while and he was a mechanic in the navy, keeping the officers' jeeps running."

"Travis?" She cringed inside. "I can't fathom him hurting his brother, let alone smashing his skull."

"Don't go soft in the head on me, Granny," Jake teased.

She made a face at his black humor. "Really, Jake, what motive would he have?"

"One of the oldest—jealousy. Travis wanted Izzy and now he has her."

"You think?" She considered. Izzy had loved Cullen for as far back as she could recall. Everyone knew that— even Travis. But who had Travis dated? She dredged up memories of him at school dances. A handsome young man—better looking than most all the others, except Cullen—standing on the sidelines or in groups with other boys who'd arrived stag, staring at the girls, laughing, stealing out to their cars to guzzle beer.

But had he stared at Izzy more than the others?

Laura realized that if she'd wondered about Travis coming to dances alone, she'd probably put it down to an inability to dance. Or shyness. But had it been something more heartbreaking? Had Travis been in love with someone who couldn't see him for love of his brother? Had that jealousy festered over the years until he'd built such rage he'd killed his own brother?

That scenario went against everything she knew of Travis and Cullen. If anything, Travis had always protected his younger brother, fighting his fights, lying to cover his sins. Cullen returned the favor, taking the blame for crashing the family car when all the kids in town knew Travis had been at the wheel.

She couldn't see any woman coming between those two. Even so...there was no denying that Izzy and Travis were close now.

She shoved at the glasses. "If Travis killed Cullen because of Izzy, how does that have anything to do with the murders of my aunt and uncle? Or with the face cream?"

Jake rubbed his jaw. "Or with my mother's room being torn up?"

"That seemed more like an act of rage," Laura muttered, anxious that her patient pursuer was getting desperate. She shivered. "Was Travis one of the initial investors in New Again?"

Jake shrugged. "We need to find out."

They fell silent a moment. Then Laura said, "Well, my money is on Payton. He's profited more than anyone from the theft of Uncle Murphy's cream. And he has the most to lose if he can't silence me."

Before Jake could reply, the flight attendant's voice sounded, advising one and all to buckle up for the plane's imminent touchdown in Spokane.

The landing went smoothly, and within the hour, Jake and Laura claimed their bags and rented a Subaru with studded snow tires for the two-hour drive to Riverdell. Jake had spent a whole year vowing he'd never set foot in his hometown again. Now, despite the night, the falling temperatures and the icy roads necessary to reach that destination, he couldn't arrive soon enough.

The second the wheels of the airplane kissed the runway, he'd been gripped by an unnameable urgency. It tickled his nerves, consumed his thoughts. So much so, he hadn't heeded his usual prudence, hadn't looked for danger at the airport. Hadn't noticed they were being followed.

Chapter Seventeen

Night closed in around the rental car as Jake drove west on Interstate 90, leaving behind Spokane and its vast population. Laura longed to go back, to lose herself in the enormity of the crowds, the anonymity, that false safety she'd utilized this past year. But she'd made no protest when Jake insisted they leave for Riverdell immediately. She'd run away for the last time.

Jake and she had no future unless they faced and dealt with their past.

The Subaru headlights glared off the ice-crusted mounds of dirty white that hugged the shoulders of the freeway. The road wore a deep shroud of snow and gravel and lanes were indistinguishable. The studded tires crunched with every revolution. The bouncy ride jostled Laura's nerves.

Winter arrived in Mesa with subtlety; it roared into eastern Washington like a blast from the Antarctic, swept far and wide, stabbed deep and fierce, and lingered past all welcome like an uninvited guest.

Laura felt the car skid, and checked her seat belt. She was tired. It had been an exhausting couple of days. If only they could have spoken with Kim...but a third try had again netted them nothing more than her answering machine. Tension nipped along Laura's shoulder blades.

She dragged her fingers through her loose hair, glad to be rid of the wig, the glasses and the annoying contact lenses. She'd tucked them all back into her shoulder bag the second they'd driven away from the airport.

She studied Jake's profile in the faint illumination thrown by the few other brave souls traveling the freeway. With the temperature dropping and snow predicted, it was not a night for the faint of heart. Jake's mouth was set as hard as the compacted snow on the roadsides.

Every mile closer to Riverdell increased her anxiety. Yes, she was anxious to lay her hands on Uncle Murphy's cream. Yes, she feared coming face-to-face with the person who'd murdered her aunt and uncle, who'd tried killing her time and again. But that wasn't all of it. No one would condemn her for running out on her wedding day to save her life, but was that the only reason she'd run?

The car slipped on the icy road, scattering her thoughts. She was glad Jake was at the wheel. "It's a good thing I didn't try making this drive alone."

He glanced at her sideways and smiled. "You'd have been fine in the daylight."

That they could still share this camaraderie threw her. Of course, they'd been friends for many years and knew each other in ways that were deeply ingrained and comfortable. Her mind swung back to her earlier musings. To marry someone, to commit your life to his, took more than an intense knowledge of that person. It took trust.

Hadn't she trusted Jake? Had running been her only choice? Had she opted to run because she'd been afraid of a murderer *and* afraid of marriage? Her pulse leaped at the thought. Dear God, hadn't she wanted to marry? She closed her eyes, recalling the doubts she'd suffered before the wedding; she'd lost a week's worth of sleep. Why? She loved Jake.

And yet she'd hurt him in the worst possible way. She had to have been desperate to do such a thing. Laura opened her eyes and stared at the road ahead, seeing nothing as she faced a truth she'd hidden from herself for a whole year.

She'd been upset at his refusal to believe her aunt and uncle were murdered. But it was more than that, she realized now. It was because he'd dismissed her concerns as though they didn't matter, as though she didn't matter. She'd lost her trust in him before she ran away. She'd hurt him deeply by leaving, but he'd hurt her just as deeply by his negation of something that meant so much to her. She couldn't marry a man who didn't honor her beliefs.

And so she hadn't. She swallowed hard and chips of stone crumbled from the wall around her heart. The sensation felt freeing, cleansing, as though she were breathing pure oxygen.

The hell Jake and she had suffered these past twelve months found them both changed. For the better, she thought. Jake did believe her now. Thank God, it was not too little or too late. Thank God, she'd grown up enough to forgive. Thank God, he cared enough about her still to forgive her.

She glanced at him again, longing to broach the subject, to talk until they'd talked it all out. They'd discussed suspects and motives and his mother and the weather—everything, it seemed, except their feelings for each other.

She started to reach over and stroke his thigh, but withdrew her hand. She didn't want just to touch him. Didn't want to make love to him even once more if it would be the last time. She'd rather live with her memories. Before they could begin again, they needed to forget all that had gone before. They needed to start fresh, on equal footing, every touch new, every emotion based on mutual respect and trust.

Would they be given the chance?

A semi rumbled past them, the clank-clank of the chained tires rattling loudly, jarring Laura out of her thoughts. "Isn't this the exit for Riverdell?"

"Yep." Jake slowed the car, smoothly abandoning the freeway for the state road—a graveled ribbon that seemed to wind forever through dormant wheat fields, now cloaked in snow and looking in the night like an endless succession of rolling sand dunes.

Jake chose a cautious speed. This highway had no street-lights defining its width, only reflective markers sticking up from the deep snow at uneven intervals. Staying out of the ditch was a challenge.

Headlights flashed behind them.

Jake said, "Some other fool traveling this dicey road tonight."

Laura felt an odd twinge of comfort knowing they weren't alone on this creepy drive. Lots of little towns dotted the area. Some with populations only in double or triple digits. Most of them home to farmers. She glanced around. The headlights sat high off the ground. "Looks like a pickup. Probably a farmer and his family."

Jake mumbled, "Hmm."

She wrenched back around in the seat. "Do you think we'll be able to get into the storage unit tonight?"

But Jake didn't answer. His gaze was riveted to the rear-view mirror. "What the hell is that idiot doing?"

The pickup came rapidly toward them, too fast for the slick surface. Jake edged as near the road markers as was safe. The pickup stayed directly behind them, charging them with purpose. His heart jolted. Swearing, he slammed

the gas pedal. The rear wheels fishtailed, then grabbed. The
Subaru leaped forward. "Hold on! It's going to—"

The pickup rammed into the rear of the car. Laura
squealed. She pitched toward the windshield. The seat belt
cut into her chest. Metal crunched. Her neck felt snapped.
She scanned the road ahead. To her horror, she realized
the moisture hitting the windshield was freezing rain. It
clung to the wipers, rendering them ineffectual. It had to
be obstructing Jake's vision.

It would make the road slicker still. The truck struck
them again. A crushing, metal-crunching blow.

The steering wheel jumped beneath Jake's grip. Somehow he managed to keep on the road. He pressed his foot
to the gas pedal. The car responded with more speed, out-
distancing the pickup as it started up a steep incline. The
little car climbed with heart, its pace fast and steady.

Behind them the truck engine roared, sounding like a
rhinoceros readying for another charge.

They crested the rise and started down into the valley.
Laura's gaze flew to the sudden sharp drop-offs on either
side of the road, and her stomach crashed. No more fluffy-
looking fields. Here, the highway wended down a bluff
twice as steep as the one Jake lived on. Instead of desert
below, one side fell away to rocky ravine, the other to the
Yakima River.

Laura pressed her feet to the floorboard and gripped the
door handle. The pickup rammed the rear of the car, plunging it forward at breakneck speed.

Jake held the Subaru to the road. He dared not hit the
brakes. The car would spin out of control. The truck pulled
alongside, looming like a tank over the compact. Then
veered into it. Metal screeched against metal as they were
tossed sideways.

Saying a silent prayer, he jerked the wheel toward the

truck in a deadly game of push and shove, but the pickup was bigger, with more horsepower. He felt the car begin a slow slide toward the drop-off.

Laura gaped at the black band of water below. The truck plowed into them again. The car slid faster. Laura screamed.

Jake jerked the steering wheel toward the skid. The cliff edge loomed. Laura couldn't breathe. As though the truck driver sensed victory, he raced the truck past them, proceeded to the bottom of the hill and disappeared into the treacherous night.

As if in slow motion, the Subaru pitched toward the cliff. Terror banded Laura's chest, cutting off her air, cutting off her scream. The river seemed close. Deadly. Eager to receive their souls into its freezing depths. Tears sprang into her eyes. Her vision blurred.

She felt the tires grab air.

Then suddenly, the Subaru lurched. Laura was thrown against the door as the car bounded away from the precipice and careered toward the other side of the highway. Jake joggled the steering wheel again. The car straightened. Slowed. A moment later, Jake managed to stop half in and half out of a snowbank.

He tore off his seat belt and was embracing her before her mind comprehended that they weren't sailing through space toward the Yakima River. Her heart thundered so hard she could do nothing more than cling to Jake.

"It's okay," he repeated again and again. "We're all right."

The words gradually penetrated Laura's shock. She drew a wobbly breath, and shoved out of his arms, a new fear attacking her. "What if they come back?"

"I don't think they'll risk it. Not now." He brushed her hair from her forehead and kissed her there. "Because someone is coming down the hill behind us. I think they scared off our attacker.''

She spotted the new set of headlights bouncing down the road. The vehicle approached gingerly. Jake sat straighter and Laura released her seat belt. ''You think he or she saw this rig coming?''

Jake nodded. ''Damn straight. Something sent him into the night.''

The new arrival, a Jeep like Jake's Cherokee, slowed to a stop. A door slammed and snow crunched as the driver strode their way. Jake got out of the car warily. Wet snow slapped his heated face. He kept one hand inside his jacket, over his holstered gun. But he doubted he'd need it with the stranger walking toward him.

He was a well-fed man in Wranglers, a fleece-lined jacket that had seen better days and a spanking new black Stetson. Concern etched his florid face. His eyes were soft-colored, their shade indiscernible in the dim light. He extended his hand to Jake. ''Howdy. Name's Denny Sandy. You folks okay?''

''Little shaken,'' Jake said, giving the man his name.

Mr. Sandy carried a huge flashlight, which he trained on the Subaru. ''Your car's a mess. You lose control?''

''Kind of. We got tangled up with a pickup truck that slid on the ice.''

''And they didn't stick around to see if you were okay?''

''Not everybody's so neighborly these days.''

''Yeah, I know what you mean. Maybe they thought you'd be mad and shoot 'em or something.''

Jake would have liked to have the chance to shoot the jerk driving the pickup. Unfortunately, he'd been too busy trying to keep them from dying to worry about it then.

''Where you folks headed?'' Mr. Sandy asked.

"Riverdell."

"Well, Ma and me gotta drive right through there. You like a lift?"

"Thanks, but I think the car will make it."

"Not very likely." Denny Sandy shone his flashlight on the rear driver's side tire. "Looks to me like you got a bent wheel."

He was right. If Mr. Sandy and his wife hadn't come along, they'd have been spending the night right here. The Subaru wasn't going anywhere in this condition. "Guess we'll take you up on that offer."

They got their belongings out of the Subaru, climbed into the Sandys' Jeep and settled together on the back seat. At least, Jake thought, if the pickup did come back they wouldn't be there. Denny Sandy had saved their lives twice.

The snow began to fall in larger, softer flakes. Jake noticed Laura was shivering, her teeth chattering. He pulled her close, finding no resistance in her, only a feeling of rightness and belonging. It brought to mind nights as teenagers when they'd double-dated. Don had driven giving Laura and him the back seat to themselves. Would life ever be that carefree for either of them again?

Would he and Laura ever have the chance to reconnect emotionally?

RIVERDELL. The population according to the sign into town read 3,003—the same number as last year. But Laura knew of five citizens who'd moved elsewhere. Either five more people had taken up residence or the mayor hadn't bothered to update the census.

Streetlights studded the six-block-long avenue that constituted downtown, illuminating the shops, all closed for the night. They rolled up the rug here around five-thirty each evening. It was nearly ten now and most of the residents would be tucked into their beds.

It had always reminded Laura of a larger version of Bedford Falls in the Jimmy Stewart movie *It's a Wonderful Life*. The odd thing was, she'd changed so much this past year, how could the town have stayed the same? Being there felt like stepping backward in time.

Jake gave Mr. Sandy his cousin Kim's address.

As they drove through town and skirted the river, Laura thought again of the attack on the road earlier and she shivered in Jake's arms. Riverdell might resemble a sleeping child, all innocent and sweet beneath the newly fallen snow, but she and Jake knew the evil that lived in its heart.

She kept her eyes peeled for a pickup with body damage. She was no longer exhausted but wide-awake. Wired. She'd had enough near-death experiences this past year to recognize the sensation. It would hold her in its grip for a few more hours. Might as well burn it off with action. She whispered to Jake, "Once we get the key from Kim, I'd like to go straight to your mom's storage unit—provided we can access it this late in the evening."

"Sure."

The Jeep pulled to a stop before 223 Weeping Willow Lane. Laura and Jake thanked the Sandys profusely and emerged into the cold night. The snow had ceased falling, and the temperature had dipped. The moon stole from behind scurrying clouds and glinted off the fresh snow, giving the whole area a muted, eerie illumination. Cold nipped Laura's cheeks and penetrated her clothing.

She hugged herself and glanced at Kim's house. It was a narrow, two-story clapboard, with a sweeping front lawn and a wide veranda. Kim had painted it an off-white with green shutters. The walkway had been cleared before tonight's snowfall, but now sported a thin layer of white. A light shone in an upstairs window, with another, dimmer, one downstairs. They strode gingerly to the front porch.

Laura's nerves felt like live wires beneath her skin. Anticipation, she supposed. Jake knocked. They waited. Laura's breath puffed cloudy from her mouth. Jake knocked again. They grew as silent as the surrounding night. Except for the rush of the river nearby, they heard nothing. No one moved inside. She heard no footsteps hurrying to answer the door.

Jake turned toward her. "This is really odd. She was expecting me yesterday. But she hasn't called. Not at all like our curious Kimmie."

Laura nodded. It was totally out of character for his cousin. Her uneasiness raised a notch. "Maybe Kim took something to help her sleep. A lot of flu-type medications cause drowsiness."

"Maybe." He turned toward the pot next to the door. "She's always kept a spare key here."

"Ah." He found it and let them in. The house smelled of peach potpourri. Laura glanced around. How like Jake's cousin to go to extremes with a theme. Kim had decorated in peach. The living room was neat, like Kim herself. Cute and neat. Her parents had given her the deed to this two-bedroom house for her graduation present. She'd barely made it through high school, and college had not been an option for Kim. Nor a dream.

Practical to a fault, Mr. and Mrs. Durant had hoped she'd have a leg up on bagging a husband if she had land of her own. But as far as Laura knew, Cullen was the only man Kim had ever wanted, and he'd belonged to Izzy. At least on the surface.

Laura rubbed her cold hands together, recalling that Kim confided to her once that she'd "dated" Cullen twice behind Izzy's back—which Laura took to mean she'd slept with him. She supposed Kim thought having him for a night was better than not having him at all. It saddened her to think that Kim would throw her life away on a man who would never return her love—who would take advantage of the love she felt for him.

"I wonder if Kim knows yet that Cullen is dead," she said softly.

Jake shook his head. "I hope not. God knows how she'll take the news. It might be better if she hears it from me."

"Kim?" Jake called out, moving toward the staircase that divided the living and dining rooms. "It's Jake. Where are you, cuz?"

He climbed the stairs. Laura waited below. She heard Jake opening doors and calling his cousin's name. Then she heard him swear. With her pulse skittering, she ran to the stairs, taking them two at a time.

When she reached the bedroom, Jake was on the phone. "Send an ambulance to 223 Weeping Willow Lane. And hurry."

Laura edged past him and spotted Kim sprawled on the floor. An empty prescription bottle lay near her outflung hand.

Chapter Eighteen

Doc Van Sheets, Father Wisdom, Daddy Comfort—the Know-all, Cure-all, Wizard of Riverdell—seemed world-weary. Drained of perspicaciousness. His brown hair was grayer than last year. It was cut too short to be mussed, but looked rumpled nonetheless. His kind blue eyes held the ache of someone who'd seen too much tragedy in too short a time. "Had to pump her stomach."

Jake's heart was in his throat. Kim had been treated at the hospital, then brought back home with round-the-clock nursing care, due to a lack of availability of hospital beds. "Will she be okay?"

Doc made a face. "Physically, she's gonna be fine in a day or two. Emotionally, I recommend professional help. People bent on suicide keep trying."

"But why?" Jake scowled. "Why would she try to kill herself?"

Mel stroked his thin gray mustache, which was silvery at the tips. He seemed to chew over what he should say. Finally, he asked, "You knew she was smitten with Cullen Crocker?"

"Yes." Jake frowned, realizing he'd taken his cousin's infatuation with Cullen as little more than a crush she'd soon outgrow. He cursed himself for the short shrift he'd given her feelings. He'd done a lot of that in the past. Especially to the women in his life.

He rolled his neck, easing the tension gripping those tender muscles. He'd paid for his callousness in heartache and loneliness. Too much hindsight and too little insight. He prayed to God for a chance to redeem himself. To prove he'd changed. "I suppose the whole town knows."

Doc nodded. "More'n likely. She pretty much wore her heart on her sleeve. I called her about Cullen myself this afternoon. Thought it'd be cruel to have one of the old hens tell her. Would have come in person if I'd known she'd do something as foolhardy as this. Miserable thing, unrequited love. Glad I had the good sense never to fall under old Cupid's spell."

Good sense? Or bad luck? Jake pressed his lips together. The huge hole in his heart was beginning to mend. He had hope for a future with Laura, he supposed, and he now realized that life was better with love and all its accompanying baggage than without it. Would Laura and he find their way together again? Or would a killer rob them of that? "Can we talk to her, Mel?"

"Probably be a waste of time. She's still pretty out of it."

Jake wasn't about to be put off. "This is kind of important. We wouldn't ask otherwise."

"It have something to do with Cullen's murder?"

"Maybe."

"Then I suppose you can try. But I don't want my patient upset, so I'm afraid I can't allow Laura to go with you. No offense, Laura. But when Kim thought Cullen had dumped both her and Izzy to run off with you, you became a real sore subject for her. I'm not sure she understands that didn't happen."

"That's all right." Laura sighed, the sound heavy in the

muted hallway outside Kim's bedroom. "We'll straighten that out when she's feeling better."

Jake wondered how long it would take to straighten out the rest of the folks in Riverdell—if Doris Handley, the nurse Doc had tending to Kim, was any example. She had gazed at Laura with veiled hostility, had spoken curtly. By now she knew Laura hadn't run off with Cullen, but leaving Jake at the altar was still an unforgivable offense in the eyes of most of Riverdell. Doris included.

Doc said, "I'm glad to see you back here, where you both belong. Just sorry that it's under these circumstances."

"I'm sorry about Cullen, Doc." Jake knew the old man felt as though he'd lost a son and almost a daughter tonight.

Mel grimaced. "I know, boy. Whole town is mourning. Come on, let's go see how she's doing."

Jake followed the doctor to Kim's room. Ms. Handley, a muscular woman as tall as Doc, handed Kim over to Mel and left them alone, joining Laura in the hall. Jake hated subjecting Laura to such antipathy. She'd endured enough distress for one night. He gave her an understanding smile. She assured him silently that one misguided nurse couldn't get the better of her.

When he entered the bedroom, Doc was walking Kim around the perimeter, trying to keep her on her feet and awake. They'd come close to losing her. She wasn't out of the woods yet. He glanced away from her and his policeman's mind took in details he hadn't noticed earlier.

To his utter shock, photographs of Cullen littered every surface and half the walls—as though Kim had built a shrine to him. A clammy chill swept his insides. Rooms like this belonged to stalkers. Kimmie, while no stalker, showed the classic signs of obsession. Would she have eventually stalked Cullen if she could have found him?

The thought raised his hackles, and once again, he cursed himself for not realizing Kim was this close to going over the edge. Doc led her back to the bed, allowing her to sit a moment. Jake sat down beside her. Kim seemed as fragile as a kitten, her auburn hair as limp against her shoulders as her limbs on the bed. Her deep-set hazel eyes were unfocused and looked sunken and small without the severe makeup she loved. She muttered something indecipherable. Then more clearly, she said, "Culn."

A sob tore from her throat and clutched Jake's heart.

The doctor grimaced at him. "We really need to keep her awake. Maybe you should wait until tomorrow."

But Jake had the unerring feeling tomorrow would be too late. "I'll walk her a bit. Just let me ask her a couple of questions. If I can't get a sensible answer, I'll try again later."

The doctor nodded and stepped aside. Jake helped Kim to her feet, propping her against him. She moved sluggishly. "Kimmie, you gave us quite a scare."

She glanced up at him. "Dake." The word came out thick as though her tongue were swollen. "Culn."

"Yeah, I know…I'm sorry, cuz. But don't dwell on that now."

"Culn."

Jake urged her to keep moving. "Kimmie, I need the key to Mom's storage unit."

She heaved a sigh, as though even breathing were difficult. "Kee?"

"Yes, the key to the storage unit. Where is it?"

Her eyelids fluttered shut, and her thick auburn lashes lay like brush tips against her pale cheeks. Jake feared she'd dozed off. But she continued to walk with him. She wrenched her eyes open. "Decks."

Decks? Did she mean desk? "Your desk?"

"Hmm," she muttered, nodding as though her neck and head were connected with a single thread.

"What desk?" He didn't recall seeing a desk in the house.

She didn't answer, just stared at the floor. He held his breath, waiting with growing impatience, fearing Doc would terminate the interview. But she lifted her gaze to his, those hazel orbs golden and clear, as though the drug was beginning to wear off. She looked sorrowful and desperate.

"Culn."

Doc clamped his hand on Jake's shoulder. "I think that's all you're going to get out of her for a few hours, son. Let's let her be until some of the barbiturate has dissipated."

Jake wanted to protest, but the doctor insisted. He called the nurse back inside and handed Kim over to her, with instructions to keep her walking. He led Jake out into the hall. Laura's shoulders sagged with relief, as though the nurse had given her a harder time than he'd imagined.

She looked at him expectantly. He mouthed "downstairs" at her. Laura followed the two men to the first floor, then hung back as Jake saw Mel to the door.

Distracted, Jake wanted to find Kim's desk and get the key to his mother's storage unit. He scanned the living room. There was no desk here. He hadn't seen one in her room or the other bedroom. Maybe he'd jumped to the wrong conclusion. Maybe "decks" meant something else entirely.

On the porch, the doctor said, "Ralph will want to speak with you first thing in the morning."

"I want to speak to him now, Doc," Ralph Russell bellowed, barreling up the walk.

Jake's earlier sense of urgency attacked him anew, knotting his stomach. The last thing he needed was another roadblock. And this one was huge.

Doc hurried down the steps as Ralph joined Jake on the porch. Jake shook hands with his former boss.

Ralph asked, "How's Kim?"

"Better. Doc says she'll be good as new in a day or so." Jake stepped aside and invited him inside. Everything about Ralph Russell was average, from his clipped brown hair and chocolate eyes to his height and weight to his even features and mild voice. Everything—except his brain. Ralph was a cautious man, a methodical one. He fitted questions and answers the way others did jigsaw puzzles.

The second he was in the door, his eyes landed on Laura and narrowed. He wasn't surprised to see her, Jake realized. "I suppose Don and Susan told you about Laura."

Ralph shifted back to Jake, his smooth brown eyebrows lifting slightly. "They had a tale to tell. I suspect she's why you knew Cullen hadn't left town, and I figure you won't mind telling me your own tale. "Why don't we sit down?" Ralph gestured to the twin love seats facing each other in the tiny living room. Taking charge was as natural to the man as reading a crook the Miranda.

Laura pulled Jake back, fear wrecking havoc with her digestive system. She whispered, "I don't trust him. What if he killed my aunt and uncle?"

Jake leaned in close, so that only she could hear him. "Even if he did, he's the law in this town. Investigating murders is his job. His right. I say it's time we find out which side he's on."

"I haven't got all night, you two." Ralph withdrew a memo pad and pencil from his pocket.

Jake and Laura settled down on the love seat opposite him. Jake said, "Where are Don and Susan now?"

"I didn't get an itinerary." Ralph poised the pencil to write. "I think we can start with how you knew Cullen might have been murdered."

Laura told him her story, omitting self-incriminating details such as the theft of Sunny Devlin's car, the securing of false identities and any other crimes she'd committed to stay alive.

Ralph wrote on the tablet, quickly filling and flipping pages. "Don says you're claiming someone murdered the Whittakers for that formula Murph was so damned excited about just before he died."

"Yes." Laura nodded, her pulse skipping a beat at his admittance that he knew of the formula.

"But, Jake, you and Don investigated that."

"We may have missed something," Jake admitted.

"Or someone could have doctored their reports," Laura suggested.

Ralph's expression blackened. He didn't like his department or his men's honesty questioned. But Laura had forgotten that he'd never allowed his own prejudices to close his mind to other possibilities. The truth was what counted. Her Uncle Murphy had admired and respected Ralph's sense of fair play since they'd been boys. He would want her to trust him now.

"What proof have you got?" Ralph asked.

"Isn't it proof enough that someone keeps trying to kill me?" She told him about the pickup truck that had tried running them off the road earlier that night.

Ralph frowned, alarmed. "You get a look at the license or the driver?"

"No," Jake answered. "The windows were too dark and I was too busy trying to keep us on the road."

"It's a small town. I'll put my sources on the lookout for a battered pickup. What concerns me now, though, is why they're so intent on shutting you up, Laura. If it's just your word against Dell's. Hell, your claims won't hold up in court." Ralph's gaze was shrewd. "So, what else have you got?"

Praying she really could trust him, Laura told him about the sample bottles.

Ralph listened, his expression going from thoughtful to unconvinced. "Even if this cream and the analysis both still exist, Dell could claim they created theirs first."

"But they didn't," she protested, realizing that was exactly the line of defense Dell's attorneys would argue. "Uncle Murphy labeled the dozen sample bottles with the name Venus Masque and with the date—a full two months before Dell even started production of New Again. I know because I ordered the ingredients for both of them. Besides, Uncle Murphy's handwriting can be verified."

Ralph looked hopeful. "If Murph and May *were* murdered, then by God, I want whoever did it. Where are these sample bottles?"

"In my mother's storage unit." Jake placed his warm hand over her cold one. "I'm not sure where that is. Kim handled it for me and she's in no shape to tell me much about it now."

Ralph inched forward on the love seat, a slow grin forming. "She put Ruthanne's stuff in storage at Dell. I helped her."

"At Dell?" Laura gaped in horror. "Good grief, that's like putting hens in a fox den."

Ralph's grin folded. "Payton turned one of the warehouses into storage units for his employees. Kim used hers for Ruthanne."

"Then Kim did say desk," Jake said. He started up out of his seat. "Her desk at work."

Ralph stood. "Seems to me we should try to locate those sample bottles pronto."

Jake agreed. "But how? It's the middle of the night. We can't get into Dell at this hour."

Ralph smiled. "You can if you're the chief of police."

STANDING ON A KNOLL that overlooked the town and river, Dell Pharmaceuticals had started life as a private airport. Vapor lights illuminated the fenced acreage surrounding two hangars and the low-slung concrete-block structure that served as the main plant. This building housed the offices on its entrance level and two labs belowground in a basement and subbasement. All three buildings were painted a soft gray, with the Dell logo—a bright-purple squiggle—across their top quarters.

Laura, Jake, and Ralph strode up the snowy walkway and were greeted by Payton Dell himself. Strands of his white blond hair stuck out beneath his WSU baseball cap. He had the tanned skin of a man who lived outdoors, the lean body of an avid runner and the face of a hawk, his features pinched and birdlike. His green eyes looked huge behind his wire-rimmed glasses.

Laura shuddered inside. But as usual, Payton's forbidding appearance had nothing in common with his affable nature. He greeted them profusely, as though they'd come to pay a social call. As though they were potential customers. He knew otherwise. Ralph had already told him of Laura's claims against New Again.

Payton said, "Come in. We've been waiting for you."

"We"? Laura thought. But she forgot it the moment

she stepped into the elegantly appointed foyer of Dell Pharmaceuticals. The scent of eucalyptus hit her immediately and roused memories of her workdays here. She could see nothing new or changed about this part of the plant and it seemed odd. Her life had altered so drastically this past year, she supposed she expected everything else to be different someway or other.

A figure stepped from the shadows and Laura's breath caught. "Izzy."

"Hello, Laura."

As usual she wore green, this time having chosen jeans, sweater and cowboy boots. On closer inspection, Laura saw that red streaked the whites of her eyes. Apparently, she, too, was taking Cullen's death hard. She gave Laura an apologetic smile. "I behaved very badly to you. I hope someday you'll find it in your heart to forgive me."

Laura blinked. She was here with claims that the Dell family had stolen her uncle's formula for a skin cream that had heftily lined their pockets, yet both Izzy and Payton were being gracious. She didn't trust either of them. But she could play the game. "Someday is today. I'd just like this all behind me."

"And the sooner we get those sample jars analyzed, the sooner it will be," Jake declared, striding to his cousin's receptionist desk. A moment later he held the key for Laura to see.

Payton said, "The storage units are in the two hangars. Kim's is in the north one."

The hangar had been insulated, wired for heat and divided into dozens of individual storage units. Jake unlocked the door and stepped inside with Laura. The others followed.

Her gaze swung to the sea of cardboard boxes. They dominated the shelves that lined the side walls and monopolized the floor in the center of the room. Furniture was stacked against the back wall and draped with old blankets.

The unit had a ransacked look to it. Laura's chest ached. Had someone gotten here ahead of them? Or had Payton and Izzy gone through the storage before they arrived? Either way, she had the awful feeling that her evidence was gone.

With a heavy heart, she began turning toward Jake, but something silvery on one of the shelves caught her eye. Wrapping paper. Wedding paper. Her pulse kicked up two beats. It was the paper she'd wrapped the sample jars in. She took a step toward it.

"What the hell is going on here?" Travis Crocker's voice stopped her cold. She pivoted. Everyone else had, too. They all seemed to be staring at his drawn gun. He wore his night watchman's uniform.

Izzy stepped toward him. "Honey, what are you doing here? Payton told you to take the week off."

"Sorry. I thought you were burglars." Travis's handsome face flushed with color and he returned the gun to its holster. He glanced at Izzy. "I couldn't sleep. Had to do something. Looks like I'm not the only restless soul. Why are you all here this time of night?"

Payton said, "Laura seems to think I stole the formula for New Again from her uncle. We're looking for the proof."

Jake said, "It might help solve Cullen's murder."

"Oh?" Travis glanced at Ralph. "Is that right?"

Ralph shrugged. "Guess we won't know if we can't find the cream."

"I have found it," Laura said, sounding surer than she felt. With her insides turning to mush, she crossed to the shelf and grasped the box. It was her box. Hope and fear collided inside her. Saying a silent prayer, she lifted the lid. Four green plastic containers nestled in its depths. Tears sprang to her eyes and relief nearly buckled her knees. She clasped the box to her thundering heart and faced Jake. "They're here."

"Good," Ralph barked. "I want an analysis done immediately. Can you get someone down here tonight to do that, Payton?"

"I anticipated that." Payton lifted his hat and scratched his head. "I have someone coming in."

"Actually, that won't be necessary." Travis had his gun out of its holster again. He grabbed Izzy and pointed the barrel against her forehead. "All of you move back, or I'll blow her brains out."

"Travis?" Izzy squeaked. "What are you doing?"

"Shut up," he said between clenched teeth. "Chief, Jake, put your guns on the floor and kick them to me."

Ralph complied immediately, but Jake hesitated. Travis jammed the gun hard against Izzy's temple. She yelped. Jake took his gun out of the holster, set it on the floor, then kicked it toward Travis, stepping in front of Laura as he did so. "Trav, I know you're distressed about your brother—"

"He's not distressed about me." Cullen Crocker appeared in the doorway like a resurrected ghost. He picked up Jake's gun, motioning him to move out of the way as he stepped toward Laura. "Give me that box."

"Cullen!" Izzy fainted and fell from Travis's grasp.

"Forget about her," Cullen instructed.

Travis aimed the gun at Payton. "He said to let her be."

"Give me that box, Laura," Cullen insisted. "I've spent a year chasing it down. I want my reward."

"You? You're the one who's been trying to kill me?" Laura forced away the shock that kept trying to grip her.

If she gave in to it, she'd lose her evidence, maybe her life. She'd come too far and fought too hard to buckle under now. "But why?"

"Money, of course." He reached for the box again.

Laura still held it to her chest with one hand. She shoved her free hand into her purse. She easily found what she sought, palmed it and pulled her hand free. She made Cullen come to her for the box. The moment he grabbed it, she zapped him in the gut with the stun gun. He dropped to the floor like a felled tree, landing on top of Jake's gun.

In the second Travis took to react, Jake grabbed the stun gun from Laura and went for him.

Laura scrambled for her precious evidence. A shot rang out, deafening in the small enclosure. She glanced up at Payton. He stood frozen as though riveted by shock, his eyes on something behind her. Fear ripped through Laura as she lurched around. Her gaze flew to Jake. Something about his stance struck her as odd. Then she saw the gaping hole in his shoulder. She screamed.

Forgetting the box, and the gun in Travis's hand, she rushed to Jake. She reached his side and caught his arm as his knees began to sag. Ralph grabbed him on the opposite side and they lowered him to the floor. Laura yanked off her coat and bunched it against Jake's wound with all her might. "Jake? Jake!"

His face was etched with pain. Terror filled every ounce of her. Blood pumped out of him at an alarming rate.

Travis stepped over her and snatched the box of Venus Masque samples from the floor, then helped his brother to his feet.

"The poison," Cullen muttered, reaching into his pocket. He withdrew a glass vial and dropped it on the floor. It shattered, spilling its liquid contents. His male-model face twisted in an malignant grin.

Travis said, "It's a quick-acting, poisonous gas. Good-bye, you bunch of losers."

The brothers rushed to the door, doused the lights and stepped outside. The click of the lock resounded through the storage unit like a death knell.

A foul odor filled Laura's nostrils. She choked, coughing. "We have to get out of here. Payton, is there another way?"

He answered in between coughs. "No. I wanted each unit to be secure unto itself."

Laura's fear swamped her. Jake was losing blood at a rapid speed. And the poison was making her sleepy. This, then, was the end. Jake and she would not be given their chance for happiness. She bent close to his ear. "I love you, Jake Wilder."

"I love you, Laura," he managed, but his voice sounded weak.

Outside the room, she heard muffled sounds, like gunfire, then screams. A second later, her eyes fluttered shut and her hand on Jake's wound went slack.

Chapter Nineteen

Laura opened her eyes slowly. Her head pounded as though it had been struck with a gong. Her tongue felt thick. She was in bed, in a room smelling of antiseptic, a room with stark white walls. She shoved up on her elbows and glanced around. Three of the five other beds were occupied by Izzy, Payton and Ralph. It was a clinic, she realized. Doc's clinic.

Dear God, Jake! Where was he? She lurched up, too anxious to be contained by the splitting ache in her head. Or the intravenous line taped to her arm. What stopped her was a nurse, the same woman who'd been tending to Kim Durant earlier. "You're not going anywhere yet, Laura. You've got to get all the antidote."

"Where's Jake?" Laura's mouth was so dry the words came out strangled.

"He's in surgery. Doc said to tell you not to worry."

Not worry? How could she not? "But he lost so much blood."

"I know." Doris Handley expected patients to obey her. She urged Laura back against the pillows. "Don Bowman donated and Doc had Jake's type on hand. So, he'll be okay on that score."

Don? How had Don known? She realized how imma-

terial that was. A sob filled her chest. She'd never had a
reason before now to like Don. But at this minute she
thought she loved him. The nurse's words resounded in
her head: *he'll be okay on that score.* But what about the
gunshot wound?

Worry squeezed her heart. What if all Doc's efforts
failed to save Jake? What would she do without him? An
awful ache traveled her body, reaching into every part of
her. Laura lifted up again. "How long has Jake been in
surgery?"

"Couple of hours now."

"Is that good or bad?"

"Try not to worry."

Laura fell back against her pillow, giving in to the sharp
throb at her temples. Doris took her pulse. She frowned.
And wrote something on a chart. Laura was amazed at how
gentle she was. How nice she was being. Something had
changed since the uncomfortable hours in the hall at Kim's
house. "How is Kim?"

"She'll be okay." Doris grinned this time, showing
even white teeth. The perfect advertisement for the Milk
Industry. "She's turned into a real heroine."

Laura frowned. "Huh?"

"She's the reason you're all here...safe and sound."

"I don't understand. Just how did we get here?" Laura
tried to recall anything about a trip to the clinic. Nothing
came to her. "The last thing I remember is being locked
in the storage unit."

"You were rescued thanks to Kim...and me." Doris
beamed as she tucked Laura's sheets tighter. "About half
an hour after you and Jake left the house with Chief Russell, Kim started getting coherent. She'd been repeating
Cullen's name since I got there. We all just thought she
was upset about his death. But she told me Cullen was

alive, that he'd forced her to take the barbiturates after she'd told him where something called Venus Masque was.

"I telephoned Doc right away." Pride shone in Doris's doe eyes at her own role in this adventure. "Apparently, he located Don and Susan and the three of them rushed to the plant. As I heard it, they encountered Travis and Cullen in one of those hangars, trying to escape.

"Some shots were fired, but no one was wounded and Don made short work of them. Then he and Susan handcuffed them inside their own truck. I got to the plant in time to see that. That pickup looked like the loser in a stock-car elimination race."

Laura flinched. So it was Cullen who'd tried running them off the road. The Subaru had been the real loser, she thought, relieved that the Crocker brothers were behind bars and were both alive to stand trial and pay for their crimes. "Did they recover my box of samples?"

"I don't know, dear."

Laura realized she didn't really care, either. All that mattered now was Jake. She spent the next hour praying, clinging to the engagement ring he'd given her. Eventually, Doris told her Jake was out of surgery and in the recovery room.

But another agonizing hour dragged by without further word. Her headache abated and Payton and Ralph began sitting up and talking. Doris regaled them with her tale of heroism. Izzy finally came around. She'd inhaled the most poison because she'd been unconscious and it had afflicted her worse because she was physically smaller than the rest of them. Laura watched her recovery with immense relief, but her eyes kept swinging back to the clinic door.

Suddenly, it banged open. Her pulse lurched. Doc wheeled Jake into the room on a gurney. The surgical nurse helped Doris transfer him to the bed beside hers. She tugged the needle from her arm and hurried to Jake's side.

Doc smiled at her. "You seem a bit anxious for someone who once abandoned this young man."

Laura realized he was teasing her and he wouldn't be if he wasn't confident Jake would recover. The tension freezing her insides began melting. "How is he?"

Mel stroked his mustache. "Lucky. The bullet went through the fleshy part of his shoulder. He can expect some minor nerve damage, but otherwise, he'll heal fairly rapidly. His youth and good physical condition are in his favor."

The other patients began sitting up. All, Doris reported, had responded well to the antidote.

"Including Jake," Doc added.

"Hey, don't talk about me like I'm not here." Jake's gaze locked with hers and her heart filled with joy.

"Bossy as ever, I see." She grasped his hand and kissed his forehead.

Don and Susan came through the door. They saw Jake and hurried over. Doc held up his hand. "Don't look so worried. I haven't lost a patient in the last eighteen hours." He chuckled at his own joke and received wry grins from everyone in the room.

Don moved to the opposite side of the bed from Laura. His craggy face was haggard. "Sorry we lied to you, partner. We were afraid Laura intended to hurt you a second time and we decided the only way we could prevent that was to find out whether or not her story had any credence."

He didn't look at Laura and she felt the old tension between them rearing inside her.

Don said, "But we knew if we told you we were coming to Riverdell, you'd balk."

"Damn straight," Jake said.

"We came to find what we could. Ralph let us reexamine the Whittaker file, but we couldn't find anything new. However, we did discover the dentist's office had been broken into. Files disturbed. The *C*s and the *F*s. After Doc told us tonight about the John Doe with the crushed skull, we got hold of Dr. Peterson, the dentist, and went through the files. Someone had exchanged Cullen's original dental records with Frankie Forks, a ranch hand who'd gone missing last year. He was last seen drinking with someone who fits Cullen's description shortly before they both disappeared."

Susan stepped up beside her husband. She held the box of Venus Masque samples. "We owe you a huge apology, Laura. You were leveling with us all along."

Laura made no attempt to retrieve her box from Susan. She didn't want to let go of Jake's hand.

Don nodded, gazing at her now with apology in his muddy-river eyes. "I was hoping maybe we could wipe the slate and start fresh. We don't want to be shut out of Jake's personal life."

Laura felt a warm glow inside. Forgiveness was a wonderful tool. Maybe even Izzy and she could find their way back together. Why not Don and Susan and she? She smiled at them. "You saved our lives tonight. I can never forget that. As far as I'm concerned the slate is clean. I'd like to be friends, too."

OVER THE NEXT WEEK, Laura helped play nurse to Kim and Jake, both ensconced in Kim's house. Kim wasted little time bounding back to her old self, but Jake had to be more cautious. He and Laura had a deeper healing to face—the hashing out of the personal reasons the wedding hadn't come off. Laura's heart clutched with fear that they wouldn't manage to work past their private issues.

On the first day, he was too exhausted for their long overdue talk.

On the second day, she brought up the subject. Jake thought he'd faced and beaten the hurt and accepted his part in the blame for all that went wrong. But examining the cause instead of the effect was like opening a wound that wasn't healing. All their bottled-up hurt and distrust spilled out. Tempers flared. Pride ruled.

On the third day, Laura admitted her misgivings. Jake admitted his culpability. They apologized, forgiving each other, but felt awkward and exhausted, overwhelmed by the expenditure of too many emotions.

On the fourth day, Laura awoke with a sense of well-being. She realized she'd finally forgiven herself.

On the fifth day, they met in Kim's dining room with Payton. Ralph and he had had the two skin creams analyzed. Laura sat next to Jake. Payton took the chair opposite them. Kim left them alone and disappeared upstairs.

Butterflies collided in Laura's stomach. She reached for Jake's hand, finding comfort in his strong grip. She addressed Payton. "You said a subtle difference was found between the two skin creams…?"

Payton again wore a baseball cap, this one with a Mariners logo. "Yes, Murphy's cream includes an ingredient that is usually found in disinfectants."

"Disinfectants?" What would disinfect— The thought burst as she recalled the "wonder cleanser" that her uncle had invented and sterilized his bottles with in order to reuse them. He'd worked on a shoestring budget—recycling because he couldn't afford new. "Are you saying my uncle's cream wasn't used as the basis for New Again?"

"No. It was." Payton lifted the baseball cap and scratched his head. "Cullen sold it to me as his own."

She opened her mouth and slammed it shut. The one man she'd trusted with the cream was the very one who'd stolen it in the first place.

Payton said, "He duped us all."

"Me, *most* of all." Laura grimaced.

But Jake rubbed his thumb across the back of her hand, a warm, loving touch that conveyed such support she knew she needn't dwell on past mistakes.

He said, "How do we know Cullen didn't infect all Laura's sample bottles?"

Payton shrugged. "I don't think we'll ever know. Ralph says he's not talking."

But Laura had given Cullen access to only one of her bottles. That was why he'd been after her to find and destroy the rest of them. No, the disinfectant had to be in Uncle Murphy's bottles.

Dear God, Ruthanne had been using that cream for nearly a year.

She squeezed Jake's hand so hard he winced. "Are there any side effects with my uncle's lotion?"

Payton propped his elbows on the table. "Only if the cream is stored in plastic—which this has been—then a chemical breakdown occurs. Prolonged use can simulate in the user the same symptoms as Alzheimer's."

"Oh, my." Laura felt sick to her stomach.

Jake swore. They looked at each other, and she could see all the awful possibilities occurring to her were also occurring to him. She asked, "Will it cause permanent damage?"

Payton adjusted his glasses. "According to my lab chemist, once use of the cream is stopped, the affected person will eventually recover completely."

Laura felt a thrill, but warned herself not to get her hopes up. They would have to discuss this with Doc. And she suspected it would be a while before they'd know for sure whether or not Ruthanne actually had Alzheimer's.

Payton said, "As to the formula, I had no idea that Cullen and Travis stole it from your uncle, but since Dell's cream is based on Murphy Whittaker's formula, I would like to offer you fair market value compensation, retroactive, and, of course, a percentage on past and all future earnings."

He passed Laura a piece of paper with an amount on it. She could probably sue Dell and win, taking all the profits. But money wasn't her motivating factor and this offer was indeed generous. "I'll accept, under one condition."

He nodded. "Anything."

"Rename the cream."

Payton wrinkled his nose, looking as though he had something distasteful in his mouth. "Venus Masque?"

"No. Eclipse—it was how my aunt and uncle both described it. Ruthanne, too."

"You could advertise it," Jake suggested, "with something like, 'feel New Again with Eclipse.' That would tie in the old name with the new."

Laura gave him a loving smile.

Payton nodded. "I think I can live with that."

"Then we have a deal." Laura shook hands with him.

Kim came downstairs as soon as Payton saw himself out. "Well, tell me."

Laura filled her in on the outcome of the meeting and on the possibility that Ruthanne might not have Alzheimer's after all. Kim expressed distress at her part in her aunt's diagnosis and suffering, but was as buoyed as they were by the news the effects of the cream would eventually wear off.

Jake kissed Laura's cheek. "I have more good news. Doc says I can leave here in two more days."

Kim frowned. "Darn, I'm going to miss you guys."

"We'll miss you, too." Jake told her. Kim seemed like a new person since her near-death experience at the hands of the man she'd thought hung the moon. She had more confidence and no longer hid her pert face beneath a layer of makeup. Jake felt sure she was on her way to recovery.

On the sixth day, Laura traded her jeans and sweater for the hottest outfit available in Riverdell's one clothing store. The skimpy red dress fitted her curves as much like a second skin as the scant red panties it covered.

Jake's glance started at her spiky red heels, lazily, approvingly, climbed her bare legs, her hips, her breasts, her neck, her mouth, until their gazes collided. He released a low whistle.

"You like?" Laura sidled to his bed and sank onto the mattress.

"Oh, yeah."

His voice held a husky note, but it was his eyes she noticed most. No more hurt. No more distrust. Just pure, accepting love.

Her heart took flight, a feather on the wind, no longer weighted down with doubt or distrust, but floating on pure, fearless love.

Boldly, she stroked his face, accustoming herself to the feel of his scar, the texture, relishing the freedom, the right, to touch him so possessively. "Did I ever tell you your imperfections make me weak?"

Before he could answer, she trailed quick little kisses down the length of his scar. He moaned so quietly it whispered from him, hot against her ear.

"Oh, babe, I've missed you."

"I've missed you, too," she murmured, lifting her head.

The heat in his eyes fanned the fire building inside her. He caught her face in both hands and pulled her mouth to his. If his imperfections made her weak, his kiss made her liquid, breathless. She pulled back, joyful. The need inside her blooming too quickly. She'd waited too long for this moment, ached for it too many lonely nights, to rush.

Jake's hands curled insistently about her upper arms, but she resisted his tender urging to continue the kiss. She wanted to touch him and taste him and look at him. His hair needed cutting and fell provocatively about his arresting face. His sweeping chest was bare, half-hidden by the blanket, his shoulder decorated with a clean bandage, his breastbone covered with crisp curly ash-blond hair.

She shoved the blanket to his waist and watched a fire flare through his eyes. She began kissing his chest, from one side to the other, reveling in the smell of him, the taste of him, in the delighted groans each brush of her lips pulled from him. She wanted more. She wanted his naked flesh touching hers. She sat up and untied the string at the back of her neck, then holding the dress up with one hand unzipped the back with the other. She stood and let the dress slither to the floor.

His Adam's apple bobbed. His tongue slipped across his chiseled mouth as though he had a mighty thirst that needed quenching. She sat again as he lifted off the pillow to meet her. Beneath his smoldering gaze her nipples hardened with a fluttering tingle that sent shivers of anticipation through her. His hands cupped her breasts, the pads of his thumbs brushing back and forth across their sensitive centers until she could contain a cry of joy no longer.

It spilled into the room, a tune as old and treasured as the first written song. Sweet music to Jake's ears. He gathered a mouthful of breast, languishing in the favorite delicacy. He heard her breathing quicken and his urgency returned with such speed it was all he could do to contain his need. He tossed the covers aside. He wore nothing but his desire for her. She sighed, smiling, her gaze a caress against his engorged flesh.

But it wasn't enough. He gathered her hand and pressed it to him, then he slipped his fingers into the waistband of her panties, a red strip of lace that yielded to his determined touch. His intimate invasion was greeted by a thick tangle of curly hair, more silken than the red satin covering it. He slid his hand lower and found her liquid center.

She gasped as he identified the sensitive tip of her womanhood, massaging it with tender, demanding strokes. Then he slipped his finger inside her.

Laura's body constricted, the climax hitting her quick and hard and sweet. She closed her eyes and let the sensations spill through her. When the ride slowed, she rose, skimming her panties down her hips and stepping from them.

She wore only his ring. It adorned the finger he'd placed it on so long ago. He noticed it now. Kissed it now. "I love you, woman."

Laura thought her heart might burst with happiness.

Jake's gaze crawled hungrily over her, found her face, the teal of his eyes darkening to the hue of a tropical pool. He caught her arms again, intending to sweep her beneath him. But a flash of pain crossed his face as he strained his wound. She urged him back on the pillow. "Be still, love. Let me do this."

Laura straddled him, locking his legs beneath her, lowering her head to stroke her tongue over his hard, sleek shaft, cherishing the feel of him.

"Oh, Laura." He gasped. "Now, babe, now."

With her gaze locked to his, she raised her hips, then slowly, purposefully, sank onto his throbbing need; the joining filled her heart as his sex filled the very core of her.

She rose and fell, rose and fell, each thrust deep and hot. Tiny star bursts tingled through her. Her breath came fast and quick, her pulse picking up the ever-increasing rhythm, lifting her higher and higher.

She cried out his name as the speed of her pleasure licked her blood to flames and burst in one gigantic fireball that exploded to her fingertips, her toes, her scalp.

The quiet that followed held a comfortable, easy peace and Laura knew without doubt that at long last Jake and her dreams aligned as truly as the stars and the planets. Their hopes spiraled around them, fitting together in an interlocking twist of life and love, of trust in each other, in their future.

As he stroked the birthmark on her inner thigh, she thought of her uncle and aunt. She felt certain they were smiling at Jake and her, happy that they'd found their way back to each other.

Jake reached for her again. She belonged in this man's arms, his bed. If ever she ran again, it would not be from him, but with him.

And on the seventh day she did. Jake and Laura eloped.

Take 2 bestselling love stories FREE

Plus get a FREE surprise gift!

Special Limited-Time Offer

Mail to Harlequin Reader Service®

3010 Walden Avenue
P.O. Box 1867
Buffalo, N.Y. 14240-1867

YES! Please send me 2 free Harlequin Intrigue® novels and my free surprise gift. Then send me 4 brand-new novels every month. Bill me at the low price of $3.34 each plus 25¢ delivery and applicable sales tax, if any.* That's the complete price, and a saving of over 10% off the cover prices—quite a bargain! I understand that accepting the books and gift places me under no obligation ever to buy any books. I can always return a shipment and cancel at any time. Even if I never buy another book from Harlequin, the 2 free books and the surprise gift are mine to keep forever.

181 HEN CH7J

Name	(PLEASE PRINT)
Address	Apt. No.
City	State	Zip

This offer is limited to one order per household and not valid to present Harlequin Intrigue® subscribers. *Terms and prices are subject to change without notice.
Sales tax applicable in N.Y.

UINT-98

©1990 Harlequin Enterprises Limited

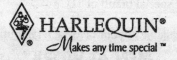

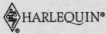 

CANCELED

RETURN TO SENDER

RETURN TO SENDER

RETURN TO SENDER

*Sometimes the most precious secrets come
in small packages...*

What happens when a 25-year-old letter gets
returned to sender...and the secrets that have been
kept from you your whole life are suddenly
revealed? Discover the secrets of intimacy and
intrigue in

#478 PRIORITY MALE
by Susan Kearney (Aug.)

#482 FIRST CLASS FATHER
by Charlotte Douglas (Sept.)

Don't miss this very special duet!

HARLEQUIN®

I N T R I G U E ®

Look us up on-line at: http://www.romance.net

HINRTS

HARLEQUIN®

I N T R I G U E®

COMING NEXT MONTH

AVAILABLE THIS MONTH:

Look us up on-line at: http://www.romance.net